ırd

'This is a wonderfu ... ıant. As with Howard Norman's other work, the story takes time to develop. At times his characters inhabit each other's lives; elsewhere they seem divorced from reality in a way which exalts them above the ordinary. He packs the text with significant moments, pausing only to catch recalcitrant details . . . The dialogue is rich, precise, and expressive' – *Glasgow Herald*

'This is a novel of images and scenes and dazzling revelations, all calmly filtered through the precise but never quite ordinary vision of a unique writer whose fascination with the offbeat has created another quietly outstanding novel' – *Irish Times*

'Norman, like DeFoe's uncle, is "enticed by bold acts of the imagination" towards the creation of a morally subtle and continually inventive novel' – *Sunday Times*

'Norman's fiction raises itself to a laceratingly shrill emotional pitch. The final epistolary stages are wholly compelling, and the all but casual build-up of narrative tension acquits itself in an ending which is daringly assured' – *Independent on Sunday*

'A distinguished novel whose shocking conclusion, inventive narrative and atmospheric depiction of a small cast of characters will gain a wide readership' – *Books Magazine*

'. . . this book is so delicate that it'll batter your heart into little tender pieces' – *Elle*

'Norman's novels prove exquisite, like pieces of folk art whose simplicity postpones a sly impact' – *GQ*

'[Norman] has mastered a narrative voice so dry, so laconic, so humbly self-denying that the most muted gestures can have the force of a scream' – *New York Times Book Review*

'Masterful . . . An impressive and admirable achievement which will buttonhole the reader from the first sentence' – John Banville, *Washington Post Book World*

'Thrilling in the chances it takes with tone and structure, and utterly memorable in the settings it evokes and the characters it creates' – *Chicago Tribune*

'The concepts of belonging, stewardship, "ennoblement", "truce", guilt, and survival are brilliantly dramatised in this breathtakingly readable novel. Wonderful fiction' – *Kirkus Reviews*

'A delightful book, warm, delicate . . . the relationship between DeFoe and Uncle Edward is the book's great achievement' – Andrew Miller, author of *Ingenious Pain*

'[Howard Norman] is one of the more interestingly enigmatic writers around these days . . . [*The Museum Guard*] fairly glimmers with the originality of his complexly tragic vision' – *New York Times*

Howard Norman's two previous novels, *The Northern Lights* and *The Bird Artist*, were finalists for the American National Book Award. In 1997 he received a Lannan Award in fiction. He lives with his family in Vermont and Washington, D.C.

Also by Howard Norman

The Northern Lights (1987)

Kiss in the Hotel Joseph Conrad (1989)

The Bird Artist (1994)

THE MUSEUM GUARD

HOWARD NORMAN

PICADOR

First published 1998 by Farrar, Straus & Giroux, New York
First published in Great Britain 1999 by Picador

This edition published 2000 by Picador
an imprint of Macmillan Publishers Ltd
25 Eccleston Place, London SW1W 9NF
Basingstoke and Oxford
Associated companies throughout the world
www.macmillan.co.uk

ISBN 0 330 37010 3

1 3 5 7 9 8 6 4 2

A CIP catalogue record for this book is available from
the British Library.

Printed and bound in Great Britain by
Mackays of Chatham plc, Chatham, Kent.

For Jane and Emma

For Melanie Jackson

"Let us shut off the wireless and listen to the past."

—Virginia Woolf

THE MUSEUM GUARD

An Honorable Profession

The painting I stole for Imogen Linny, *Jewess on a Street in Amsterdam*, arrived to the Glace Museum, here in Halifax, on September 5, 1938. I had left my room in the Lord Nelson Hotel at 6:45, and gotten to work at 7 a.m. in order to help my curator, Mr. E. S. Connaught, install a new exhibition, "Eight Paintings from Holland." Mr. Connaught did not go in for lofty titles, the way they did in some museums.

We set to work unpacking the crates. The Dutch all got Room C, the Margaret Glace Memorial Room, named after the founder's wife. To me, it was a mystery why Mr. Connaught chose to put a painting here or there. He asked me to hang *Jewess on a Street in Amsterdam* on the south wall between windows, where you could glimpse Halifax Harbour. He must have had an intuition for that painting in that spot, because when it was on the wall, he said, "Perfect."

In the Glace Museum, there are only the large rooms, A and C, both 18' × 22', and Room B, 8' × 21', which is more a connecting hallway. Though Room B has a certain importance, because it is where the permanent collection resides. There is a bevy of watercolors and oils by Canadian artists. Among them is a trapper's shack, a totem pole above a rocky beach, a blind cellist, and a very unhappy-looking nude. And there is also an oil, 18" × 12", *The Glace Museum*, which was painted by Simon Glace, the museum's founder. The scale is off in this painting, I noticed. The schooner masts meant to be in the background—the wharf is actually four blocks from the museum, which is on Agricola Street —seem to jut directly up from the roof. Otherwise, it is a nice painting.

I always tried to study up, learn enough about our new paintings to answer basic questions. But I was a guard, not a tour guide. That was Miss Helen Delbo's job. She also taught Art History at Dalhousie University.

All that October, I was the guard farthest from the front door, in Room C. The other guard was my uncle, Edward Russet. He worked in Room A. We could both see the entirety of Room B, so shared jurisdiction.

When all was said and done, "Eight Paintings from Holland" took two hours. After we got all the Dutch on the walls, Mr. Connaught clutched his hands behind his back and toured the room. This was a ritual of his. He stood in the middle, next to the bench donated by Mrs. Yvonne Glace, niece of the founder and herself an amateur watercolorist. She did not have work in the permanent collection. Mr. Connaught revolved slowly, chewing his lip. Bifocals on, then off, then on again. He is a tall man, with completely white hair. A week earlier he had turned fifty; I had gotten him a tie pin, which was what I could afford on my salary. When deep in concentration like this, he had the tendency to rub the sides of his head and jaw, as if kneading bread dough. My uncle could do an expert imitation of this. Mr. Connaught has a tired, intelligent face, thick eyebrows also turned white, and can sometimes display a look of genuine bemusement. Studying the museum walls, he often puffed out his cheeks, sighed with sudden torment, and said, "No —lower that one. Put that one over there," and the like. So, now he appraised the Dutch. But in the end, he left the paintings exactly where he had me first put them. "Let me get used to this arrangement for a few days," he said. "I'm slightly troubled by the positioning of the still lifes. Too many still lifes on the same wall can be deadening. But it's fine for now." He walked over to me, put his hands on my shoulders, closed his eyes, opened them again. "Therefore, DeFoe," he said, "these are your new charges." As if it completed a formal agreement that I would die on behalf of any and all the paintings, we solemnly shook hands. "By the way," he said, "Mrs. Boardman won't be attending the bookstore today. She's quite ill, I'm told. You'll have to sell postcards." Then he returned to his office, just behind the small bookstore, to the left as you walked in the front door. The door had a brass ram's-head knocker; before 1920, when the museum opened to much ribbon-cutting fanfare, it was Simon Glace's private mansion.

About 9:15, Mr. Connaught left for a fund-raising lecture across the harbor in Dartmouth. I unlocked the doors to the public at 10 a.m. The way he or I did every morning, except Mondays, when the museum was closed.

My uncle stumbled in about 11:00, maybe 11:30. His over-all dilapidation was more familiar than alarming. He had on rumpled black trousers, a white shirt, not tucked in, sleeves rolled up unevenly. Black shoes, no socks, and it was quite chilly out that morning. His extra guard uniform, pants and suit coat, I mean, still on their hanger, where the hotel laundress, Mrs. Klein, had put them, was slung over his shoulder. He had puffy, bloodshot eyes. His face looked swollen. His entire countenance was racked with drink and insomnia. Despite how wrecked he looked, here again was the inescapable fact of how handsome he was. With unkempt, but richly thick black hair, like a young man's. He was forty-eight years old. And despite the stubble beard, slumped shoulders, it was uncanny how much he looked like my father. My father had been the elder by two years.

My uncle glanced around at the new exhibition. "I'm nearly twice as old as this boy here," he announced, more to the Dutch than to me. "And look at his scowl of disapproval, will you?" He was slurring. "I have lived life tenfold what my nephew has, or ever will."

He then laughed off his insult and condemnation, all of it made worse because it was so true. He walked up to me, cuffed my chin, embraced me, falling heavily against my chest. "Oh, come now, DeFoe," he said. "You know how I talk."

"Mr. Connaught's over in Dartmouth," I said. "He won't be back until after lunch. Better go into the custodian's room and clean up a little, Uncle Edward. Take a nap."

"I see the Dutch have invaded, eh?" he said. "I'd intended to help you get them on the walls. But Natalie forgot to set the alarm."

"Who's Natalie?"

He studied me a moment. "No matter how bad I might look today," he said, "nephew, you look worse. I mean, sure, you're all neatly packaged, as per usual. Ironed your tie, and all that. But what *happened* to you last night? Oh, oh, oh, Imogen, was it? Wouldn't let you sleep with her again. Another night of howling at the moon, I suppose. We'll discuss it later. We'll have an old-fashioned uncle-and-nephew talk."

Locking my arm in his, I guided my uncle to the custodian's room, located next to Mr. Connaught's office but with a door leading directly in and out of Room A. He lay right down on the cot. The room also had a deep washbasin with a movable spigot. Mops were upright in a bucket, scrub brushes hung on a cork board. I kept an iron, bought with my own money, in the cupboard. A wooden ironing board with an asbestos coverlet and collapsible legs was behind the door. A radio was on the shelf. The custodian, Mr. Tremain, came in three nights a week to mop floors, wash the inside windows, dust the frames, tidy up the office and bookstore, clean the washrooms. Weather permitting, on Monday mornings he got out a ladder, bucket, and sponges and washed the outside windows.

Before I could bring a glass of water to him, my uncle was asleep. I closed the door and went back to Room C.

Had Mr. Connaught seen him come in late that day, he might well have cornered my uncle and shouted, "Tardy!"—a dunce-cap child's word, my uncle called it. Mr. Connaught had reprimanded my uncle in public any number of times. One day, my uncle might be ten minutes late, the next day not show up until noon, then immediately take his half-hour lunch. One time, he began his workday at 1:30 p.m. and said to me, "I just took my lunch, or else I would've been in at one sharp." There was just no predicting. He would be absolutely punctual two, three, even four weeks in a row. Though more than three weeks of punctuality inevitably resulted in lots of truancies—another of Mr. Connaught's words. In 1937, my uncle was tardy every day in January. One day mid-January, he did not come in at all. At 5:00, Mr. Connaught emerged from his office and said, "No doubt Edward was just too worn out from his—how does he put it—amorous investigations. With a hotel employee, as usual, isn't it? A Matilda, or Isabel, isn't it? Or Altoon, wasn't it? He doesn't stray far from home." My uncle also lived in the Lord Nelson Hotel. I was in Room 22, my uncle in Room 34. One floor apart.

The odd thing was, when Mr. Connaught dressed my uncle down, his face up close to my uncle's, announcing, "You're docked a full week's pay, every last penny!"—still, my uncle simply took his medicine, bowed, and said, "Very well, my liege," or some such extravagance, then repaired to his assigned room. "Since I earned and expected such punishment," he said after one such drubbing, "why lose my temper over it?"

By the time, in 1936, I began as a guard, my uncle had already worked thirteen years for Mr. Connaught. He had hired Edward after being curator merely a week. Before that, my uncle had worked in the baggage room of the Halifax train station. The only other previous guard, Trevor Salk, whom I met once, had retired to Peggy's Cove. Anyway, from early on, I sensed that Mr. Connaught and my uncle liked each other, and that that fact made for mutual irritation. My uncle took advantage of Mr. Connaught's tolerance. Any fool could see that. In turn, Mr. Connaught seemed to have no limit of tolerance toward my uncle. So there it was. Their give-and-take. Or, as regarded my uncle, his take and take and take. In the museum I think that my uncle's most desperate satisfaction was to flaunt tardiness and not get sacked. To flaunt tardiness in order to *prove* he would not get sacked. That is my best guess. By and large, I would say that my uncle was a good museum guard. Though he would hiss—I mean a loud *Hsssss!*—and shake his head back and forth at a museumgoer for no reason the museumgoer, or I, for that matter, could detect. Quite often, on some whim or other, he would retreat to the custodian's room, leave the door slightly ajar, then turn the radio up full volume. I could easily name a dozen such behaviors. At dinner one night in the hotel dining room—I had been a museum guard for over a year—my uncle said, "I don't much like working around people. Or paintings, for that matter. But what's my choice in a museum? I just do my best." Mostly, I felt that you had to shrug off his quirks, work around his irritabilities, try and ignore his violations, even when they were not at all comical. After all, he had all those years of museum guard experience. He had gotten me the job. I had learned a lot from my uncle.

I know this is leaping ahead. But as it still pertains to my uncle and Mr. Connaught, I'll tell it. Late one morning, roughly six months after I was hired, Mr. Connaught beckoned me into his office. He sat behind his desk. I sat in a chair directly across. "As far as your uncle is concerned," he said, "I know you've already seen much for yourself. With a colleague like Edward, you'd have to be blind not to. Seen his rather personal interpretation of how to carry out his guard duties. And I'm not sure what he has, or hasn't, told you about his years at the Glace. For example, did you know that Edward single-handedly looked after the museum for the two weeks I was in St. Rita's Hospital recuperating, never mind from what?"

"No, sir. I did not know that."

"Of course, later I found out that Edward had simply locked the doors, put up a sign that said CLOSED FOR RENOVATIONS, and taken a paid holiday. Spent I have no idea how. I was not amused. Especially in my weakened condition. After a very difficult night's thinking, I came to see it as the action of a man who knew his own limitations. You see, to Edward, the prospect of being responsible for the museum on his own must've simply overwhelmed him. Not to mention, he was drinking with great dedication in those days. I believe he's cut back a bit, hasn't he?"

"Some nights."

"Back then, we employed but the one guard. That was Edward. When the Board of Trustees was informed what

he'd done—one of them had dropped by midday for a visit, surprised, to put it mildly, to see the doors locked—well, I was put on probation for a year, Edward having been my hire. Very much a public humiliation. What's more, I had to argue fulsomely against Edward's being sacked."

"Maybe I shouldn't ask, but why did you keep him on?"

"Why *do* I, that's the question, isn't it? And right to the point, DeFoe, hiring you was my way of keeping Edward employed. Because we simply had to have another guard. Because Edward, paid full-time, you see, is at best half a guard. I mean by that, he's so often occupied somewhere outside the museum during working hours. Edward and I have what may be called a truce. We have an ongoing *truce.* Yes, I'm comfortable with that word. You have to first have a battle to come to a truce, now, don't you; in our case, hundreds of battles. Perhaps in a strange way, it's brought us closer. It's not a friendship. It's a—*vigilance.* As a museum guard, Edward—well, I'd started out with higher expectations. Let me put it that way. I'd expected him to practice the basic courtesies. To stay alert. To not quote Ovid Lamartine at whim to the museum's visitors. The radio personality Ovid Lamartine, whom Edward is so obsessed with and dedicated to. And to not eavesdrop and then take personal umbrage at what he hears. If Edward overhears an opinion about a painting he disagrees with—have you noticed?—he's quite likely to shout, 'Stupidity!' Oh yes, that, and worse.

"Even more directly to your question, why keep him on? I know that by nature Edward is not cut out for museum guarding. So, yes, how strange that my sympathies should so cloud my professional judgment, eh?"

"Well, I don't know what he'd do without this job, Mr. Connaught. He wouldn't go back to the train station. I know that much."

"I blame only myself. The museum is a small place. And Edward's shenanigans certainly can make it seem infinitely smaller. Perhaps you've felt this. I just don't know; I hired Edward without a reference or proper understanding of his nature. That wasn't his fault. He didn't put anything over on me. He just applied for the guard position. His nature, which revealed itself from day one on the job. And his nature keeps revealing itself with remarkable persistence, wouldn't you agree?"

"I couldn't put it any better."

"I mull all of this over now and then. Mull, mull, mull. But mostly the working days just pass."

"He respects you, though. My uncle does."

"He's said that?"

"He used the word 'respect.' We were sitting in Halloran's Restaurant when he used it."

"I suppose that's a reward for patience. Have I put you in an awkward position, hearing of my woes with Edward? I hope not."

"He's my uncle. He raised me. But I'll keep what you've said to myself. You didn't have to say it. You must've had your reasons."

"Being a museum guard is an honorable profession. From what I've observed so far, you're treating it as such."

"Thank you."

"Don't get me wrong, DeFoe. I like Edward, God help me. Very fond of him, in ways I've had to invent specially. Maybe that's at the center of my keeping him on. I've had to remain inventive in my sense of tolerance. It's just habit now, I suppose. Your uncle and I have worked in the same rooms for thirteen years. We've hung any number of fine exhibitions, and some of lesser quality. The Glace is our common address. And yet I'm as familiar with his life outside the museum—the exception being what reports of nighttime adventures he foists on me in my office—familiar as I wish to be. Not much at all. And I've never had Edward to my sister's and my home for Christmas dinner. Or any holiday otherwise."

Exhausted, hung over as he was, in a quick appraisal my uncle had seen right through me. "Another night of howling at the moon"—he was nothing if not crudely perceptive, my uncle. The fact was, the night before had been one of Imogen's and my worst in a year. The celibacy and quarrels. Plus which, Imogen had suffered one of her unpredictable, stupefying headaches. She had finally fallen asleep. But no sleep for me. I felt disheveled of mind, body, soul, everything, I suppose, a person can feel disheveled of. Still, again, my uncle was right: my guard uniform—black suit coat, trousers, white shirt, black tie, I *had* ironed my tie—was all neat, trim, and pressed, as Mrs. Klein would say. My black shoes were shined right up. Above my suit coat's breast pocket, my name tag, DEFOE RUSSET, was perfectly horizontal. At 6:00 a.m. in my hotel room, I had shaved, shortened my sideburns a touch, taken a bath.

Yet all morning I smelled Imogen on my skin. From having lain next to her, our chests pressed together. Her work shirt was neatly folded on her bureau. Imogen's bureau had six drawers. I had folded the shirt myself. She never would have folded it. All day I smelled her perfume, as well. Imogen's sweat, her cigarettes. And maybe it was frustrated longing that made this worse in particular, but I—well, it was more a floodtide of memory, from having slid my finger inside her that brief allowed moment. "Brief allowed moment" is a phrase Miss Delbo used during her guided tour of French military paintings; what, exactly, she was referring to I cannot remember. I think it was philosophical, about Life and Death in battle, what is given you can just as suddenly be taken away. In bed, I had *asked.* I had said, "Imogen, is this all right?" and Imogen said it was all right. But then she immediately cried out, as if happening upon an untoward incident, something she could not abide. She cringed. "What could you possibly be *doing?*" she had said. Her voice seemed to have the entire room's worth of distance in it. Still, it had startled me. She then drew the sheet up around her shoulders, pulled it entirely off the bed, and fled from her bedroom to the kitchen, the next room over. She sat at the kitchen table. After ten or so minutes I said, "Imogen?" But she only stiffened. An hour went by, then another. She smoked cigarettes and kept refilling her glass with ice cubes from the icebox, then with water from the sink. The sheet was still wrapped around her.

"Bad day at the cemetery?" I finally asked. You see, from 1929 to 1938, when she turned thirty, Imogen was caretaker of the small Jewish cemetery on Windsor Street, owned by the Robie Street Synagogue and located ten or so blocks from Citadel Park, downtown Halifax. In fact, the day before, when I stopped by the cemetery to see if she was up for dinner and the cinema, she had said, "New grave this morning. Mrs. Esther Rossman. That makes a total of one hundred eleven." Imogen was familiar with every cemetery resident on a first-name basis, plus the grass, weeds, shrubs all around. She took great pride in this.

Anyway, I had asked bad day at the cemetery because I was venturing out. I was attempting a conversation. Even though we had been intimate for two years, quite often I found I had to circle around her with words, trying to detect her mood. Even lying next to her in bed, pitch-black room, or a strip of light from her kitchen floor lamp showing under the closed door, she did not always seem directly approachable. And I wondered, too, why she insisted the bedroom door be closed when it was just the two of us there.

"It so happens," she said, "that today I got a lot done." She stood up, still wrapped in the sheet, poured another glass of water, sat down at the table again. "I got a lot accomplished. Working on my hands and knees like I do, DeFoe, is one of the only times I get to *think.* I mean, truly think. Weeding, or alone in bed in the dark. A washcloth over my eyes just after a headache; or a cold washcloth helping me to get rid of it. Sometimes, you know, it seems I'm only allowed to live life between headaches. I don't expect you to understand. Anyway, I can't really think when you're in my apartment. Not really. You don't realize it, but it's a decision I make: either I talk with you or I get the privacy to think. I imagine some people can think with somebody else in the room. I'm not like that. I should have canceled our date this evening. I really should have. Because, as we sit here, this very moment, I have a new, very, very difficult phrase to think over, and I'd like to get started on it as soon as possible. It's a phrase Miss Delbo said to me when she was visiting her mother's grave two days ago."

"Can I at least hear it?"

"You may, but you have to listen carefully. It's just one sentence, but it's got a lot of parts to it. 'Life is made up of dramas of the soul's estrangement and reconciliation.' My God, it is deeply complicated."

"I'd need a dictionary."

"Hours in the dark with my eyes closed is what it'll take to figure it out. Now maybe, just maybe, Miss Delbo was accidentally quoting someone. She reads a lot of books, you know. But to me, it sounded original. Directly from her. Miss Delbo has truly original thoughts."

"She's always struck me as intelligent, all right."

Imogen walked over and kissed me on the forehead. "Please don't take personal offense or make a fuss, DeFoe," she said. "But I do honestly wish you'd leave now. I'm not a bit hungry for dinner. We'll do something together later this week, all right?"

But I did not leave her apartment until 5:30 a.m. She shut the bedroom door and thought over her phrase. Then she came to bed. But we did not sleep together, yet we did

everything else. And all day in the museum I smelled Imogen on my skin. I thought I had washed all traces of her lipstick from my ears, neck, chin, nose, back, legs, and its fragrance may have faded as the day went by, but it did not disappear. Between 10:00 a.m. and when my uncle got there, I had taken up my post in Room C. I stood awhile next to the corner chair. I moved to the bench. I stood up. I straightened *Jewess on a Street in Amsterdam* maybe half an inch. I had taken notice of its alignment but not yet of the painting itself. In fact, I had taken only scarce notice of any of the Dutch. I looked out the window at the wharf. Rain clouds were scudding in over the historical schooners, the ones for tourists; you could pay a fee and spend time on board. My hair was neatly combed. I sat down on the bench again. I stood up. I went back to the window. I was agitated.

I went into the custodian's room to check on my uncle. He was still sprawled asleep. During the years we shared a hotel room as I was growing up, not to mention the dozens of times he had fallen asleep in the custodian's room, he often looked more unhappy and distraught in sleep than even in his worst mood awake. At first, this struck me as unnatural, but it became familiar, since he was my uncle. Now, in the custodian's room, his pinched, gritted expression of alarm, his mouth set hard, haunted me. It was exactly that expression he had had on the morning of July 23, 1921. The morning my parents, Cowley and Elizabeth Russet, died in the crash of a zeppelin at the fairgrounds in Fleming Park.

My parents had each paid 50¢ to ride in the gondola, to float and drift over Halifax, the harbor, then back to the park.

That day I had been sitting with my uncle on the porch of the Lord Nelson Hotel. My uncle was already living there. We had chosen the porch because he had read in the newspaper that the zeppelin's route included the sky directly above the hotel. It was a hot day. Coffee after coffee, my uncle was working off a binge, and I was having a sandwich and a root-beer float. He was just about to scoop a bite of my float with his spoon when a man—I remember he had a handlebar mustache and the sleeves of his sweat-soaked white shirt were rolled up to the elbows—ran up the steps and shouted, "Is there a Dr. Moore here?" Across the crowded porch, Dr. Moore stood up, removing his cloth napkin from his collar. "Here!" he shouted back, his hand raised like a schoolboy's. "Is it my daughter?"

The mustached man stood on a chair. He choked up mid-sentence, but managed to say, "You're needed at the fairgrounds. There are bodies everywhere!"

What happened next, I can never forget. I yanked at my uncle's sleeve. "I want to see! I want to see!" But he lifted me entirely out of my chair. At age eight, I was a slight boy, and he stood me right on the table. He embraced me so hard I thought that he would break my ribs. He held on and it frightened me. I felt the plates and silverware under my shoes, heard the near and distant pandemonium of voices, saw people running from the porch, which was empty of everyone but us in a matter of seconds. My uncle then held my face a few inches from his and said, "Do *not* move, DeFoe. You wait right here. You'll be fine. Sit down, and don't move an inch, understand?"

My uncle ran into the hotel. I kept standing on the table; it afforded me a view of people fanning out along South Park Street, into the Public Gardens. I saw a few men and women call horse-drawn carriages, waving money at the drivers. With all the commotion, all the people zigzagging and shouting, two horses reared, whinnied hysterically, and one started backing up its carriage; the carriage tilted, and both driver and woman passenger leapt out. I remember thinking, Something terrible is happening to all these grown-ups. The horse actually backed the carriage up the remaining length of the park; the driver was chasing it, waving his arms, which may have made things worse. An old pastry chef, Dunsten Brooking—my uncle often got him to concoct rum-filled cakes—wearing his chef's hat and spattered apron, hurried right past me, then into the street. I followed his hat bobbing among the rosebushes, until it disappeared across the park.

In a few minutes my uncle came back. There was a woman with him. I had seen her at the hotel. On occasion, my parents would drop me off and I would do my school homework at a corner table, while my uncle played cards with the bellhops and kept an eye on me. I had seen my uncle kiss this woman near the electric lift. She was very pretty, with red bobbed hair. But awfully nervous now. My uncle set me down on the porch. "Now, DeFoe," he said, "this is Altoon Markham. We're good friends. She's going to be your good friend, too, okay? And she's going to stay with you while I—. Grown men and women are needed at the fairgrounds. Do you understand?"

"I'm going with you."

"No, I'm afraid you can't."

"We'll get along just fine," Altoon Markham said. She was squinting hard, forcing a smile.

"At the fairgrounds some people fell down," my uncle said. "I'm going to help pick them up."

"Okay. I'll stay here. But tell Mother and Father where I am. I don't want them to think I'm alone. You know what they're wearing, Uncle Edward. You'll find them. My father has a new haircut."

"I know he does," my uncle said. He kissed me on top of my head.

"Sweet darling," Altoon Markham said. "I'll get you some ice cream. The cooks and waiters have all left, so ice cream's ours for the taking. We'll go be ice cream robbers, this one special time, all right? Cake, too."

"It's your birthday, isn't it?" my uncle said.

Altoon's expression changed quickly from puzzlement to exaggerated agreement. "Why, yes. In all this excitement, I almost forgot my own birthday. And wouldn't you like to celebrate with me, DeFoe? A little party, just the two of us?"

"Don't let him out of your sight," my uncle said.

He pushed a number of wadded-up dollar bills into Altoon Markham's hand. He looked at me sternly, lovingly, and with a hint of pity, which I noticed because I had never seen quite that look before, and it made me want to hold Altoon Markham tightly, even though she was a perfect stranger. "Altoon has a shortwave radio in her room," my uncle said. "It gets London—all sorts of faraway cities. Ask her to show you how it works, okay?"

"If I like it, will you get me one?"

"It's a deal. I promise."

"Okay," I said. But by this point both my uncle's and Altoon's faces betrayed enough to let me know that something very, very wrong had occurred. My uncle ran from the porch.

"Edward has nice shoes," Altoon Markham said, a statement so at odds with every emotion I felt at the moment that I relied on it.

"I was with him when he bought that pair," I said proudly.

"Which shoe store, Kerr's?"

"Yes, ma'am."

"My my—well, I'm sure you helped pick them out. And don't you and Edward both have good taste, then. Let's sneak into the kitchen now, all right?"

She took my hand and we walked through the abandoned lobby into the restaurant. She pushed open the white swinging door into the kitchen and walked to the freezer along the back wall. Opening the freezer, she took out containers of three different flavors of ice cream. She glanced around and found what she was looking for. "And there's my cake!" she said, pointing to a chocolate cake that already had candles on it. Of course, it was not her cake, there were only half a dozen candles. It was not her birthday. All this occurred to me much later. But Altoon and my uncle had promoted this lie in order to make the distraction more intimate. It worked, because when Altoon said, "Dunsten Brooking especially put so few candles on it to make me feel better about getting older," I believed her. My uncle had often intimated that everyone who worked at the Lord Nelson Hotel—bellhops, waiters, laundresses, chefs, desk clerks, cleaning ladies—were one big family. They knew secrets about each other, but the secrets never went beyond the porch steps, never got out into Halifax at large. So I felt that Altoon Markham had confided in me. I put my finger to my mouth and said, "Sssshhhh," like I would never tell anyone, ever. Holding the cartons of ice cream, she walked me over to the cake.

"How about we sit at an indoor table?" she said.

"Fine by me," I said. I looked over the flavors. "I'd just like vanilla."

She returned the other two cartons to the freezer. "I'll carry the cake, you take the ice cream. Pick any table that's neat and clean."

A few tables had abandoned lunches on them. I chose a table near the parkside window. Altoon set the cake down, scooped out ice cream onto each of our plates.

"It's the custom that I make a wish," Altoon said, "but guess what?" She reached into the pocket of her white smock, took out a matchbook, and struck a match. Lighting the candles, she said, "I'm going to let you make the wish, DeFoe."

"My stomach hurts."

"Why, DeFoe, and you haven't even had a bite of cake and ice cream."

"I know. But my stomach hurts. I don't want to make a wish."

"Well, eat an eentsy bit of cake. Then we'll go up to my room. I'll let you find all sorts of countries on the radio." She closed her eyes. "I'll wish something for you, how's that?" She blew out the candles. She cut a slice of cake for each of us. By this time, my stomach was cramping; I actually clutched at it, and Altoon bent over me and said softly, "Come now, darling. Let's go upstairs, all right?"

"I want my mother and father."

"Edward's gone to find them."

We went up to Altoon Markham's room, which, I remember to this very day, was number 43. I saw the big radio on top of her bureau, but had lost interest in it. I lay right down on Altoon's bed. It had a quilt rather than the standard chenille hotel bedspread. I noticed right away that Altoon kept her room homey. I was suddenly exhausted and fell asleep. When I woke up, Altoon was ironing a shirt. "Sleepyhead," she said, smiling. "I've brought my work up here, from down in the laundry. I was out of the room just a few minutes. I wouldn't have left you alone for too long. The bellhops helped me lug this stuff upstairs."

There were four or five baskets of laundry on the floor.

"You were out like a light," she said.

"Is my uncle back yet?"

"Not yet, I'm afraid. I mean, I'm not afraid, and he did telephone to say he'd be a while longer. Are you hungry?"

"It's dark out."

"It got dark while you were sleeping. You slept as if it was already nighttime, DeFoe. It surprised me. I thought maybe you were sick. I felt your forehead, but no fever."

"My parents were out late last night. I stayed up in the hotel lobby till all hours. My uncle was playing cards. It might have been the latest I ever stayed up."

"That explains it, then," Altoon said, humoring me.

"Probably my mother and father are still helping to lift people up. They're like that."

"Are you hungry?"

"No. And I'm sorry I ruined your birthday party."

"You didn't ruin it at all, young man. This is nice for me. Just the two of us. I think this is nice, don't you? A birthday party, just minus the cake and ice cream is all. You're very good company, DeFoe. Asleep and awake."

"My mother and father would like you."

"Thank you. Do you help out with the ironing in your house?"

"Not with ironing. Not yet."

"You're old enough to."

"I guess you're right."

"How about this as an idea? You give me the birthday present of letting me teach you how to iron? You might need to know someday."

"That's what you want for your birthday?"

"Good practical know-how. Someday a woman will admire that in you."

"My mother will, I bet. She'll be surprised I know how to iron."

"Actually, I meant when you were much older."

"That's a lot of clothes you have to iron."

"I do this much every single day, six days a week. But I have some seniority. I can choose which day of the week I'm free. It doesn't have to be on the weekend, either. I like walking around Halifax on a Thursday, for instance."

"You must do my uncle's clothes, then. Since he lives in the hotel."

"Yes, in fact that's how we met, Edward and I. He came downstairs to complain about how I'd ironed his shirts, and I told him they were ironed perfectly well. That was our very first conversation. Quite romantic, eh?"

"My stomach feels much better."

"Strong enough for a lesson now?"

"I think so."

Altoon stood behind me at the ironing board. Mainly she taught me shirts, at first guiding my hand as I ran the steam iron over a sleeve, back, between buttons. "You learn by doing it," she said. And within half an hour, I had taken over. Though Altoon kept adding detailed instructions, depending on the type of shirt. "Always check for missing buttons," she said. "Sprinkle on too much water, you can actually get deceived and singe a shirt." Things like that.

"How old are you today?" I said, folding a shirt the way she had just taught me, setting it in a basket. She was sitting on the bed, paging through a magazine, but still looking distracted.

"Well, I'm thirty-one."

"My mother is thirty-three. My father is thirty-three."

"Oh dear," Altoon said. "Excuse me." And she hurried into the bathroom, shut the door, ran the water in the sink, trying to drown out her crying. But she did not. I kept on ironing a shirt. It was a blue work shirt, the kind my uncle wore at the train station. Hearing Altoon's sobbing, I did not forgive myself for asking how old she was. My own mother had warned me, "Don't ask a woman her age."

When she came out of the bathroom, Altoon's face looked dreadful. "Can I just lie down on the bed with you, DeFoe? Darling. We've only just met. But I know your uncle Edward quite well. He wouldn't mind. There's nothing shameful about it, really, is there? It's as if I'm your aunt. You can think of it that way. Worn out after so much ironing, aren't we? Come over here, all right? It's nighttime. Time to sleep. If you can't sleep, just lie here with your eyes open."

I crawled over the bed to where Altoon had lain down, and she turned off the bedside lamp and embraced me. In the pitch-dark. Then, in a short time, by the way she was breathing, I knew she had fallen asleep. I lay awake awhile. But finally—I think because I had made myself sick and exhausted with nervous premonition—a few moments later, I readily slept. And when I woke again, my uncle was lying asleep crosswise at the end of the bed. I shook him awake by the shoulders. "What took so long? What took so long?" I said. "Uncle Edward—"

He sat up. "Oh, DeFoe." Altoon was sleeping soundly. "Nephew, I've got some bad news."

And then he told me.

I sat in the same place on the bed for at least an hour. I could not stop shaking. Not crying, shaking. I had the quilt wrapped around me. It was not cold in the room. It was a summer night. The only thing I remember saying was "I ironed all those shirts." My uncle went downstairs and returned with hot cocoa; he added a healthy dose of rum, which helped knock me out. The three of us slept with our clothes on, there, on the bed. I woke up once in the night, groggy, alarmed, and thought, for an embarrassed moment, that I had crawled into bed with my parents the way I used to when I was three or four. The radio woke me up early the next morning: ". . . the zeppelin fell in flames to the ground about 12:25 p.m. Terrified spectators—" I turned it off. I saw that my uncle had moved to the rocking chair. He was still asleep. Altoon was gone. The ironing board and iron and folded laundry were nowhere in sight. I went downstairs to the lobby. The newspaper, on its metal stand, had blaring headlines:

ZEPPELIN CRASH KILLS 18 PASSENGERS
AND 5 ON GROUND
Captain and Crew Perish in Accident
at Fairgrounds

The funeral was a week later. I remember that across the cemetery grounds another victim of the zeppelin crash was being buried. And when I walked with my uncle and Altoon Markham past that funeral, a boy about my age, standing in front of the casket, caught my eye, and we just stared at each other a fleeting instant. It is odd to admit, but I named him. From that day forward, in my memory, I called him Paul. I do not in the least know why. The name just flew into my head. That night, lying in my bed—and maybe this is just how an eight-year-old would think—I wondered if he had named me.

Then I was living with my uncle. On any average morning before the zeppelin, I would have woken in my own bed, in our house on Brighton Street, and heard my mother and father talking in the kitchen. Suddenly I was in a different life. Now I woke on the sofa in my uncle's room at the Lord Nelson Hotel. I slept on that sofa for the next eight years. My uncle sold my parents' house. With the exception of a few photographs of my parents and me together, mementos of my first eight years were stored in boxes in the hotel's basement, an 11' × 14' area surrounded by wire mesh. I continued on at the same school. I had the same pals. School nights I did homework at a table not twenty feet from where my uncle played cards in the lobby. I did my mathematics, my geography, my Canadian and world history. The bellhop Jake Kollias, an old friend of my uncle's, assisted with my geography now and then. "It's a hobby of mine, anyway," Jake said. "I've always loved maps. Always wanted to go on an expedition somewhere exotic. But all I do is go into the electric lift and come out again, and carry luggage for world travelers."

A year after my parents died, my uncle married Altoon Markham. I spent a lot of time with her. She liked to walk in the zoo, the botanical gardens. In the summer, she drove me out to the beaches to swim. My uncle would never accompany us. I don't think he knew how to swim. Altoon had the darkest red hair I had ever seen, or have since seen. Anyway, when she abruptly left for Saskatchewan and I asked why, my uncle answered with another question: "How could she prefer Saskatchewan?" Then he insisted we drop the subject. Another redheaded woman, Constance Marchand, replaced Altoon in my uncle's life, almost immediately, as far as I could determine. Constance might have been in my uncle's life before Altoon left. In turn, Constance was overlapped by Helene Fouset, who was quite tall and had black hair, and liked to sit doing crossword puzzles, looking up now and then to watch my uncle play cards. She liked the lobby as much as he did. Both Constance and Helene were employed by the hotel but did not live there. My uncle did not marry either of them.

What else?

No food ever in our hotel-room refrigerator; every meal eaten in the hotel dining room, Halloran's, sometimes in the café in the train station. What else, what else—? Sitting at a table, the lamp illuminating my schoolbooks, the musty hotel lobby, my uncle joking and arguing with the bellhops, the grandfather clock in the southwest corner. The sound of cards being shuffled. Falling asleep head down on the table. Waking to the sound of cards being shuffled. My uncle saying things like "Let me waft a little of Abigail's perfume over at you, boys, get you all distracted, and place a bet that'll keep me in steaks for the rest of my days." Abigail Broyard. I forgot about her. She followed Helene. She was very nice. And I remember, when I was fourteen, a new man was behind the night desk. His name was Zachary Barth. I was doing my homework one evening, Abigail Broyard was reading a book across the lobby. I heard Mr. Barth say to a woman who had just signed her name in the registry, "See that kid over there? He's at the same table every night. He's orphaned. Remember the zeppelin crash?" My uncle heard this. He immediately got up from cards, walked behind the counter, took Zachary Barth, who was much larger than my uncle, by the ear—I could tell it hurt a lot, his face was all squinched up. My uncle pulled Zachary Barth into the back room. When my uncle came out, he bet on a hand right away and lost a pile of loose change and bills, and laughed a little too loudly at his luck. Zachary Barth, on the other hand, did not come out for at least ten minutes. When he finally appeared, he held an ice pack to his jaw. "Get to work!" he barked at a bellhop. It was Alfred Ayers. But the woman who had just registered had gone up to her room. There was nobody's luggage for Alfred to attend. So he just went out on the porch for a smoke.

I dropped out of school at age sixteen. My uncle and I never discussed this. His response was to get me employed in the luggage room at the train station. "Now, what with your new job," he said, "you should think about a place of your own." And a week later I was living in room 22. My uncle had paid a month's rent for me in advance. Which he admitted he had won at poker. "What's the difference?" he said. "Alfred and Jake—they've known you since you were a nothing pipsqueak. All the bellhops, they would've pitched in for your rent anyway, if I hadn't taken it off them at cards. So don't get all guilty and philosophical. A month's rent, what's the big deal? I'm your uncle, so there's no strings attached."

Imogen Linny

My first day as a museum guard, September 19, 1936, was also the day I met Imogen.

At 8:30 a.m., my uncle stood by with an overwrought, somber expression, as Mr. Connaught, dressed in his customary finely cut suit, listed for me the basic courtesies. He had written notes down on a piece of museum stationery.

"Now then. Every visitor is 'Ma'am' or 'Sir,'" he said. "No exceptions, no matter how they're behaving. Should someone touch a painting, first off give them a polite warning. Most people, you'll find, are utterly surprised. They don't even realize what they've done. Often you'll find that's true. Now, when reprimanding a child, do it gingerly, then notify the parents, if the parents aren't standing right there. Sometimes it's a nanny. As a guard, you're perfectly within your rights to scold. Be a presence of authority." He checked his list. "Disorderly persons of any ilk," he continued, "do not get a second chance in my museum. Get them to leave, *directly.* Of course, use your best judgment. Avoid an argument. Arguing is beneath a museum guard. Keep your voice at an even keel. However, should things—and this happens; rarely, but it happens—should things get out of hand, retain Edward's help. Wake him up, if need be, but ask for assistance. Do you have any questions, DeFoe?"

"No, sir."

"Anything to add, Edward?"

My uncle shrugged. "He's sharp, Edgar. He'll get the knack of it, two, three days."

Mr. Connaught perused the list again. "Oh yes," he said. "Two more things. We've never had a painting damaged." He slid the list into his suit coat breast pocket. "And, lastly, DeFoe—we've never had a theft."

Then Mr. Connaught and I shook hands. I shook hands with my uncle. To me, it was a wonderful, private, professional moment. My uncle went into the custodian's room. We heard the radio come on. We heard my uncle switch stations, settling on classical music. With the radio, my uncle had unpredictable preferences. I went into Room C. Mr. Connaught joined me there. "DeFoe," he said, "I left one thing out. Because it's a sore spot, which I didn't want to mention in front of Edward. It's water under the bridge, for the most part. It was the incident of the *Cupid.*"

"*Cupid?*"

"I'll let Edward tell you about it. It definitely was not the best day in this museum's history. Edward was at the very top of his form that day. The incident concerned Edward and our esteemed tour guide, Miss Delbo. And several visitors."

"All right," I said. "I'll try to work it into a conversation."

"I mention it because it's the only time a complaint was ever filed. So, you see, you're now part of an institution that's earned high public opinion. Live up to it."

"I'll do my best, Mr. Connaught."

Mr. Connaught offered a taut smile, then returned to his office. At 10:00 my uncle closed the custodian's door behind him and walked into Room A, standing near the front window. He stared out onto Agricola Street, a rainy morning. Mr. Connaught unlocked the front door.

The instant Mr. Connaught closed his office door, my uncle walked into Room C. "Let's go to Halloran's after work," he said. "To celebrate your first day guarding. No matter how well or badly it goes. My treat."

"That's generous of you."

"We'll talk about this and that."

The morning went smoothly. Nothing I considered an incident. Oh yes, I had walked in on someone smoking a cigar in the Men's, but did not have any knowledge if it was allowed or not. Cigar butt in the toilet. Ashes in the sink. Nasty glance from the old fellow. Nothing. Nothing at all, really. Up to noon there had been thirteen visitors. I know, because my uncle showed me the clicker. Whichever guard worked in Room A held a little clicker. It kept count. At the end of the workday, the clicker was to be set on Mr. Connaught's desk. He registered each day's number in a ledger, balancing it against the amount of money in the 25¢ admissions box. We did not click in children under the age of twelve. My first day, I heard my uncle outright ask a young girl, "How old are you?" Her mother said, "None of your business," then put a dollar bill into the slot; even if the girl was over twelve, that still would have meant a fifty-cent donation.

Room C had an exhibit of twenty landscape paintings from around the world. The largest was, I would guess, 18" × 20". It was from Spain.

At about 11:30, when there was a lull in visitors, my uncle walked up to me. "What do you think about these landscape paintings you've been guarding with your life, DeFoe?" he said.

"It's like traveling. I mean, I've never been out of Halifax, as you know."

"All these trees. They make me want to get on a train to Toronto," he said. "I much prefer cities. I like when paintings of city life come in."

"Well, this one—" I pointed to a Dutch landscape by Jan van Kessel. I remember thinking I was about to pronounce the name wrong, but pronounced it anyway. "It's by Jan van Kessel. The fields and—"

"You don't pronounce the *J*—as in *j*unk," my uncle said. "Jan begins with a *Y* sound, is how you pronounce the Dutch. You don't want to embarrass yourself in front of a patron, DeFoe. You need to brush up on your foreign pronunciations. That's part of museum guarding. Having basic knowledge like that. The rest you can leave to tour guide Delbo."

"All right. Well, anyway, you asked, and I feel that so far it's been interesting. I haven't had to give out any warnings. No reprimands. And there's only one, maybe two, landscapes I would not like to see in person. I'd like to lie down and take a nap in that exact place by the river, in that Japanese scroll–like landscape over there." I pointed to the opposite wall. "With the white birds."

"Those birds look as if they could do you some damage, though. Some kind of heron, I think. Or Japanese crane. Elegant, sure, but with sharp talons, and look at those beaks. I don't know. I wouldn't care to fall asleep near them."

"It's a peaceful-looking place, if you ask me."

"Now, now, DeFoe. Don't get too personally involved with the paintings. Don't get all lost and daydreamy, stay alert, eh? We'll no doubt get a school group in here in a week or so. You've got to really keep on your toes with that."

"The Japanese one's very peaceful, but I'm not falling asleep on my feet, Uncle Edward. Plus, I had two cups of coffee this morning at the hotel. I'm wide-awake. I'm noticing everything."

"You want to take your lunch first? I suggest a sandwich from a vendor in the Public Gardens. The park's nice and quiet, I find. Of course, there's the old stand-by, the porch of the Lord Nelson."

But I had already turned toward the front door, where a young woman, dressed unlike the average museumgoer (in all my first morning's experience), overalls, a blue shirt, a black, somewhat threadbare sweater, work shoes, had just come in. She had red hair tucked up under a kind of flat knit hat, shaped almost like a beret. I admit, I boldly stared.

My uncle turned to see what I was looking at. "Oh, her," he said. "Yeah, she comes in now and then. Delbo tells me she caretakes the Jewish cemetery. I personally haven't exchanged two words with her. I did notice once that she rebuffed small talk from another museumgoer one day. So I thought—I recall thinking—two things. Dark red hair like that tends to drive me a bit to distraction. And that she and I probably have something in common. We don't want to be bothered by other people in a museum." My uncle laughed at his own speculation. Then he turned back to the business at hand. He reached into his pocket, took out a penny. "Okay, then, let's flip for who goes to lunch first." He flipped the penny into the air, then clapped it between his hands.

"Heads," I said.

My uncle lifted his top hand, said, "Tails. I'll be back in half an hour, give or take."

My uncle walked past Imogen and stopped near the postcards. "Mrs. Jonatis," he said, "want anything? Tea?" Mrs. Jonatis was the volunteer working in the bookstore at that time. She was about sixty and had what at first glance appeared to be a helmet of silver hair. She had a pleasant smile, was courteous to every customer. "I make it my job to read the inside covers of every single book in our bookstore, to make sure I know what the subjects are," she told me late that morning, after Mr. Connaught had introduced us. "It was Miss Delbo's suggestion." Even in that limited space, she seemed to bustle about. She kept the store in perfect order. She dusted the postcards and postcard rack every morning.

"No, thank you, Edward," she said. "I'll just nibble on my usual scone. And my mineral water specially prescribed. Doctor's orders, you see."

"Right-o, then," my uncle said, affecting an outsized British accent. He left the museum.

Imogen—though I did not know her name yet—passed right through Rooms A and B, and began looking at the paintings in Room C. I stood in front of the Japanese landscape. Imogen moved over in front of the Jan van Kessel painting. Then she turned and said, "You're new here, aren't you?"

"Yes, ma'am."

I had boldly stared at her, I admit. She turned away from me. "You're a little too close to the Dutch landscape there," I said. It just flew out of my mouth. It was not true at all.

Imogen stepped closer to the van Kessel. "I've visited this museum before," she said, facing the painting. "I know how to behave. I like looking at paintings and I'm a personal acquaintance of your tour guide, Miss Delbo. Professor Delbo. In fact, she herself suggested I come look at this exhibition." Now she walked directly up to me. "Since you're new here, I won't tell your curator how rude you are. Besides—." She looked at my name tag. "DeFoe Russet. Guard Russet. How did you mean, 'too close'? Too close for your comfort, maybe. But not for mine. I was quite comfortable. All I was, really, was lost in thought. Which is the best way to be about anything, paintings included, wouldn't you agree?"

I was tongue-tied, and recalled what Mr. Connaught

had said just a few hours before. "Arguing is beneath a museum guard." I did not say that out loud.

"I had a headache," Imogen said. "It went away. Now it's come back. Boy oh boy, a new guard, and he makes that kind of accusation, 'too close.' "

"This is my first day."

"How long have you been standing in this very room?"

"Three hours, about."

"In this Dutch painting, you see that rake leaning against the barn? I could use a rake like that. I often get very very practical ideas from paintings in this museum, besides just liking to look. I'm going to make a little sketch of that rake and see if my superiors can get one like it for me. It'd be good for getting behind bushes, between gravestones and the like. I work at the Jewish cemetery."

"I was told that."

"Told what?"

"Where you work."

"By whom?"

"By my uncle. He's the other guard here. Who told *him* was Miss Delbo. I haven't met her yet."

"My name's Imogen Linny."

"That's a nice name."

"I didn't get too close, Mr. Russet."

"No, in fact, you didn't. I was trying out a reprimand, but I wrongly applied it. My apologies."

"Would you mind guarding another room while I finish looking at the rest of these landscape paintings." She looked through Room B into Room A. "Besides, it looks as if your uncle's disappeared. You're the only guard now."

For a reason unbeknownst to me, I immediately said, "All right." Me, a museum guard, taking up a visitor's request to leave the room.

"By the bookstore would be far enough."

And that is where I stood, next to the postcard rack. Now and then I looked over at Imogen. She stood in front of each landscape, the Dutch and German ones the longest. Others she looked at for a mere few seconds, seemed to dismiss them outright, even shook her head back and forth. I did not know her at all. Yet, already, I wondered what her exact opinions were. Of the paintings. Of me. In front of the Japanese, she glanced over at me, then back to the Japanese. She took out a handkerchief, leaned forward, brushed something from the lower-left-hand corner of the canvas. It was a gesture that violated museum etiquette and yet was clearly harmless. Instead of uttering a word to Imogen, I said to Mrs. Jonatis, "I need a drink of water."

"Well, you know where the drinking fountain is, young man," she said. "Who's to stop you?"

The fountain was next to the bookstore. I took a drink of water, then walked into Room C. Imogen had completed her tour of the landscapes. "You may not yet be much good at guarding," she said, smiling, "but, Mr. Russet, do you know what? You're at least ennobled."

"How is that?"

"Just by standing all day in this room. You're guarding ennobled objects. Paintings. Drawings. Whether you like them individually or not— They're ennobled things. So guarding them ennobles you. Is how I see it."

"I take it that's a compliment."

"You may want to think of your job as ennobling from now on."

"I'm sure I'll come to think of it in a lot of ways."

"Well, I've made my mind up about each and every one of these paintings. I've got to get back to work now. I'm a working girl. I work at the Jewish cemetery, as I mentioned."

"On Windsor Street."

"That's the only Jewish cemetery in Halifax, isn't it?"

"Yes."

She closed her eyes a moment, sighed, then opened them again. "If you come by the cemetery some day after work. I get done about 5:30. Come with an opinion, Mr. Russet. About that painting there—." She pointed to the van Kessel. "Then let's see if we agree. If we agree, you may ask me out to dinner."

"I'm not supposed to have personal conversations like this. In the museum."

"Well, stop it, then."

"Anyway, what makes you think I'd want to see you again?"

"If I'm wrong, I'll know, because you won't show up."

"You might want to look at the Flemish drawings in Room A."

"Oh, I don't like those at all. I was here last week to look at them. Goodbye, then, Mr. Russet."

After Imogen left the museum, I got a rush of feeling about the postcards. I suddenly wanted to send one. I walked to the postcard rack to look them over. As I turned the rack, I realized that I did not have any friend or acquaintance or relative to send a postcard to. "We have a nice selection, eh?" Mrs. Jonatis said. "It's nice to familiarize yourself with them." She whispered now: "The young woman whom you were speaking with. That's a lovely, lovely young woman. Now *she*—as opposed to some I've seen on the walls here —*she's* a young woman somebody should paint a portrait of."

That evening the dinner my uncle and I had together started out just fine. We left the museum at 5:15 and walked to Halloran's on Robie Street, a small family restaurant with indoor and outdoor tables. It specialized in steaks. Steaks were not cheap, but we were celebrating. It was a balmy night for September. As we walked, I remember, there was a breeze with the smell of brine coming up from the harbor. We sat at an outdoor table. "Remember, I'll pay," my uncle said. "My treat. A new occupation's a big deal. And so is my covering the check!" He cuffed my chin, as he was wont to do since I was a boy. A waiter came to our table and we ordered right away.

"I appreciate that you're paying," I said. "I'm broke and I could eat a horse."

"We should've gone to Vizenor's, then. Rumor has it, a horse anywhere in the Maritimes breaks a leg ends up in Vizenor's galley."

Our steaks each came with a baked potato. We had ordered extra fried onions, too. The waiter held a bottle of red wine in front of my uncle. My uncle looked at the label and nodded his approval. The waiter corkscrewed out the cork, poured my uncle a little wine, my uncle tasted it and said, "*Magnifique!*" The waiter said, "Very good" and filled both of our glasses, then went and stood just outside the door. He slouched, one foot up against the wall, unlit cigarette in his mouth. "To your new job!" my uncle said, holding forth his glass. We clinked glasses. "May it change your life for the better!"

"I hope it does, too."

"We should eat together here more often, DeFoe. The waiters know me. They don't mind how badly I pronounce the French, and wouldn't say so if they did mind."

We ate and did not talk much. We went through the bottle of wine. We looked at people on the street. Finally, my uncle said, "It's wise to invest in an extra guard uniform. Top to bottom, I mean. Except shoes. You only need one pair of shoes, comfortable ones to stand in all day, naturally. I have two uniforms, as you know."

I swept a few bread crumbs from my trousers. "Where do you suggest I go?" I said. "Back to Mayhew's, where I got this one?"

"Sure. Sure. Except the tailoring is sloppy. With your second suit, try the tailor over on McKeldon Road. Hebrew fellow, name of Myerhoff. He has a thick accent, mind you; even if a word's got only one syllable. Polish, I think. Or somewhere near Poland. I don't know. Our stalwart curator, Mr. Connaught, told me years ago that Myerhoff's the best tailor in the Maritimes. He even brought in a magazine article called 'The Best Tailor in the Maritimes,' all about Myerhoff."

"I'm convinced. I'll get a second suit right after I'm paid."

"You need any money to hold you over till then?"

"No, but thanks."

"Make sure you cover your rent, then buy the suit."

My uncle ordered another bottle of wine. "So, nephew," he said, "since we're talking about this and that. Honestly, what'd you make of Edward Connaught's 'courtesies'?"

"I'll try and keep them memorized."

"That's a good idea, sure."

"For the most part, they sounded like common sense."

"Well, you're just starting out. Museum behaviors can be surprising."

"You've warned me about a thing or two already, remember? How's your steak?"

"Fine. Just fine. I was surprised to hear you ask for yours rare. That really surprised me, DeFoe, after a hundred well-dones. And don't forget, I took you out for your very first steak, when you were aged nine, a year almost to the day after your mother and father died."

"Ordering it rare caught me unawares, too. It turns out it wasn't a mistake, though. I'm enjoying it."

"That's good."

"What'd Mr. Connaught mean, the *Cupid*? He whispered something about a Cupid. He called it an 'incident.' "

"Oh, he did, did he?"

My uncle sighed deeply, then let out his breath in

shorter sighs. He looked highly annoyed. He took a bite of steak, chewing it with great deliberation. He ceremoniously replenished our wineglasses full up and, holding his glass, leaned back in his chair. Then, forcing a calm into his voice, he said, "Look, DeFoe, I *know* you're worrying over your new job. But believe me, it'll be fine. I had so much confidence in you today. Your first day; so much confidence I could go into the custodian's room, listen to the radio, no worries whatsoever. I'm proud of you. You've got poise. I mean that."

"I didn't think my worry was showing."

"It is. It is."

"Thanks again for getting me the job, by the way. I had no qualifications to speak of."

"Well, it's laughable, don't you think? Edgar Connaught must've been a bit hard-pressed to consider *me* a good reference."

"You're the only reference I had."

"I simply said you'd catch on fast."

"That's all it took?"

"To get the interview. See, I knew the job was going to be advertised widely in Halifax. I had to get a jump on it."

"I owe you a lot."

"I added to Connaught that it wasn't your fault we were related, uncle and nephew. I assured him we were different as night and day."

"What'd he say to that?"

"He looked relieved."

"You got me the job in the luggage room at the trains, too."

"If I don't know that, who does?"

"Seems jobwise, at least up to age twenty-eight now, I'm following in your footsteps."

"Small as they are."

I took a sip of wine, then a sip of ice water. "What happened with the *Cupid*?"

My uncle looked out-and-out exasperated. He stood up, motioned to our waiter, a young, lanky man badly in need of a haircut, I thought. He might well have been from Paris, France, the way he spoke French with the other waiters. He did not speak Canadian French, I knew that much. Halloran's was not even a French restaurant. They were lucky to have authentic French waiters, possibly from Paris, if that is what they were. Having got our waiter's full attention, my uncle pointed to a newly cleared table. He got the waiter's nod and stepped over and sat down at the empty table. I looked at the waiter, who shrugged, as if to say, "What can I do?" I sat down across from my uncle.

"Uncle Edward, are you having dessert?"

Our waiter cleared the dishes from our former table, but brought over the bottle of wine and the wineglasses. I ordered coffee.

"DeFoe," my uncle said, hand over his heart, "my apologies. Heartfelt. Here it's your first seven hours on the job. First day of guarding. Plus, your new boss piques your curiosity. *Cupid*. He didn't have to bring up a bad memory. I'm your uncle. I raised you from eight on. I am very, very proud of you. And then Mr. E. S. Connaught, in his own devious, and I'd add *sly*, way, tries to lower me in your opinion. Demote me in your opinion. You must've felt embarrassed on my behalf, eh?"

"Forget I ever asked."

My uncle sat in silence a moment, half brooding, half alert to the people walking by on the street. He glared at a few passersby. He could ambush a person with a menacing look; I think he worked at it, looking as if he was blaming somebody for something. The waiter brought us each a cup of coffee. My uncle drank more than half his cup, which was steaming. Then some excited memory caught him. He sat stiffly upright, loosened the knot of his tie, then slid his tie off. He crumpled it into his trouser pocket. Now he was ready to talk. "One time," he said, "we had this painting on loan. You saw it once when you came to get me for lunch. It was called *The Temptation of Saint Hilarion.*"

"I even remember the painter's name, because you told me I pronounced it wrong. Dominique Papety."

"Papety, that's it!"

"It was part of that exhibition on saints. Paintings of saints had come in from all over the world. Five or six countries."

My uncle now got so worked up, he shifted to another chair. "And do you remember poor Saint Hilarion himself?" he said. "He was leaning back against some rocks. Boulders. Holding out his arms"—my uncle now was demonstrating—"like *so.* He had on a brown robe. Thickly pleated. And there was a woman tempting him. She was standing right

in front of Saint Hilarion, tempting him. She had on a nightgown you could see through."

"More a silk chemise."

My uncle twisted up his face. "Oh, I see." He scowled, held his scowl for a long time. He polished off his wine. The waiter came by and refilled our coffee cups. My uncle slowly lifted his cup to his lips. He was working through a thought, trying to keep from blowing his top. I knew all the signs. The way he clenched his jaw. The way he would not meet my eye. And how he slowed his movements and gestures down to nearly a standstill. In a certain mood, he could take a full minute to sip his coffee, the cup already at his lips. A sign that he was truly irritated, which he was now. He could not bear to be contradicted by anyone, least of all by me.

"Are you an art historian now?" he finally said. "Whatever *you* call the garment, it was *see-through*. And what makes you such an authority on women's underthings? Silk chemise. What was her name, your former lady friend—oh yes, *Cary*. Was a silk chemise part of her nighttime wardrobe?" He had gotten overly upset and knew it, and was now trying to back up a few steps in the conversation, get on a different footing. He raked back his hair with his fingers. "As for the woman who was tempting Saint Hilarion," he said, "her see-through garment was knotted around her, below the waist. And she didn't have any top on at all. None at all, DeFoe. One hand was brushing back her hair, the other hand was like she was yawning—a big, cat-stretching yawn. And her nipples were pointing right at Saint Hilarion."

Our waiter, who had been standing nearby, now moved to just inside the door.

"There was a little table of fruit and wine between them," my uncle went on. With even more enthusiasm. "Out there in the wilderness, a table. The thought occurred to me—I remember this thought occurring: that Saint Hilarion lugged a table everywhere he went. Anyway, they were all alone, just the two of them. And Saint Hilarion could not avoid this temptress. And if you could put words into his mouth, he looked to be saying, 'No! No! No!' "

I read a Chinese proverb once; it might have been in a fortune cookie, in the Chinese restaurant located in an alley off Asphodel Street. *Open up enough doors,* the proverb said, *eventually a tiger will leap out.* Talking with my uncle, say for more than half an hour in a row, any subject might prove a fatal door. At our second table of the evening at Halloran's, I drank a little more coffee. I weighed my words a moment. Then I ventured forth.

"Miss Delbo had this idea about Saint Hilarion," I said. "I read it in the catalogue she wrote, when I was studying up on Glace Museum history before my interview. None of what I studied ever came up in the interview, by the way. Anyway, Miss Delbo said it was as if God was watching. I'm not quoting exactly here, just summing up her ideas. That God kept a close eye on saints, a closer eye than on anyone else. God was judging Saint Hilarion. And so Saint Hilarion *had* to refuse. Or else he wouldn't've stayed a saint."

"Oh, oh, oh, oh," my uncle moaned. He flattened his hands out on the table and seemed to be inspecting his fingernails, almost entranced by them. He then tightened his hands into fists, opened them flat again. "I've heard Miss Helen Delbo lead museum tours for six years now," my uncle said, his voice ratcheted down an octave, which put me on edge. He sipped some coffee, breathed oddly, as if catching his breath. "Saint Hilarion, nephew, was a *coward*! Or else he couldn't get his pecker up"—coffee sprayed from my uncle's mouth—"there's no nice language for that. And I'll tell you exactly what I heard from a little girl, not some intellectual tour guide from Dalhousie University—.

"One day in the museum, when *The Temptation of Saint Hilarion* was in Room C, a genius of a little girl, no more than age seven, eight at the most. She looked up close at Saint Hilarion's predicament. She stared at him. She stared at his temptress. She took it all in. Then she tugged at her mother's sleeve. She was so upset. She said, 'Mother, what's *wrong* with that man? Does he have the flu or something?' "

"How loud did she say that?"

"Loud enough to turn heads. I mean, this little girl was far too passionate for museum etiquette, DeFoe. Plus which, it was true, Saint Hilarion was pale as paper. Pallid skin, sunken eyes; oh, life was just too much for him at the moment. And he was out-and-out turning this woman down *flat*. He was volunteering for celibacy."

"It's a religious painting, Uncle Edward. Come on, you know that. You've stood for hours with religious paintings. Being a saint is complicated. There're books about it. I noticed one right in the museum book store, about religious paintings. Three hundred or so pages. Now, you have to admit, that many pages has to make it more complicated than whether Saint Hilarion had the flu."

"Flu or not—" And now at least my uncle lowered his voice, but he did not look around Halloran's. It was crowded and cheery. "Flu or not, I have *f*—."

I recoiled, clasping my hands over my ears. "Please—."

"All right, Jesus! *Slept with*—," he said in a mockingly dainty whisper. "Slept with women when I had a *deathly* flu. Matilda, who worked at the Lord Nelson? You remember Matilda. Well, she and I slept together five weekday nights in a row, and we *both* had the flu. DeFoe—look, calm down, will you?"

"*Me* calm down?"

"You're disagreeably out-of-sorts, what with your new job and all. My only point was, Saint Hilarion exercised poor judgment."

The waiter brought us five choices on the dessert tray, and both my uncle and I pointed to the pineapple upside-down cake at the same moment. "I'm afraid we only have one piece left," the waiter said.

"Why'd you offer it to both of us, then?" my uncle said.

I waited a week before going to see Imogen. Though I admit that I had thought about her every day in between. On September 26, I was about to leave the museum when my uncle said, "Want to go to Halloran's? Or to the train station. Our old boss, Billy Tecosky—William—he says you never come around anymore. He'd like to see you. The three of us could have dinner."

"I'm otherwise occupied tonight." My uncle used that phrase when he did not want to describe the actual goings-on in his life.

"What could it be, what could it be?" he said. "None of my business, I suppose."

"It's nothing yet. Nothing to speak of."

"Well, good luck every minute, with nothing to speak of. If luck's what you need."

"With this young woman, Uncle Edward, it might take more than luck."

"Well, nephew, the evening will either go well or badly. Save your life or end in disaster. Often, I find there's little in between. Or I don't want the in between."

"I'd just like to have a nice dinner. If we go, it'll be to Halloran's was my idea."

"Okay. I get it. I won't be eating at Halloran's, then. You can count on that. You will not look over and see your old uncle."

"I'll come clean with you, Uncle Edward. It's the young woman who came in last week. You said you'd seen her in the museum before. She's the caretaker of the Jewish cemetery. Her name's Imogen Linny, by the way. I'm going over to see her now."

"She's a looker. If she's a looker in those work clothes, just imagine—. Maybe I was wrong about her not wanting to be bothered by other people."

"I don't intend to bother her. I'd like to talk at dinner is all."

I walked across town to Windsor Street, then a few blocks to the cemetery. I had passed it many times but never noticed a caretaker at work. The cemetery was crowded with gravestones, on thereabouts an acre. It had an iron fence, a big supply shed near the front gate. It was almost dusk when I got there. But Imogen was nowhere to be seen. I stepped in through the gate. Then heard, "Why, hello, Mr. Russet." It was Imogen's voice, but more hollow than in the museum. "In the shed." The shed door was wide-open. I stepped over to it. "I hope I didn't startle you," Imogen said from inside the shed. "I'm just about done working through a headache. I sit in here to work through headaches, you see. Two minutes or so, I'll be ready to come out, okay?"

"Take as long as you like."

"Wander around a bit. There're some old stones here."

"Some other time maybe."

I stood near the gate until Imogen emerged. She walked over to me. We might have struck an onlooker as an odd pair, me in my guard uniform, Imogen in her gardener smock, dirt-stained knees, trowel sticking out of her back pocket. "Follow me," she said. "I have something to show you." I followed her through an aisle of gravestones. We stopped in front of one that read *Agi Delbo / 1859–1930.* "This is Miss Delbo's mother," Imogen said. "And next door here"—she touched the grave to her immediate left—"is my mother. Now, I don't have a Jewish name. Linny. My father wasn't. My mother's side was Jewish, from Holland. That's one reason I went to the museum. To see the two Dutch landscapes Miss Delbo said I should. She said some people harbor deep memories of places they've never actually been to—but where their mother lived. Memories you inherit in the womb, she said. When I was looking at

the Dutch landscapes, though, I didn't remember anything to do with Holland. I racked my brains, but all I came up with was a pair of tourist wooden shoes my mother brought back from Amsterdam, maybe when I was three or four."

"Where's your father buried, then?" My question somehow felt strangely intimate, yet warranted, considering that Imogen had introduced me to her mother in the way she had.

"Oh, he's across town," she said matter-of-factly, as if her parents being in separate cemeteries was quite natural. "When I was a child, I overheard them make that decision. One night after dinner. I was in the playroom. We lived on Kastan Street. I was about ten or eleven, I guess. I don't think they had any trouble being different religions in marriage. My mother went to synagogue. My father went to a church. Anglican. I accompanied my mother till I was about sixteen, then I stopped. They died when I was twenty."

"What hit me hardest, when mine died—I was eight. It was in the zeppelin accident, in Fleming Park."

"I *remember* that. My God! That was something."

"Years and years later, I thought, no matter how old you are, when your parents die, you're an orphan. Most people think of 'orphan' as only describing a child. But you could be sixty when suddenly it happens, you feel orphaned. That's hardly an original thought, I know. But it was pretty shocking when I first thought it nonetheless."

"So here we are, then, Mr. Russet. Having our second conversation ever. Now we've both been orphaned. One orphan plus one orphan equals—what?"

"You're right. It's a pretty dismal subject. I'm sorry. Dismal way to get to know each other."

"Oh, I don't know."

"Well—anyway."

"Sit down. It's okay to lean against the stones. I do it all the time."

I leaned against Miss Delbo's mother's gravestone; Imogen leaned against her mother's. We stared straight ahead, then looked at each other and burst out laughing. Though neither of us gave a reason.

"As for the painting by Jan van Kessel—," Imogen said.

"You pronounce the Dutch language very well."

She took off her cap and held it in her hands. She took the trowel from her pocket, put the cap on it, and spun the cap around. Then she set both on the ground. "So, then, what's your opinion?"

"On my first day at work—after you left, I looked at it a long time. I said to myself, Everything I know about paintings, really, is based on my uncle's opinions. He's the other museum guard. He's lived with paintings, I haven't much yet. In fact, at dinner that night he and I got into an argument about a painting, and it surprised me that we did. So what did I think of the Jan van Kessel landscape? That guarding it up close for the next two months, maybe I'll find the right words for how much I admire it. But I'm no art historian. I'm just a museum guard."

"Fair enough."

"What's your opinion of it?"

"Well, it's a peaceful scene. The swans. The river. The hills. When I said as much to Miss Delbo, she said, 'The river has terrible secrets.' "

"If they're secrets, how'd she know they were terrible?"

"I asked her that very same thing. That *very* same thing. And she said, 'A river never saves someone from drowning, does it?' I had to think that over a long time. I sat up in bed half of one night thinking about it. I still don't know all of what she meant. All I do know is that it disturbed me. That brilliant Miss Delbo looks at a river in Holland and drowning comes to mind."

"Whatever comes to mind just does. You can't help it."

"Miss Delbo's got a lot of ennobling things that come to her mind. Far more than most people, I'm sure about that."

"I haven't met her yet."

I do not know if I would be justified in calling our courtship usual or unusual. I had little to compare it to. But I saw Imogen at least two or three evenings a week. We went to dinner, the cinema, I walked her home. I sat with her at the cemetery on Sundays, when she earned overtime pay. We spoke on the telephone. From all that, I felt hopeful, but after six months had still not set foot in her apartment. One night I suggested that we join my uncle for dinner at the hotel. "I'd rather not, DeFoe," she said. "Not just yet. Meeting family is no small thing. Let's wait." My uncle, however, kept after me. "What'd you tell her about me?"

he would ask. "That I have horns?" I had to keep inventing excuses why Imogen did not want to meet him. He teased and cajoled. "What's her favorite thing—you know, *favorite*." You see, he always went into bedroom details about his "lady friends," as he called them. He would walk right into whichever room I was guarding and start right in, "Matilda let me do this or that," or, "Matilda did this or that. You could've knocked me over with a feather." He did not care if a museumgoer got an earful, either. Sometimes I think he preferred an audience. Whatever was or wasn't true, he was animated and seemed happy in the telling of it. Though he would stop—reluctantly—when I asked him to.

I did not have a lot of experience. The one woman I had slept with previous to Imogen was named Cary Milne. When I was working at the train station, one bitter cold night, slush all down the streets, I was assigned to carry this lovely but quite jittery woman's suitcases out front to the taxi stand. She was slim, with dark brown hair and a pale complexion. Very pretty, I thought, on first sight. It was snowing heavily. The streets had iced up. No taxi in sight. In fact, eventually almost an hour passed before one showed up. In the meantime, we sat on a bench inside and talked. Anyway, Cary's was the first woman's body I had fully seen, other than in paintings of nudes when I visited my uncle at the museum. We did sleep together quite often, each time to my grateful surprise, and this went on over about eight or nine months. But I did not ever feel much *more* in love with Cary Milne than I had in the first month of our courtship. And I never finally determined what I was courting her *for*, since we never got around to speaking of marriage.

She worked in a shipping office and I walked her home five nights a week from the wharf, and saw her on Saturday night as well. Then, one fine day in the middle of August 1935, Cary asked me to meet her on the porch of the Lord Nelson Hotel. At about six o'clock she walked up arm-in-arm with a man who looked to be about forty. "DeFoe," she said, her voice full of nervous cheer, "how nice to run into you here. I'd like you to meet Boyd Jessup, my fiancé. Boyd—as I told you—has been all over the world. As you know, he's just come back from a year in North Africa. I showed you his letters. You admired the postage stamps, remember? He's been all throughout Asia, too. He's—his *profession*. Well, he's in aviation."

"You never did tell me," I said.

"Well. All right, then," Cary said. "Boyd, shake hands with DeFoe."

Boyd held out his hand and we shook hands. "From what Cary wrote, I owe you thanks for walking my bride-to-be home some nights," he said. "Not that your city of Halifax is dangerous. Compared, say, to Cairo. Still, it was kind of you, old man."

"Think nothing of it," I said.

"Enjoy your tea," Cary said. Then they went inside the hotel restaurant for dinner.

That night, at the height of stupefying humiliation and self-pity, I sat brooding in the hotel lobby. My uncle was playing cards with the bellhops as usual. He sauntered over, handed me a glass of whiskey, and said, "This drink's equally paid for by three bellhops and your uncle. Sympathetic men, who sympathize. And who wish to say, 'If she wasn't worth dying for all along, don't kill yourself over it now.' Have a nice meal, on the house. A big steak dinner at midnight with us, right here in the lobby. To celebrate the fact that life doesn't provide happiness too easily." I looked over at the card table. Jake Kollias, old Paul Amundson, Alfred Ayers, each held up a glass. All of them lived in the hotel. The head chef, Maximilian Cheuse, who also lived at the hotel, all but burst through the kitchen door, carrying a tray full of steaming steaks, potatoes, and two bottles of wine. My uncle slapped me on the back and said, not loudly enough for the bellhops to hear, "You might feel like crawling into a hole, nephew, but go along with this for their sakes, eh?" I stood up and walked to the table with my uncle. With a dramatic sweep of his hand, Jake cleared the table of cards, poker chips, a little money. My uncle pulled up a chair for me. We both sat down. Max Cheuse served us dinner, then sat down and ate with us. Boisterous at 2 a.m., we disturbed a hotel guest, who came down the stairs in his pajamas, robe, and slippers, hair mussed up, face drawn from sleep. He surveyed the lobby and said, "You boys are loud, but who's there to complain to?" He had a good attitude about it, I thought. Jake asked him to join us, but he declined and went back upstairs.

Sometimes memory comes undisturbed. For instance, I can wholly remember Imogen's and my first night in bed, while so many nights after are in a fog. Individual moments come back, sure, but that first night is like a page I've memorized from a book. Up to that night, we had had intimacies, but with our clothes on. We had sat up late in her apartment, kissing. After two months of that, we took items of clothing off, but then stopped. On a number of such nights, I might then iron her blouses and knickers, and she might wait out a headache in the darkened kitchen, a cold washcloth or ice pack against her forehead. Or we would talk. Or listen to the radio. Or she would read a book suggested to her by Miss Delbo. A history book. Or a book borrowed from the museum. By this time, I had met Helen Delbo, had listened to at least two dozen of her museum tours: school groups, wealthy patrons, visiting professors of art, dignitaries, and so on. Or the Halifax Women's Art League.

I remember the night was February 7, 1937, because it was my birthday. We had dinner at Halloran's. "Your birthday present's at my apartment," she said when we were finished. "I made a cake—so we don't need dessert here." We left Halloran's and walked without speaking to her apartment, which was on the third floor of a building at 29 Quinpool. It had a bedroom, a cramped sit-down kitchen, a bathroom, and a living room with two large windows. Her view of the harbor was partially blocked by another section of her building. The apartment was not all that homey. But there was a row of photographs of Imogen as a child, others of an older Imogen with her mother and father. The bedroom was overfurnished, whereas the rest of her apartment felt sparse, even neglected. The bedroom had flower-print wallpaper. A four-poster bed, a bureau, a padlocked wooden heirloom trunk, a big oval mirror, an armoire, and three small braided rugs. A bedside table. A standing lamp was next to a wooden chair with a hand-sewn scene of nurses attending patients in an open-air hospital in India (to the left of the hospital structure was an elephant with a jeweled saddle). "That's an interesting chair," I said, after looking around the apartment. She did not respond, only looked wistfully at the chair. Then we sat in ladder-back chairs at the kitchen table. Imogen brought out the birthday cake. "It's got lemon frosting," she said. "My mother's recipe." There were thirty candles on it, one extra for good luck. She lit the candles. She turned off the kitchen light. "Make a wish," she said.

I blew out the candles.

We sat in the dark. The radio was on: piano music.

"Well, here we are, then," Imogen said.

And that sentence we both interpreted to mean we should be in another room, and then we were. In her bedroom Imogen put on lipstick, and we began to kiss while standing up. She turned off the bedside lamp. If I remember right, she took off more of my clothes than I did of hers, but we both ended up with none on, and she said, "Please close the door." Now, it is not just because it was our first time and a certain nostalgia is attached. Not just that. But as I mentioned, the memory of it remains clear; it was the most honest night in bed we were to have. Since we knew nothing about each other, naked, I mean, everything was a revelation. Imogen could say, "That's very nice," and I felt that it was meant. I said things, too. After we had finished for the first time that night, Imogen stretched out over me, her breasts pressed against my back, which I admit was heaven. We fell asleep like that for a short while. I remember, it was unusual for me to dream something wonderful, unheard of to wake and have it actually going on. Imogen said, "I'm going to find every place I left lipstick on you and leave some more." I did not say no. Later, we slept and woke again. Imogen lay with her head against my chest and gave me advice about my life in the museum. I did not mind at all. It was nice to talk in the dark.

"I've been thinking, DeFoe," she said. "When I get caught up in one or another corner of the cemetery, you know what I do? I purposely go to the opposite side. Somehow it makes a difference. You must feel Room A or C gets pretty small, I bet."

"Sometimes I go into the custodian's room and splash cold water on my face."

"How about this? You check your watch, and every fifteen minutes you stand in a different spot. Or guard a new painting close up. Or go bench to window. In whatever combinations all day long. See what I mean?"

She was kissing my ears, then my chest, and when I answered, I scarcely recognized my own voice. "It could really work. Because only half a year into the job—a job I might want my whole working life—already I was getting concerned, especially on slow days. It's not that you have to stay so alert when it's just you and the paintings. But a museumgoer could walk in at any second."

I felt Imogen suddenly sit up. "You might want to be a museum guard for thirty more years?"

"I might. What do you think of that?"

"You aren't proposing marriage, are you? Are you asking would I be willing to live with a museum guard? Are you?"

She moved to the edge of the bed.

"Hey, you just got tired of me and went to the opposite side."

"And you see, it worked. Because I'm interested again." She rolled over and kissed me deeply, reached down; we kissed more, and she slid onto me. "Oh, I was just kidding about marriage," she said, then moaned.

Truth was, I had not made a wish. No wish was best, I thought.

In the middle of the night I woke to find Imogen sitting at the kitchen table. The radio turned down low. Faint streetlight in through the window. She had a robe on and had eaten a piece of the lemon cake. "Darling, want a piece—it's my mother's recipe. Did I mention that?"

"You did. And yes, I'd like one."

Imogen put a slice of lemon birthday cake right in my hand; when I was done eating it, she sat on my lap and kissed and licked each of my fingers. I did not ever want to leave her apartment. "You've been asleep over two hours," she said. "Do you want to do it here or back in bed?"

"Here," I said. But Imogen had figured that out; her robe had already slid to the floor.

All the following day in the museum I put Imogen's strategy to the test. Except I made it every half hour, not every fifteen minutes. I went from the center bench to the window that looked out onto the wharf. I went corner to corner. I stood next to each of the landscapes in turn. After work, as my uncle and I walked to the hotel, he said, "DeFoe, I couldn't help but notice you were restless as a kid on a scooter. Now, me, I sit in a chair reading the newspaper. To conserve my strength."

"I had a new destination every half hour. It wasn't my idea."

"Whose, then?"

"Imogen Linny's."

"Ah-hah! Well, if it keeps you—on your toes, eh?"

"There were a lot of people in today, don't you think? How many, by the way?"

"Fifty-one. Good thing you were so alert."

"Good thing, yes."

"Have you two listened to Ovid Lamartine's broadcasts in bed?"

"No."

"The radio at all, then?"

"In the kitchen. Her kitchen."

"His broadcasts are important, DeFoe."

"I know it."

"When you listen to him in bed, let me know, will you? It'll give me some hope for your future together. It's nice you have someone. You haven't had—an amorous *companion*—. Maybe we'll all have Ovid Lamartine in common."

"I'll ask Imogen if she wants to listen some night."

"That'd please me no end."

"Fine."

"Does she have a radio in the bedroom, even?"

"She has one radio, Uncle Edward. She happens to keep it in the kitchen. I just told you."

"It's just a matter of pulling the plug, carrying it into the bedroom. You could make the time for that simple chore, between doing whatever."

"Enough, please."

"Radios at a pawnshop are cheap. To get one for the bedroom. Say you don't want to get up and go into the kitchen. Lying there, entwined. You could at the same time let Ovid Lamartine educate you about Europe."

We got to the hotel. My uncle went to the back of the lobby to sit with the bellhops Jake Kollias, Alfred Ayers, and Paul Amundson and have a drink. I went up to my room. I had an hour before I was to meet Imogen for dinner. Cold, snowy night coming on. I quickly bathed, changed into brown slacks, woolen socks, undershirt, dark blue shirt, gray sweater, overcoat, scarf, black shoes, galoshes. I went downstairs, stepped out onto the porch of the hotel. Then I set out for Halloran's. The wind spun snow in a dizzying fashion, right at my face the entire ten or so blocks. When I got to the restaurant, I saw Imogen through the window. She was at a table near the kitchen. She had on a charcoal-colored dress. More fancily dressed up than usual, even than for my birthday, I thought. I did not know why. I think she just wanted to be. I had eaten in this restaurant a hundred times before I had ever met her. Now its light was welcoming in an entirely different way. Imogen looked beautiful. Her two braids were held up by jeweled clips. I had seen the clips on her bureau. I would never ask if the jewels were real. They looked old-fashioned to me; they might have been her mother's.

It appeared that Imogen had only just arrived. The waiter was hanging up her coat and Imogen was blowing into her cupped hands, rubbing them together. We kissed hello. We kissed when we clinked wineglasses together. Over coffee at the end of dinner, she said, "We could still make the cinema. But if we aren't in bed together in ten minutes, I'll die." From there it became an even more ennobled evening.

I woke up at 8 a.m. Sometimes you can feel it snowing out, even if the shades are drawn. Have to get home, change into my uniform, get to the museum early, I thought. Mr. Connaught wants to rearrange some drawings in Room A. I got out of Imogen's bed, got dressed, found Imogen sitting in the kitchen. "How about a coffee?" she said. "I made a cup for myself."

"Please."

She was in her nightshirt and robe. She poured me a cup of coffee, and I sat at the table with her. "You didn't think I got you a present, did you? Well, I did. But it took us half the night last night, just to get to the cake."

She set a small package on the table. It was gift-wrapped in red paper. I opened it. It was a tie pin. "It's nice," I said. "And I need it. My uncle told me to get one when I first became a guard, but now I'm glad I didn't."

"It's practical in two ways. It'll hold your tie nicely. And it's what I could afford on my salary."

"Thank you, Imogen. I'll wear it every workday."

"You know that chair you admired?"

"The one with the elephant?"

"It belonged to my parents."

"You looked sad when I mentioned it, so I dropped the subject."

"My parents' names were Grace and Quinn," she said. "I was twenty-three when they died. We lived two blocks apart. I was already at the cemetery by then. I got the job when I was twenty-two and was happy to get it. I had no upper-level education to speak of. My mother was friends with the rabbi at the synagogue. I told you she attended. My mother had heard that the previous caretaker, Mr. Grenwald, was about to retire, the job was up for grabs, so my mother asked out-and-out directly. I was good at gardening. I'd planted a lot of gardens in the neighborhood, and even got paid for it sometimes. Mr. Grenwald tried me out. I apprenticed with him for a month, then he kept an eye on me for two more months. The summer went by, and he recommended me for the job. I think he'd been convinced it was a man's job, but then got otherwise convinced. And from the start I liked it. You know—Miss Delbo told me—Jews in the Old Country called the cemetery the 'Village of the Still-Living.' I'd like to be remembered by loved ones so strongly in that way, as if I'm still here, wouldn't you? I would."

"I talk to my parents now and then. I'm twenty-nine years old, and I talk out loud to them."

"One orphan plus one orphan equals what, do you think?"

"Just us sitting in your kitchen. Nothing more or less."

"They died three days apart, from infections they got in India, my parents."

"India?"

"My aunt Maggie, my mother's sister. She was a nurse in India. My parents went to visit. Maggie never got sick. After my parents died, she did have a number of nervous breakdowns, she called them. She brought my parents back by steamer. India to England, then to Canada."

"Do you still see her?"

"Maggie? Well, she quit nursing and became a stenographer at the courthouse in Yarmouth. She went back to night school for it. I saw her quite a bit during that time. But then she married a bookbinder, and they moved to Vancouver, British Columbia. Each month I get a newsy letter. But I haven't seen Aunt Maggie in, let's see now, four years this past Christmas."

"At least you're in touch."

"I don't know why I keep this chair. I mean, it's as if they'd been sitting in a chair that predicted their fates. That hospital scene."

We drank coffee and did not talk for a while.

"Well," she finally said. "You don't want to be late for work."

"I'm in heated rooms all winter, at least."

"I do just fine. I keep very busy. I never get cold, really. Plus there's the café, the Fish & Chips. I get tea whenever I want. My hours are my own, really. As long as I get my work done."

"I better go now."

"DeFoe, happy birthday, yesterday." She put the tie pin into my trouser pocket. "Want to go to the cinema? There's an American shoot-'em-up."

"I said I'd have dinner with my uncle. That would be about 5:30. Want to join us?"

"No thanks. But I'll meet you at the Robie Street, seven o'clock."

"See you then."

"As for India. The chair, and all of what I told you. I just thought you should know those things about me."

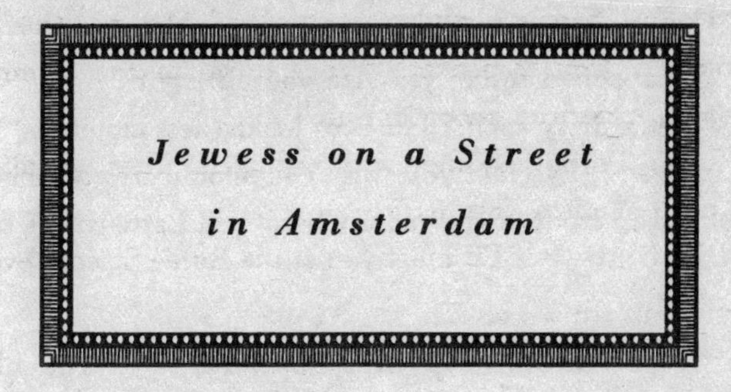

Jewess on a Street in Amsterdam

Back to when *Jewess on a Street in Amsterdam* arrived at the museum. Actually, the day after: September 6, 1938. My uncle did not get to work until eleven o'clock. I was in Room C. My uncle tucked himself behind the wall dividing rooms B and C, held out his arm, and waved a woman's undergarment; "knickers," he had raised me to call them. He tossed the knickers on the floor of Room C. They landed near my feet. He walked into Room C and collapsed to the floor.

Down on my knees, I slapped my uncle's cheek, lifted him a little by his shirt, slapped him again. He groaned and opened his eyes. "Smelling salts," he said.

"I don't happen to have any."

He clutched my lapel, breathed sourly into my face. "Did you hear Ovid Lamartine's broadcast last night?" he said. He was nearly sobbing.

"I caught some of it."

"Were you with Imogen?"

"I happened to be, yes. Are you all right?"

"Just a dizzy spell." His eyes looked less clouded. "You and Imogen—I've *told* you this. You should be goddamned transfixed in front of the radio when Ovid Lamartine's talking."

"Well, we weren't."

"It's all heating up in Europe, he says. The black shroud is about to descend. National Socialist Shithead Party. Listen, nephew. Last night Ovid Lamartine predicted Canada will go to war. Not tomorrow, maybe. Not the next day or next year, even. But eventually. And it'll be with Germany again. Canada in good conscience will not be able to stay out of a world war. DeFoe, my only nephew, you're a young man. You'll be called up to serve."

"I'll serve, then. Do you think Mr. Connaught would hold my job for me if I came back? I might do you proud in Europe. Did you ever think of that?"

"DeFoe, if you take life seriously, you take Ovid Lamartine seriously. I still cough from mustard gas, the Great War."

"You told me that. Though I've never personally heard your mustard-gas cough."

"You've heard it. You just didn't recognize it as such."

"I've seen your uniform, though. Uncle Edward, maybe Ovid Lamartine's wrong this time. I know he's in the thick of it over in Europe. But maybe his fortune-telling's a bit off."

"No sir. Never. Mark my word. You'll have to leave Canada. You're my only nephew, my bloodline once removed. Your father would never forgive me if I let you die in Europe. Or your mother. She wouldn't forgive me, either."

"You're talking through your hat."

"The hell I am. If there's a conscription, I'll put you on an airplane and sit next to you. Where'd that one painter go, an exotic South Seas island? Gauguin. The native women posed naked for him; wasn't it Tahiti? You could go to Tahiti. That's far enough out of Canada."

"Can you sit up?"

"I think so."

My uncle lifted himself to a sitting position, then more or less shinnied up my legs. He was wobbly on his feet. "Not a lot of people realize," he said, "but Canadians were in the mustard-gas trenches." He took a few uncertain steps, then leaned against the wall between two Dutch paintings. "Where's Connaught?"

"Over to Dartmouth. He's not due back till mid-afternoon."

"Get me a glass of water, will you?"

Praying that no museumgoer showed up, I went into the custodian's room, turned the spigot, waited for the rust to clear, then filled a coffee mug. I brought the mug to my uncle. I picked up the knickers. My uncle saw me stuff them into my suit-coat pocket.

"And how was your evening last night, DeFoe?" he said. He drank the water, dribbling some down his shirt. "What did you do with Imogen, and where's your souvenir of it? I brought *you* a souvenir from my evening, now, didn't I?"

"A dead mouse on the stoop to show me a night's work, eh?"

"Now, now. Mine was named—Natalie." He pronounced the name slowly, holding the last vowel as if it had permanently shaped his mouth a different way. "French-made, directly from France, Natalie is. First, I played cards with the bellhops, as per usual. Nothing new in that now, is there? Routine's my life's blood. Later, I had dinner with Natalie, right in the hotel. Lovebirds right out honest in front of everyone, waiters, cooks, bellhops, people she sees every day, since she's a housekeeper. Responsible for the top three floors of the hotel, which job is nothing to sniff at. She's given room and board. We went into her room. We shared a small bottle. We shared a bath."

"Do I have to hear this?"

"We shared a bath. She has a radio next to her bed. We didn't turn the radio on just yet. First, we conjoined. I fell right asleep. When I woke up, I heard Ovid Lamartine's voice. I know his voice better than I know my own. I sat up and listened to the rest of the broadcast, right on to the end. National Socialist bungholes. Bastards, DeFoe. Ovid was in Brussels. It was one of his bravest reports yet. I fear for his life. I had the covers pulled up to my neck on my side of the bed, but bless her heart, Natalie did not on her side. She wanted to—I mean, she reached over for me. But what Ovid Lamartine was saying upset me too much."

My uncle handed me the empty mug. His fingers had smudged up the wall between paintings.

"Some men shrink on the vine because of alcohol," he said. "Me, it's because of radio news that's horrific. I went

limp as a sardine in a can, nephew, and Natalie leaned over and unplugged the radio. Which, for all my being upset, was still a lovely sight to behold. But the thing is, I do not allow Ovid Lamartine to be interrupted. Her radio or not, it doesn't matter. So I said to Natalie, 'Do not cut Ovid Lamartine off like that ever again.' *Jesus,* mid-broadcast like that. Natalie went in for a cooling-off bath. I plugged the radio back in. Through the door she said, 'You have me here, and you have the radio, and you made your choice. When the broadcast is done, get out.' As she soaked—and I respected how she handled the situation—Ovid Lamartine proceeded to scare the hell out of me. Things heating up in Europe. Which made me take out another bottle. Which put me in the condition you now see in front of you."

"Thanks for sparing me every little detail, Uncle Edward."

"I've constantly told you the facts of life, since you were eight."

"Look at you. Reeking, and there's money stuffed into your pockets here."

"I must've won at cards. I'm a regular at cards with the bellhops, you know."

"If there's one thing I know, it's that."

"I'm familiar at the Lord Nelson. Who are you familiar with, DeFoe? The bellhops and waiters know you, sure, but otherwise, who else? Who are your friends? You never mention friends. Except for me. Except for Imogen Linny. For how long have you two been associated? Two years, about. Am I right? And from what you tell me, as a friend she's doubtful. Unreliable; because what kind of friend could she be, doesn't let you sleep with her on a regular basis? I mean, take Natalie, for instance? She hates the radio, but she's my friend. Imogen does not let you sleep with her, am I correct?"

"Imogen is none of your business."

"Why won't you ever answer that question? It's a simple yes or no. It's got no philosophical implications whatsoever, that question."

He slumped back to the floor. "Put the CLOSED sign on the door," he said. "Then let me sleep for an hour, I'll revive. DeFoe, just do it!"

He shook his head as if profoundly disappointed that I could not grasp how tormented he was over Ovid Lamartine's broadcast. Or how difficult was the compromise he had to make, sleeping with Natalie, a woman who could not sympathetically share the radio with him. How it all disturbed him so deeply. And he was right; all I really saw at the moment was the need to get my uncle cleaned up before Mr. Connaught got back. I knew my uncle's expressions. From the floor, he viewed me with a kind of hopeless disgust. He took off his suit coat and wadded it up into a pillow, turned his face away, stretched out, and almost instantly dozed off. I took the money from his pockets and counted it. One hundred eight dollars. That was close to three months' hotel rent, if he used it for that. I stacked the bills neatly, then tucked them into my back pocket. I went into Mr. Connaught's office, took the CLOSED sign from its peg. I double-checked Mr. Connaught's desk calendar: yes, just as I remembered, there was a school group scheduled for the afternoon, to be led by Miss Delbo. I walked over and

hung the CLOSED sign face-out on the entrance-door window. I thought, Why not just roll my uncle into the custodian's room, keep the museum open. Because what if an important patron should stop by? Yet I just walked back to Room C and let my uncle sleep.

For the next hour, almost exactly until 12:25 by my watch, I perused the Dutch paintings. I heard rain on the roof; the museum's outside brick walls needed to be scrubbed, dirty rivulets of water ran down the windows and I knew would dry in streaks.

Six of the Dutch paintings were still lifes; pleasant enough was my private opinion. Bowls of fruit, vases, bottles, a partridge hung on a nail by twine. And there was one called *Self-portrait in Artist's Studio*, by Cees Rietveld. I studied the tables; there were six different kinds of Dutch tables, and I noted how each was constructed, their fine tooling, the whorls of wood, enviable craftsmanship, all of which was the best part of the still lifes for me. The still lifes neither made me stifle yawns nor feel suddenly more alert; they would be reliable companions in the museum, all the hours I would be spending in their company. I did not expect any real surprises from them. *Still Life with Pears*, for instance, did not make me see pears in a new way, or actually get hungry for a pear. "If a viewer doesn't respond to a painting," Miss Delbo said during a tour, "the fault is not the painting's." Well, with these particular Dutch still lifes, I therefore felt at fault.

The largest of the paintings, 3' × 4', was called *Sunday Flower Market*. I do not have the advantage of Miss Delbo's vocabulary, but this painting, first glance onward, caused me all kinds of upset. I knew from the start that guarding it was going to be difficult.

The average museum visitor might not realize it but at times a guard takes a painting very personally. It happens now and then. Of course, with my uncle, he took every painting personally; he took every minute of every day personally, paintings included. My uncle and I got together with a group of guards from other museums two or three times a year. Usually, we would meet at a pub near the wharf. Just for a bowl of soup, mugs of ale, conversation. Naturally, the subject of standing all day with paintings came up. "Sometimes you just can't help that a painting offends," a guard named Ivan Kirsten said one night, eight or nine museum guards at the table. Ivan worked at the Dalhousie University museum; it had some French and Spanish drawings, and African tribal sculptures, plus some paintings by professors.

"The flip side of that is sometimes true, too," Mitchell Down said. He was a guard from Toronto who had retired to his wife's family home in Halifax and who joined us for all our get-togethers. "There was a nude in my museum in Toronto. I think she was Italian. My God, but she required me to constantly daydream I was taking a cold shower!"

There was laughter all around, but I knew what both Ivan and Mitchell meant. As a guard, you had emotions. You got to know paintings better than you got to know most people in your life. Speaking for myself. Though, of course, I did not have a wife or children, as many of the guards did.

Anyway, when I first stepped back, then up close to

scrutinize *Sunday Flower Market*, a current of anxious revulsion went through me. So powerful was this feeling that if it was not for *Jewess on a Street in Amsterdam*, I would certainly have asked my uncle to switch rooms. It would have cost me fifty cents per day, our agreed-upon price. This agreement came about because of a still life that had arrived to the Glace from Australia, a month after I began as a guard. It depicted a bowl of peaches on a splintery table, and above the table, nailed to the wall, was a kangaroo pelt. The kangaroo's head, I remember, kind of lolled to one side, and it had glass eyes. The painting was to hang in Room A, my uncle's room, for six weeks. But my uncle simply could not bear the painting. I do not know why he came up with fifty cents a day. But I found it a fair amount to switch rooms. I needed the extra money. And the painting did not bother me much at all. "Another minute would've ruined eating peaches for the rest of my life," my uncle said. That was his logic. It was fine by me.

"Being a museum guard requires personal restraint," Mr. Connaught once said, after I had offhandedly remarked about a watercolor. I do not even recall what I had said. "But naturally you'll form opinions about our works of art. Keep them to yourself. I'm not interested."

After five minutes or so of looking at *Sunday Flower Market*, my opinion was: Get me out of here. First, I had caught sight of the dwarf swathed in rags, with his nose pushed to one side of his face. He was crouched under a flower bin, over to the far left side of the painting. He was clutching a knife, about to stab up under the belly of a goat. The goat was harnessed to a wooden four-wheel cart. A boy—he was three or four years old, I would guess—sat in the cart, holding on to its sides, as if trying to keep his balance, though there was a wedge of wood under a wheel to keep the cart fixed in place.

This little boy had curly blond hair and a small cap on his head, and a pinched smile. He had on church clothes, I thought—the "Sunday" in *Sunday Flower Market* came to mind. At least they did not look to me like play clothes. Then again, I had never been to Amsterdam, so did not know what Dutch children wore day to day, let alone to church. You have to trust a painter's knowledge on such matters. (But I knew it was Amsterdam, because on the metal plate screwed to the frame it read, *Sunday Flower Market,* followed by *Amsterdam.*) The boy was holding a bouquet of red-orange flowers with big petals. His mother and father were standing next to the cart, the boy's face had a resemblance to both of them. The parents were dressed in their Sunday best, too. The father looked proudly at his son. He did not know that, just under the bin, something evil was just shy of occurring. One more second—I could almost hear the goat's bleating. That dwarf really got to me. I kept returning to him. Knobby skin, rag bandages, and he was also munching on a flower. His knife no more than one inch from the goat now.

The painter's name was Peter Lely. I am not a thinker here, only a describer—but, again, my most private opinion was that Mr. Lely had painted a waking nightmare, or maybe one he himself had actually had in the middle of the night. But what difference did it make what I thought? Miss Delbo's words rang in my ears: "Should you condemn a painting for displaying excess emotion, perhaps you simply don't possess enough emotion to match." She was referring to me—not on purpose. I wished that Miss Delbo was there. I wished that she would start up a tour. I could eavesdrop. I could get my ignorant opinions refined.

Wincing away from *Sunday Flower Market*, I saw that my uncle had worked off his shoes, rolled against the wall, yet was still asleep.

I walked over to *Jewess on a Street in Amsterdam*. I opened a window, breathed in the cool, rain-filled air. I closed the window. I stepped back.

The painting was about 2' × 2', I would estimate. It had a simple wooden frame, with a brass plaque stating the title, and *1931*, the year it had been completed. The artist's name was Joop Heijman. Joop Heijman had printed his name in yellow paint, in small letters at the lower-right-hand corner.

The Jewess of the title was walking in some old quarter of the city, though I did not know if all of Amsterdam had a similar appearance. She was pushing along a bicycle. Also, she held a loaf of bread.

The street sign read HERENGRACHT. A tall, antique metal birdcage hung in a storefront window, and the cage was reflected in a wavering twin in the canal—"wavering twin" is from Miss Delbo's description of a lamppost reflected in a puddle, in an altogether different painting.

Directly to a viewer's left, behind the Jewess a few steps, was a solid red-brick storefront whose window had a darker red awning, with black petaled trim. In the window were all sorts of toothbrushes. The toothbrushes made me laugh. They quickly put me in a good mood. But then I looked close up at the Jewess's face; I was sunk from that mood in a second.

Because it struck me as a face of desperate sadness. Those are my own words.

I stood as close to the painting as I could without touching it. Me—a guard. I reached out then and touched the woman's face. And I did not flinch back my hand or warn myself.

I studied her face. I thought, She is in difficult straits. I thought, Something is tearing her up inside. Joop Heijman knew some truth about her. I jump ahead a little here, but later, during a tour of the Dutch paintings, Miss Delbo said of this Jewess (I wrote this down; like Imogen, I often jotted down things Miss Delbo said, though I never told Imogen): "One gets the shocked sensation that a secret resides here. Not, perhaps, a secret the artist made up and then expressed accordingly on the woman's face and in her bearing—but a secret already there, in whoever the model was. *If* she was a model and not born entirely out of Mr. Heijman's imagination. Yes, perhaps the artist Joop Heijman caught a real woman in a moment of utter preoccupation, thinking about her secret. Therefore, he has painted that very preoccupation."

Whether or not Miss Delbo got such ideas from books about paintings or thought them up herself, I do not know. She was either right or wrong about a "secret," and Joop Heijman was not there to tell us which. But what I felt was envy. I envied Joop Heijman. I envied his knowledge of the woman on Herengracht, envied his knowledge about life in general. Because what did I know about, really? Museum guarding. And I knew about steam-ironing clothes and folding them neatly. I knew how to spend almost the exact same amount of money per month. The exception being if Imogen asked to go out to a restaurant and then to the cinema on the same evening, followed by a coffee. Luxuries I could ill afford but never said no to. I could not refuse Imogen. She made even less money than I did. And my rent at the Lord Nelson Hotel was six dollars a month less than her own rent.

I was not so much disturbed that the Jewess had several features like Imogen's, either, such as dark red hair, the shape of her face, which still showed something of childhood roundness that was contradicted by a tense, worried expression. No, it was more that the Jewess reminded me of how little I really knew about Imogen. Directly compared, that is, to how much Joop Heijman seemed to know about his subject. It was the first time in my life I was fully aware of wanting to be someone else. I wanted to be Joop Heijman. And I easily convinced myself, then and there, that Joop Heijman was in love with the Jewess he painted. Any fool could see that. Look how lovely she is. Look with what sorrow, tenderness, and detail he has painted her. If he was not in love with her when he started the painting, surely he was when he finished. Maybe he had lost her. Maybe he had glimpsed her and desired her in the worst way—Miss Delbo never used the word "wanted," she always said, "desired" when talking about romantic paintings. Modern romantic paintings, or paintings from other centuries, some with Cupids in them.

The woman herself was slim. Her hair had tinges of a lighter rust color, little spinnings of paint along her neck. Her hair was tied up, as if absentmindedly, in a black handkerchief. She had fair skin and very tired, drawn eyes, shadowed by sleeplessness—now that, most definitely, she shared with Imogen. She had on a faded brown dress with a black hem. It seemed such a melancholy dress for such a lively street, a sunny day. She wore black shoes tied up to the ankles. And she carried a loaf of bread. In my estimation she was twenty-eight or twenty-nine. Thirty at the most. On closer inspection, I changed my mind: she was not pushing the bicycle along but was standing still, contemplating a wooden sign, HOTEL AMBASSADE, that hung by two short lengths of chain out in front of a white brick hotel.

Did she not want to return to her room in the hotel? Did she want to rent a room and not go back home? Did she have enough money to rent a room? Was she even from Amsterdam? Did she have someone waiting in Room 5 or Room 9 or Room 15? It took me aback; here I was, a museum guard speculating about a *woman in a painting,* after all. And asking myself intimate questions about her. I went into the custodian's room and splashed my face with cold water.

Drying my hands with a towel, I remembered the two Jewish students in my middle school, level eight, I think. The two I knew for a fact were Jewish, I mean; they had mentioned it in book reports or some other presentation. I dropped out of school after ninth and have forgotten the names of many schoolmates, but theirs were Thelma Wolman and Harry Glube. And I realized I was acquainted with only one Jewish person in Halifax now: Miss Delbo. And of course, Imogen, whose mother was. (I myself did not practice a religion. I did not work on Christmas and Easter only because the museum was closed.) Of course, I was quite familiar with the Jewish cemetery by this time. I had built an extra shelf for the shed. I knew what Imogen kept in there. Trowels, shovels, spades, a lawn mower whose blades she sharpened herself. Gardening smocks, boots, gloves, seeds, flower pots, and so on. I had watched Imogen use a scissors to clip roses or daisies and place them in jars, which she set in front of neglected headstones. I had seen her nick moss out of Hebrew lettering. I had admired the shapes of the Hebrew lettering, noted the dates that told how long a person had lived. Some said things in English such as *Born in Poland, Died in Canada,* or something in Hebrew. Or a Jewish proverb, a poem, an Old Testament saying. But truth be told, it was a world, living and dead, I knew little about.

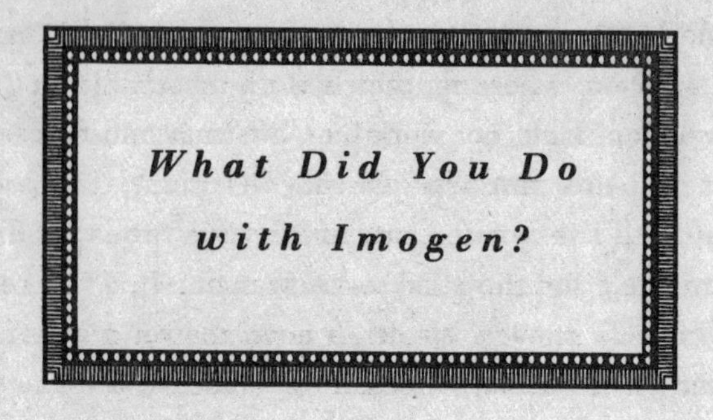

What Did You Do with Imogen?

I was lost in *Jewess on a Street in Amsterdam*, when I was startled by my uncle's voice close to my ear: "I'm a flawed man!"

I pushed him away.

"A *poisonously* flawed man," he said, slurring a bit. "Addicted to my flaws. At night, I can't be alone, for instance. Ask Natalie. If she so much as gets up for a glass of water, I turn the radio on, middle of the night, it doesn't matter. On shortwave, an announcer is always awake in some country. I need a voice. Or someone lying there not talking. Mr. Connaught thinks I whore. I don't whore. I have *companions,* who are whatever the opposite is of whore. Whoring is not one of my flaws, at present. But we all look for something to excel at, don't we, DeFoe? You, for instance, excel at celibacy with Imogen. I think about you, nephew. I think about my nephew's life. And that's my best-educated guess.

"We both excel at museum guarding, each in our own way, right? Now tell me, which thing should I put in my obituary? 'Couldn't be alone,' or, 'Was a museum guard against his better instincts'? Or maybe both. Maybe I should put both in. I've written out an obituary already. In case I'm struck by lightning or some such thing. I've even set aside obituary money. It's in an envelope, in my safe. You have the combination, DeFoe. I gave it to you a few years ago. Did you memorize it?"

"I wrote it down."

"You know what? Lying on the floor just now, I thought: A man should have a philosophy of life! What's yours, DeFoe? 'Everything neat and clean and in its own place'?"

"I don't have one completely thought out yet. And please, don't bring up again what you just mentioned."

"About your and Imogen's special arrangement?"

"You don't have any idea what you're talking about. You make something up, then act as if it's the truth and why can't I see it?"

"It's okay, DeFoe. It's all right. We all have to accept ourselves for what we are. But do you know what's the most cowardly—the *most* cowardly thing a man can say? 'I forgive myself.' That idiot, what's his name? Oh yes—Clarion Reed, who murdered that poor family down on Axel Street, then says in a newspaper interview, 'In my many years in prison, I've learned to forgive myself.' God Almighty, what a garbage mentality! Makes me want to vomit. It isn't up to Clarion Reed to forgive himself. I've worked to near-exhaustion at keeping my flaws front and center every minute of my own life. In order *not* to forgive myself."

I was about to interrupt, finally, when my uncle did an uncharacteristic thing. He peered over my shoulder at *Jewess on a Street in Amsterdam*; the painting held his gaze, and he went dumb silent. Then he said, "Now *that* is beautiful." He quickly shrugged. "Oh well, it'll be here, how long? Three months or so, eh? Hello, goodbye. The visiting paintings you love and the ones you hate stay exactly the same amount of time."

I wrapped my arms around my uncle, said, "Come on," and led him into the custodian's room. Once inside, he slumped in an exaggerated marionette way on the slat bench. Mr. Tremain had recently painted it park-bench green. I sat on the opposite side and looked at my uncle. I did not mind hearing him out a few minutes more, though I worried about Mr. Connaught. "I don't forgive myself," he said. "And I don't ask anyone else to. Right there, that's my philosophy of life. Unconditional unforgiveness toward myself. I have it down pat. I haven't done any big confessions to God to confirm it—in fact, I haven't set foot in church since your parents' funeral.

"About a year after they died, I did catch myself praying. But I prayed to your mother and father—sent them a direct message. Not to God. No, I spoke directly to Cowley and Elizabeth, whom I miss every day, and still think I see them walking on the street. I said, 'Cowley, Lizzie, if you see God, give Him my opinion that He fled. He fled. He let you die, and I don't forgive Him.' That was my prayer. Remember the funeral?"

"I remember it, Uncle Edward."

"What that reverend—I forgot his name. What he said: 'Redemption is not of this world.' Sitting in the front pew, you sitting next to me, wailing loud enough to bring down the rafters, I thought: I don't believe in the next world, either. That really puts me in a bind now, doesn't it? Because, sure enough, after they died, I often, *very* often, spoke directly to my own brother and sister-in-law in the next world I didn't even believe was there. That went on for a year. My mind was off kilter, no doubt about it."

"The bind you'll be in sooner than later is with Mr. Connaught," I said. "Come on, let's get you cleaned up."

I had shaved my uncle in the custodian's room at least two dozen times. And he had come to work dressed like an unmade bed so often I finally persuaded him to keep his spare guard uniform in the custodian's room.

"Get out of those clothes," I said.

My uncle tossed his clothes to the floor. Stripped to his underwear, he said, "Let's get on with it, then."

I lined up the shaving utensils, which I kept in a leather kit bag in the cupboard. I turned on the basin spigot and filled a small porcelain bowl full of the hottest water I could draw. I set the bowl on the bench alongside my uncle. He was sitting slumped over again. I locked my arms under his and lifted him upright. "Please hold still," I said. He shut his eyes. I ran a towel under the hot water, shut off the spigot, then wrapped the towel around my uncle's face. I took out the small wooden bowl of caked lather, dampened it, then swirled the shaving brush in it, squeezing the end to a wick. I attached the strop to the nail I had put at the end of the bench for this purpose. (I had told Mr. Tremain as much; I knew that he would have noticed the nail anyway.) I stretched the leather strop and stropped the razor.

Hearing the strop, my uncle threw off the towel. "Just end it," he said. "One swift stroke—." He drew his finger across his throat. "Come *on*, DeFoe! Show some ambition to be the senior guard, for goddamn Christ's sake!"

"Shut up, please."

I left the towel on the floor. My uncle's skin had blotched up under the heat. Leaning close to him, I said, "You could use a bath."

"You could use a day without one."

I lathered up my uncle's face.

"Natalie has sewn her name into her knickers," he said, wiping lather from his mouth. "I saw you put them in your pocket. I want them back. You have to return them to me, but there's no hurry."

I threw the knickers into the corner. My uncle's head and shoulders shook slightly with laughter, so I pulled back the razor.

"Please hold still," I said.

"The odd thing is, she used two *l*'s. I'm positive that 'Natalie' has only one *l*. Poor girl spelled her own name wrong. Maybe she was translating from French."

"I'm sure you'll correct her, when the time is right."

"So as not to insult her intelligence."

"You wouldn't want to do that, no." I held my uncle's face in my hands. "Try not to move."

For the most part, whenever I shaved my uncle, I simply imitated the barber, Mr. Ormond, whose barbershop was on Quinpool Street. It was where I got my haircut every Saturday morning at 8:30, and where I had sometimes accompanied my uncle to get his, on no predictable timetable. I more or less followed Mr. Ormond's routine, which I had observed in mirrors since I was a boy. I began just under my uncle's sideburn, left side facing me first. I worked to the middle of his chin. I then rinsed off the razor, stropped it, and proceeded in an identical fashion on the right side of my uncle's face. I tried to work at a steady, deliberate pace.

I had just dabbed more lather on his face and run a clear, clean stroke across his chin, and was holding the razor midair, when the door to the custodian's room opened.

Both of us looked over at Mr. Connaught. He was holding the CLOSED sign. He took in the scene, then calmly said, "I never got well acquainted with either of my uncles, come to think of it. Weston or Luke—Lucas. Both perished in the Great War. I've always felt that loss sharply. Never getting to know them."

He held up the CLOSED sign. "We're open again," he said. "Finish up now, please. We've got a school group shortly, and Miss Delbo. It's the school attended by the children of two of our most generous donors. It's nice you'll be clean-shaven, Edward."

He closed the door.

"Today's wages up in smoke," my uncle said.

I finished shaving his chin, evened out his sideburns, then toweled off the remaining lather.

"Right, then!" my uncle said, saluting me. "Same time, same place, how's next Thursday?"

He stood up, removed the clean uniform from its hanger, put it on. He knotted the tie in front of the small oval mirror I held. He returned the coat hanger to its hook. He put on his shoes.

I handed him the one hundred eight dollars. He peeled off two dollars and handed them to me. "Shave, no haircut—right?" I took the money.

My uncle opened the door, and with a mock bracing military gait, he walked out of the custodian's room into Room A. He halted, clicked his heels together, then sat on the corner chair. I put the shaving utensils in the kit bag, returned the bag to the cupboard, and stood in the doorway of the custodian's room. In a moment, Mr. Connaught walked out of his office. "DeFoe," he said, "take your lunch now, please. I'd like a private word with Edward. And cut it short ten minutes. I'm afraid I must insist. We have the school group."

Just as I left the museum, a cold drizzle began, and by the time I got to the sandwich vendor's three blocks away on Sackville Street, there was hail. Then it all stopped. I bought a lobster, lettuce, and mustard sandwich, plus a hot cocoa, then carried it all to the porch of the Lord Nelson. I sat at a table next to an electric heater. The bellhops Jake Kollias and Lincoln Dewis—Lincoln was half Jake's age—were sitting at another table, also next to an electric heater. "We're indoors all day, so it's nice to get some fresh air, once that hail quit, eh?" Jake said. "Care to join us?"

"No thanks," I said. "I've got things to think over."

"We don't," Jake said. "We're just eating lunch."

"What've you got there?" Lincoln said. "The sandwich."

"Lobster, lettuce, mustard."

"You're not supposed to sit on the porch eating what you didn't buy at the hotel," Jake said. "You know the rules."

"Turn me in, then," I said.

"What's important is that you *know* you're breaking the law," Jake said. "And can get away with it, on this porch in particular." He laughed, and Lincoln Dewis laughed.

"Jake thinks he's the house detective sometimes," Lincoln said.

I sat there musing about this and that. I had my coat and scarf on. Then my uncle's question "What did you do with Imogen . . . ?" echoed in my head, and as accurately piece by piece as I could remember, I went through the previous night.

I had gotten to the Jewish cemetery at about 5:30, almost dusk. The streetlamps were on. Imogen was crouched in front of a gravestone. When she saw me, she held up the trowel and waved. Then she went right back to work. She had her hair tucked up under a knit stocking cap. Looking at her, I remembered she called hers a "girl's body." She meant gangly, but I did not think of it that way. The first night we ever slept together, she remarked, "I'm nearly beautiful," when we were lying in bed. I had no clothes on; she had just put hers back on.

"Closer than you might think," I said, "to being beautiful, I mean. Just a fraction away." Actually, I thought that

Imogen was exquisitely beautiful, but I did not want to fawn, which, I had quickly learned, she hated. Hated to be too readily agreed with on any subject. So very early on in our courtship, I invented ways to almost agree.

I watched Imogen work the trowel around the gravestone which read, *Borace Rinzler 1879–1929.* It had been sunny all day. I could see that Imogen's face was sunburned. She had freckles on her chest above her breasts and would blush there easily, and it was where, in summer, she got most easily sunburned, too. There, and on her arms. But truth be told, in all the time I knew Imogen (and still today), when I dreamed about her, it was her face I saw most clearly. She had blue eyes that were not striking; they might even be called flat. "My mother had the same blue," she once said. "Like any girl, I wanted a prettier blue. But I got what I got. My aunt Maggie and a few of my cousins have them as well. Eyes are like any other bodily inheritance, DeFoe. You can't escape your family. And you—you simply make too much of my face. I let you kiss it more than's comfortable, because I know you can't help yourself. But when I look in a mirror, I see my mother and Aunt Maggie. I'd much prefer a face I felt alone with. You have a nice face, DeFoe. But I don't moon over it, do I?"

"No, that's one thing you certainly don't do."

At the cemetery I stepped up to Imogen, said, "Hello," and leaned down to kiss her on the forehead, which was smudged with dirt. But she held the trowel between us. I straightened up. Still holding the trowel, she rubbed her temples with her gloved hands and stared at the ground. "DeFoe," she said. "Darling, listen. I've been on my hands

and knees half the day. Now that's hardly unusual—but there's this headache. It's fading. But it's plagued me all afternoon."

"I'm sorry to hear that. Did you take any headache powder?"

"I didn't, no. It usually doesn't help. I've even had a headache get *worse* after the powder."

"I can get you a cup of tea."

"The headache's manageable just now, DeFoe." She touched the gravestone. "Mr. Rinzler here. His stone took over two hours of detailed work. Weeding. Gluing a cracked flower pot back up—see it? Looks brand-new, eh? I admit Mr. Rinzler's place looks neatly tidied up. Last year the Rinzler family sent me a holiday card."

"Did you get any lunch today?"

"Then there's that. On my lunch break I sat in the Fish & Chips on Quinpool, composing a letter to the rabbi, Rabbi Harry Esrig, asking for a new pair of gardening gloves. He's generous, so I don't know why I got so worked up over asking for gloves. But I hardly touched my meal. I'm not all that cheery. To top it all off, right when my headache was at its worst, who comes to visit her mother's grave but Miss Delbo. It was so upsetting, because I never want to have a headache when she's here. Because a headache's distracting. And I like to concentrate, to memorize what Miss Delbo says. Some of what she says, I mean. Not the chitchat. But things about life. She's got so much finesse. Me, I'm just clip, clip, clipping around with my clipping shears, while she's got a dictionary's worth of words on the tip of her tongue."

"She's lucky to have you to talk with, too."

"Oh, I'm *sure.*"

"Well, that's how I see it."

"You're sweet, but a lot of the truth sneaks past you."

"What a mood you're in."

"It's a mood, all right."

"Can I help you pack up your wheelbarrow here?"

"That would be nice."

Imogen gathered up her tools and put them in the wheelbarrow. She took off her gloves, tossed them in the wheelbarrow, and I pushed it to the shed. I put the wheelbarrow into the shed. Imogen cleaned off the trowel, a rake, a spade, and a pair of shears. She hung up the spade and rake, put the shears and trowel on the splintery table. She locked the shed, waved at the gravestone, "Goodbye, Mr. Rinzler."

We did not speak much on the way to her apartment. Opening her door, she said, "Well, here we are, then. I'll put on a kettle."

I saw a pile of clothes in a wicker basket on the bed. "Are those clothes already washed?" I said.

"Washed and dried—in the new machines, in the basement of my building. Help yourself."

I carried the basket into the living room. I went to the hallway closet, took out Imogen's ironing board. (I had given it to her for her twenty-ninth birthday. I had also given her two new shirts and a bouquet of flowers. I spent so much money I skipped meals over the next week.) I set up the board, filled a glass with water in the kitchen, set the glass at the end of the ironing board. I took the iron down from the closet shelf and plugged it in. I chose a blouse, sprinkled water on it with my fingers—for my own ironing at the Lord Nelson, I had purchased a pepper shaker to sprinkle water—then went to work.

Imogen sat at the kitchen table. She lit a cigarette. Watching me, she said, "Where'd that come from, your love of ironing? In all the time I've known you, I never asked."

"My uncle's wife taught me. She wasn't his wife at the time. I guess I enjoy it. Or I don't know the difference anymore, enjoy or not enjoy. Weeding around a gravestone or lying in the dark is how you do your best thinking, right? Well, for me, it's ironing."

"Your famous uncle has a wife?"

"I've wanted you to meet him, Imogen. How many times have I suggested it? You haven't wanted to."

"Well, there's the reason—he's a married man. I don't want to fall in love with a handsome museum guard who's married." She smoked her cigarette; I ironed. "Just kidding."

"Her name is Altoon Markham. She was a chef's helper and worked in the laundry when I first met her. I was ten when she and my uncle got married. She lived in the hotel."

"Where is she now, then?"

"Regina, Saskatchewan. She left less than a year after they got married. I don't know all of why."

"I bet your uncle and Altoon know why, though."

"I attended the wedding ceremony, which was in my uncle's and my hotel room. Jake Kollias—the bellhop? He was best man. A minister. The rings. Kiss the bride. But Altoon never lived with us, exactly. I mean, we never moved to a house or bigger rooms in the hotel."

"Let me guess. Uncle Edward liked to tiptoe down the hall late at night."

"Not always in Altoon Markham's direction, either, as I recall."

"That's why she's in Regina. Out-and-out adultery."

"He spent more nights with Altoon than with anyone else, is the only thing my uncle ever said. He never talks about Altoon Markham. And they never got legally divorced. I liked her a lot. I thought she was great."

"We got off the subject, though. Ironing helps you think, does it?"

"Four or five shirts later, I've come to a conclusion, or at least I've gotten closer to one."

"And what kinds of things do you think about, ironing, DeFoe? Just give me a for instance."

"Why we don't get along better."

"Oh, that. I see."

"Except I've thought about that through a hundred shirts in a row. Not all my own shirts, of course. But when I really need to think something through, I ask Mrs. Treacher or Mrs. Steig to let me do more shirts. Sometimes I even take other people's shirts up to my room. But with that subject—us getting along better, I mean—lately. It always ends up the same, doesn't it? What's the matter? It began okay. When we first met, we started out fine and normal. There was a directness between us. Some nights we'd sleep together, some not. It was going along fine, don't you think? Now, for months now, we get our clothes off and everything. Something happens. I end up here, you end up over there, in the kitchen. Ice water. Cigarettes—*thinking*.

I get to watch you think. Of late the best of it is, I get to wash lipstick off in my hotel room."

"I'm taking my bath now. When I come out, I'll try and get along better with you."

The tea kettle whistled. "I'm out of the mood for tea," Imogen said. "Want some?"

"No thanks."

She turned off the kettle. "The water got all heated up for no good reason, huh?"

"Maybe I'll have some tea later on."

As Imogen took her bath, I finished ironing four blouses, a pair of work overalls, a dozen pairs of knickers, a pair of socks. I had them all neatly stacked in the basket. There were towels and washcloths left to do.

Imogen came out of her bath wearing a robe. She saw the clothes. "You're good to me, DeFoe," she said. "In the ways you know how to be."

"I realize there're ways I don't know. But, Imogen, it's been over six months now."

"Since what?"

"Since we've been . . . intimate. You know. *Intimate.*"

"What do you mean by that word?"

"I shouldn't have said that. I shouldn't have said that. I should've said, not intimate *enough.*"

"Save yourself for your husband, my mother told me."

"You haven't. I mean, you didn't."

"I was twenty, and you know what I said back to my mother? 'What if there's no husband, eventually?' My mother hadn't expected that. She said, 'You've got a point there.' Then my father walked in. God, he was a kind man.

'What's the joke?' he said. 'Why are you two laughing?' And my mother and I just laughed so hard."

"That's a nice memory. You know what, though—we started out intimate, didn't we? And then it stopped."

"You never asked what I want or like. In bed, I mean. Eventually a man should ask a woman that. Especially if he can't discover it on his own. Miss Delbo said, 'The right question can lead to an answer you hadn't even dreamed possible.' "

"She was talking about paintings, though. Questions about paintings."

"Probably."

I went into the bathroom, picked up Imogen's shirt and denim overalls. I folded her shirt on the bureau, set the overalls in the laundry hamper. I do not know why I folded the shirt, since it was grass-stained at the elbows and needed to be washed. I should have dropped it in the hamper. Imogen took off her robe and slipped under the blanket and sheet.

"It's not even six o'clock," I said.

"A woman—right after a headache leaves—might like to have a man undress her. It's too late for that, so just come over here."

I laid my trousers, suit coat, and shirt across a chair. Imogen's robe was on the floor. "If you pick that robe up and fold it, I'll scream," she said. I took off my undershorts and got in bed.

Then Imogen began to kiss me. She smelled of lavender bath soap. The skin above her breasts had blushed from the hot water. As always, I immediately fell into kissing her back only exactly as hard as she kissed me. She kissed my ears, face, chest (I am remembering *clearly*). She kissed along the back of my neck, down my legs. She stretched herself over me. She kissed my ears; I could almost feel the lipstick shapes. "Turn off the lamp," I said.

"No."

"Should I shut the door?"

"It is shut."

Still lying on top of me, Imogen guided my hand, helped me slip my finger into her. She moaned, "DeFoe, that's nice."

"So I won't stop, then, all right?"

I looked at her face: dreamy, eyes closed, a sudden confusion. She pushed away. She pushed me away. "No!" She pulled the sheet right off the bed. She went into the kitchen and sat at the table. "What could you *possibly* be doing?" And I knew that our evening in bed had been completed.

Imogen then ignored me. That is really something to endure. Having someone you adore simply act as though you are not there. Less than a ghost. She took up a pencil and said aloud as she wrote on the back of an envelope, . . . *the soul's estrangement and reconciliation.* She wrapped the sheet tighter around herself.

"Oh, I see. I get it," I said. "Time now to think."

She studied the envelope like a palm reader. She did not look over at me once. After two cigarettes and a cup of cold tea, Imogen fell asleep at the kitchen table. It was a little past seven o'clock. I simply sat there in the bed and looked at her, my mind did not drift.

I got up finally and finished ironing all Imogen's clothes. I took her shirt from on top of the bureau. I got the powdered detergent from under the sink, washed the shirt in the bathtub, rinsed it, wrung it out, hung it on a hanger over the steam radiator.

At about nine o'clock Imogen woke up. "DeFoe," she said, "I'm not feeling too well. An old headache's back, or it's an entirely new one. I'm going to bed."

She got up from the table, went into the bathroom. I heard her rummage around in the medicine cabinet, turn on the spigot, then turn it off. On the way to her bedroom, she let the sheet fall away. Holding up a small bottle, she said, "New prescription. From that quack Dr. Lofgren. It won't help." She crawled into bed and in a short while was asleep again. I felt her forehead. She was running a low fever, I determined. I put a cold washcloth on her forehead. She was sleeping soundly. I smoothed the sheet and blanket over her.

I turned on the radio, which was on the kitchen counter next to the toaster. I listened to some music, then a news program, then more music. A few minutes after ten o'clock, I switched stations, locating Ovid Lamartine's broadcast. He had already started his report. In his preacherly voice, with its varied pitches of excitement, seldom calm, he was saying, "—this plague, this abomination of anti-Semitism, has moved, slowly but surely, from the German peasantry into the intelligentsia. Germans are ashamed of their past, intoxicated by their future, but blind to their present: Mr. Adolf Hitler. Mesmerized by this failed painter

Adolf Hitler, a genuine psychotic. There, in Germany—and I was in Germany just days ago—the echo of jackboots resounds on the streets at midnight. And midnight soon will shroud the midday sun. Darkness is descending. History is in the making. And I shudder to think what kind of history. Here is Evil, my fellow citizens of Canada. Mr. Hitler is Evil's death's-head puppet. Or perhaps we have entered a new era of unsurpassed horror: Evil is being puppeteered *by* Mr. Hitler."

I switched stations, a weather report, then returned to Ovid Lamartine: ". . . you see, we get, we have always gotten, the watered-down versions of Grimm's, and other fairy tales, from the dark forests of the German subconscious mind. Make no mistake about it, they are *cautionary* tales. Many of them, told in today's German households, warn: 'Do not go out of your houses at night, good children of Germany, pure-blood German children. Do not wander from your villages. Stay huddled in front of the hearth. The monster lurks nearby. Children of the new Germany, stay safe and warm under your bedcovers. Take heed. Take caution. Take *precaution*. Which means, take action against. And in the nightmare world of Mr. Hitler's Germany, this 'monster' is the Jews. The Hebrew people. Read Mr. Hitler's *Mein Kampf*, a degenerate book from a degenerate mind. In his twisted vision, the Jew is pariah. The cause of all troubles and woes. The Jewish people, a rich culture, a country people, an urbane people, also. A rich part of the European intelligentsia. In Brussels, I spoke with Professor—" I turned off the radio.

Ovid Lamartine's program was called *Dateline: Europe.* He was based in London, but seemed to be living out of a suitcase. He often began his broadcast: "Just back from—" Some European capital, or the home of a dignitary at which political high intrigue was discussed over dinner. In one broadcast he said, "I stand accused of bringing you more bad than good news. At times, and we are in such a time now, at times in human history, bad is disproportionate to good, and so I own up to the indictment. It's a fact of life, my Canadian brethren, that we cannot always control where the truth comes from, or how bad it turns out to be, or what it reveals about human nature." He always ended his broadcast: "Remember: as my grandmother always said, if you wish to make God laugh, make plans. This is Ovid Lamartine—*Dateline: Europe.*"

Looking up from the radio, I noticed that Imogen had thrown off the sheet and blanket. The washcloth was on the floor. I walked over and drew the bedcovers up around her shoulders again.

I fixed a pot of tea. I turned the radio back on, purposely stayed away from Ovid Lamartine. I lay down next to Imogen. Countless strange worries. I left Imogen's apartment at 5:30 a.m. No sleep at all.

That day in the museum, of course, my uncle had revealed that, while I had been sitting in Imogen's kitchen, he was with Natalie in Room 19 of the Lord Nelson Hotel. The same radio broadcast connecting us across the city. And that was the answer to my uncle's question "What did you do with Imogen?" It had been the kind of night that, no matter how familiar my and Imogen's behavior, I could never get used to it.

On the porch of the Lord Nelson Hotel, I finished my hot cocoa and sandwich. I left a small tip, just for the use of the table, I suppose, and wondered if either Jake or Lincoln would pick it up, like a bribe to the house detective. I glanced at my watch; with some surprise, I saw it was 2:18. I got back to the museum at 2:29. When I walked in, I saw that the school group's tour was in progress. Mr. Connaught was standing near his office door. He saw me, took out his watch, flipped open the cover, glanced at it, snapped it shut, slid the watch on its chain back into his pocket. I offered an apologetic look. I hung up my coat and scarf. Walking into Room B, I saw that there were about twenty children, roughly ages ten and eleven, I would say, and their teacher and two assistants. They were situated in a half circle in front of *Jewess on a Street in Amsterdam.* Miss Delbo was tracing her hand at a proper distance along the length of the canal. "I studied a map of Amsterdam," she was saying, "and this is the Herengracht Canal, which runs under many footbridges." I started toward Room C, but Mr. Connaught said, "I've assigned Edward that room in your absence, DeFoe. Just for this afternoon."

I wanted to hear what Miss Delbo had to say about the Dutch paintings, even to children. I would say "desperate" to hear about *Jewess on a Street in Amsterdam* especially. But I went into Room A.

When the tour ended and the school group had left the museum, and Miss Delbo had also left, I walked into Room C. My uncle was sitting on the corner chair. When he saw me, he produced a dunce cap he had fashioned from the newspaper. He fitted it over his head. It was too small. He pinched his mouth into a pout, then slapped his own wrist. My uncle could make me laugh.

"I'd just got out of my long consult with Edgar Connaught," he said, "and right away, there's the school bunch and that insufferable Helen Delbo."

"She's not that at all. I learn from her tours."

He did a mocking imitation: " 'Now, children. These Dutch paintings . . . notice the light . . . notice the shadowing. Notice the sadness in the woman's blah, blah, blah.' I stood there, though. A presence of authority."

"Sorry I was late."

" 'Tardy,' my boy. The word is 'tardy.' "

"Which woman?"

"What?"

" 'Sadness in the woman's—' *Which* woman?"

"What, oh, the Jewess—all right, now *that* observation I'll give Delbo credit for. But the sadness is hard to miss, isn't it? It's like telling those children the sky is gray when they can see it's gray."

"How'd the children respond to *Sunday Flower Market*?"

"I don't know. Connaught had called me back into his office to rake me over the coals a few more minutes."

"How'd it go? With Mr. Connaught, I mean. What'd he say?"

"He asked me what happened. He asked why, yet

again, I had arrived unshaven, slovenly, et cetera. Risking public embarrassment for the Glace. Then he docked my pay, naturally."

"How'd you answer him? I'm just curious."

"I tried hard to remember the truth. I told him about Natalie. I mentioned Ovid Lamartine's broadcast, how it tore me up. I spoke of the dark shroud. He understood that; he lost those two uncles. I generally caught Edgar up on my life and loves."

My uncle took off the dunce cap, unfolded it, and started to read the comic strips.

"I'll take you to dinner," I said.

"You'll pay? An otherwise poorly day ends with a miracle. Then for a drink at the Lord Nelson?"

"No, I can't. I'm going to try and see Imogen."

"Oh, oh, oh—"

"If you as much as mention her name at Halloran's—or do you want to eat at Vizenor's?—just even speak her name, I'm getting up from the table."

Next to the bookstore, Mr. Connaught snapped his fingers. "Get back to Room A, DeFoe, please. Empty of visitors or no, it's what I pay you for."

Mr. Connaught went into his office. As I was leaving Room C, my uncle said, "I've got to meet this Imogen sometime. I mean, a proper face-to-face, handshake introduction."

Miss Delbo

It turned out that Imogen and my uncle met two weeks later, September 20, 1938. Properly or improperly introduced, I would be hard-pressed to say.

My uncle had been only forty-five minutes late for work. He walked in and immediately said he wanted to guard Room C. I said I did not want to switch. We had six visitors all morning. I took my lunch from 11:30 to noon; my uncle's lunch went from 12:15 to 1:30. When he returned, he saw that there was nobody but me in the museum. So he fell asleep on the sofa in the custodian's room. When I looked in on him, his shoes were on the floor, the radio was playing softly. Mr. Connaught had a day of meetings outside the museum, which happened at least twice a month.

By three o'clock there had been only nine or ten new visitors, I cannot remember exactly. Then an old French-speaking couple came in, hand in hand, and went directly to Room C. I was guarding all three rooms. Standing between Room A and B, I looked at the couple. I would say that they were in their late sixties. They kept holding hands. Then I tried not to look at them, but was looking at them when Imogen came up behind me. She put her arms around me and laid her head against my shoulder. I was so shocked by her public affection, the tenderness, it took me a moment to realize that she was whispering, ". . . and Miss Delbo suggested I look at the Dutch paintings. One in particular. A woman holding bread."

"That old couple is looking at it right now."

Imogen let go of me, and I saw that she was dressed in her regular work clothes. Overalls. Black sweater frayed at the collar. Her shoes were caked with dirt. She walked over and stood next to the elderly couple. Without a gesture of acknowledgment or greeting to Imogen, the man and woman moved off slowly to *Still Life with Pears* and spoke in low, excited tones about it. The man put on eyeglasses, stepped back, and waved his outpointed finger in front of the painting like an orchestra conductor. The woman's speech was full of exclamation. It was as if they were remembering all the best pears they had ever eaten. It did not change my mind about *Still Life with Pears,* but at least I would now have the memory of them delighted with the painting. The woman kissed his hands. He kissed her hands. Imogen stayed in front of *Jewess on a Street in Amsterdam,* head slightly tilted to her left, brow furrowed.

Finally, the old couple went into Room A to look at some nineteenth-century photographs, an exhibition called "Faces from the Past," which Mr. Connaught and I had hung two weeks before the Dutch paintings arrived. It occurred to me that most visitors walk first thing through the museum to Room C, then work their way back to the postcards, then out the door. I could not possibly guess the reason, but it was fairly predictable museum behavior.

I stood next to Imogen. "Miss Delbo will be here any minute now," I said. "She's got a tour."

"The Halifax Women's Art League. I know. She told me. That's another reason I'm here. I've never been on a tour of hers. I'm looking forward to it."

"How did you manage to get off work so early?"

"I held off on my lunch break. But truth be told, I may not go back to work today. Nobody ever checks up on me, really. No one from the synagogue. They know I do my work. I've never played hooky, though, headache or no."

"I'm glad to see you."

"Give me a little time alone in here, okay? You don't talk to the other museumgoers as if you know them."

"But I do know you."

"Act professionally as if you don't, please."

"Fine by me. I'll be—"

"In one of the other two rooms, I bet."

I went into Room A and stood where Imogen could not see me. In a few minutes, however, she walked past. "I'm going to wash up," she said. And she went into the Ladies'.

Over the next five or ten minutes, the women from the Halifax Women's Art League drifted in, one at a time or in pairs. They each hung up their coat in the coatroom. They milled about, looking at postcards or the photographs,

not wanting to view the Dutch without Miss Delbo's guidance. The elderly French-speaking couple left the museum.

"Is there anyone to sell postcards?" a silvery white-haired woman named Mrs. Lightman (I had seen her often in the museum) said quite loudly. She was expensively dressed; her fox-fur piece had actual fox heads still on it, which made me want to laugh and cringe. It was a popular fashion around downtown Halifax. Finally, she hung up her coat. "You're one of the Mr. Russets, aren't you?" she said.

I looked over and saw my uncle peek out from the custodian's room, catch sight of Mrs. Lightman, and duck back in.

"Yes, ma'am, Mrs. Lightman. I'm DeFoe Russet. And I can sell you postcards."

"What happened to the volunteer?"

"That would be Mrs. Boardman. She's been ill, I'm told."

"Say no more. I was in the museum two weeks ago, and she wasn't here then, either. I know what that means."

"It means, I think, her illness has so far lasted two weeks."

"You're young. You don't know what you're talking about."

"Anyway, Mrs. Lightman, I can sell you postcards."

"Fine." She looked toward the front door. "Here's Miss Delbo now. A touch on the late side. But here she is."

Almost in unison like a school group, the Halifax Women's Art League—the youngest was at least sixty—said, "Good morning, Professor Delbo."

"Perhaps you know Mr. DeFoe Russet," Miss Delbo

said. "Be duly warned. He will be keeping a sharp eye on us. Stay safely back from the Dutch paintings. Unless, of course, you require a closer look." There was some laughter, although I think a few in the Art League could not quite tell whether or not Miss Delbo was joking. "Mr. Connaught, the curator of the Glace Museum, told me a curious fact. He said that quite often people who wear thick eyeglasses, when they first take them off, get disoriented. Their perception of how far they are from the painting gets skewed. Their sight might be blurry. So if they reach out to point, 'Look, how lovely that pear is,' they might, *accidentally* of course, touch the painting. So, dears, those of you needing to remove your glasses to look close up, do so well ahead of time, please. Perhaps take them off, then count to twenty. You don't want Mr. Russet here to drag you off to Citadel Prison, do you?"

"I've watched him," Mrs. Lightman said. "He's not capable of such an action. It's that uncle of his—where is he?—Edward. Now that man is capable of dragging any one of us off to Citadel, for no other reason than humanity itself annoys him. He once rudely commented on my shoes!" Several ladies nodded their recognition and approval of what Mrs. Lightman had said. "As part of humanity for eighty-one years, I personally enjoy annoying Edward Russet right back, I must admit. Never intending to provoke, only to annoy. I wore my fox-head collar on purpose today, hoping that Edward would be working, if working's what you'd call what he does. He hates that coat. If I'd seen him in the museum, I wouldn't have hung my coat up. I would've worn it, even if it was sweltering."

Imogen walked past the group into Room C and stood in front of *Jewess on a Street in Amsterdam.*

"You're a spirited sort, Eleanor," Miss Delbo said to Mrs. Lightman. "And you're going to enjoy, I trust, the Dutch paintings. Shall we, then?"

Miss Delbo led the group into Room C. She walked up to Imogen and took her gently by the hand, spoke a few words. Then Miss Delbo flicked something off Imogen's collar, held out her hands, and squared Imogen's shoulders, setting her posture upright, as if she were Imogen's mother sending her off to a formal dance. Though, of course, Miss Delbo and Imogen looked nothing alike.

Miss Delbo was forty-five. I knew this, because I saw her birthday mentioned on the August 15 page of Mr. Connaught's desk calendar: *Helen's birthday. Gift in order. (She is to be 45.)* I thought putting her age in parentheses, in a private calendar, revealed how deep down Mr. Connaught was gentlemanly and discreet. Miss Delbo was about five feet five inches tall. She had an extremely calm bearing. I knew that she enjoyed sweets; I had seen her many times sitting on a bench in the Public Gardens across from the Lord Nelson Hotel, eating an éclair or a sugar cookie, even before I knew who she was. In fact, for her forty-fifth birthday, Mr. Connaught had given her a box of fancy chocolates. She immediately opened it, offering Mr. Connaught, me, and my uncle each a piece. The box had a guide to the candies on the inside cover; in each reproduction, a bite had been taken out so that you could see the filling. It was quite a spectacle of pastels, browns, and blacks. Anyway, Mr. Connaught gave Miss Delbo chocolates, so he must have known something. Because she looked deeply pleased. I thought, for having an insatiable sweet tooth, she has such a narrow face and is so slim. Though of course, for some people, eating éclairs did not add up to not being slim. Helen Delbo was one of those. And she took obvious pride in her figure, it seemed to me. Not bold or ostentatious pride; it was more professional pride. The way she dressed, in good taste and so on, with elegance and authority, which is how she spoke, too. Now and then I had thought to sign up for one of her classes at Dalhousie University. But if I did poorly, I reasoned, then I would be embarrassed to see her in the museum. I thought myself quite capable at avoiding embarrassment. I considered it a skill of mine. Except when it came to Imogen, because I was so incapable of doing much right around her. I wanted to take one of Miss Delbo's classes, though, and at one point had even set aside money for that purpose. But I never mustered up the courage. I settled for writing down much of what she said on tours.

I thought Miss Delbo had beautiful hands; the most subtle ring still would have been a violent contradiction—that was a phrase from one of her tours. She had been talking about an American painting; at one side of the canvas, a man and woman were entwined kissing in a cornfield. But to the other side, a bolt of lightning distracted a viewer. No matter, because Miss Delbo never wore a ring. On occasion she wore a pearl necklace, but never a ring. If I had to choose a word to describe her face, it would be "alert." Though that might seem an odd kind of flattery. She never had a bounciness or false kindness in her expression; nothing, ever, you would want to glance away from. I had always found hers a face that disallowed any possibility but to look directly at it. A very honest face, never comically serious, though usually serious. She had dark brown eyes. Her black hair was most often braided up. The type of braid varied quite a bit, tour to tour. Sometimes she wore twin braids atop her head, fastened by modest pins. Always the braids were exquisitely woven, neat and careful compositions. And because she treated a tour as a formal occasion, Miss Delbo wore a not flamboyant red lipstick, "not flamboyant" being a phrase she once used to describe a particular hue in a Canadian still life.

Miss Delbo was about to start that day's tour with *Sunday Flower Market.*

"There's much to look at here," she said, standing just to the left of the painting. But then she turned toward Imogen. The Art League had already formed a half-circle around *Sunday Flower Market.* But now Miss Delbo walked over to *Jewess on a Street in Amsterdam,* and everyone followed. "No—forgive me," Miss Delbo said. "Let's begin here." And she stepped to the left side of the painting. "My apologies. But, yes, let's start with a *quieter* circumstance."

The fifteen women dutifully formed another half-circle, nobody crowding. "Please, just look for a moment. I'll do the same," Miss Delbo said, and studied *Jewess on a Street in Amsterdam,* as did the entire Art League.

One woman clicked her crutches together, adjusting herself to another angle of vision, but otherwise the museum was nearly silent.

I heard the faint static of the radio. I do not think anyone else did; my ears were tuned to that kind of thing in the museum, whenever my uncle was not in sight.

"The title is *Jewess on a Street in Amsterdam,*" Miss Delbo finally said. "The artist is Joop Heijman." Her voice had a somewhat stern, yet soothing, teacherly aspect. Then again, she often betrayed emotion, which did not seem to come naturally to her, at least not in public; it seemed to surprise her each time it happened.

Imogen tucked herself to the outside of the group. She took out a notepad and pencil.

"Mr. Heijman was born in 1878, in Amsterdam," Miss Delbo continued, "where he still resides. As you can readily observe, his is a realistic style. Sufficient, not showy—that is, trying neither to shock nor to overly please. But it tells us that the painting is fully resident in and of itself; we don't have to look elsewhere for meaning.

"Now please look at the Jewess's face: a terrible moment of indecision, I should think. Or a decisive change of heart. She stands looking at the hotel. Her mind seems utterly focused, not on the brick façade but on some life—or lack of it—inside the hotel. She is fixed in place, not able to move. Her legs seem leaden, and for the moment, the loaf of bread seems to hold the weight of the world. Who can say what she is thinking?—alas, Mr. Heijman is not here to tell us, and—how to put this?—perhaps the artist himself is the last to know certain things about his own creation.

"As for the title, *Jewess on a Street in Amsterdam.* A

pedestrian—literally—title, yet evocative, isn't it? Because truly, truly look at her. This Jewess is not so much generally representative, not so much symbolic as *mysterious.*"

"The bread looks stale—" my uncle said.

The entire group, myself included, turned toward my uncle, who had come up behind Imogen. He yawned loudly.

"This, as some of you already know, is the obviously esteemed art critic Edward Russet," Miss Delbo said.

"No, no," my uncle said, "just a museum guard."

"Just," Miss Delbo said.

"But I know stale bread when I see it," my uncle said. "I buy day-old bread at Hollings Bakery, over on Eluard Street. Even two-day-old. And in this painting what she's carrying is hardly a fresh loaf. Give credit where credit's due: Joop Heijman worked in that detail—stale bread—worked it in there on purpose. Look, don't feel bad. You can't notice everything first glance, can you?"

"But, finally, you've noticed *everything,*" Miss Delbo said. "This painting's been here, how long? A few weeks."

"Maybe you just don't know what stale bread looks like," my uncle said. "I doubt they serve it in the faculty dining hall at Dalhousie."

"In fact, they don't," Miss Delbo said. "In further fact, you're interrupting me here."

"It's my professional contribution is all," my uncle said. "What she's clutching to her breast is stale bread. Which, ladies, could mean she's been walking all night carrying a loaf of bread, not eating one bite, from the looks of it. Restraining herself, because bread, stale or not, is tempting."

I looked at Imogen, and lightning strike me dead if she was not taking notes on my uncle's interpretation, as she had been of Miss Delbo's.

"Maybe they sell day-old bread in Amsterdam as a regular part of life," my uncle said. "Maybe it's not so different from Halifax. I could be convinced of that. I could be convinced she's always got that sleepless look. Maybe she was simply up awake early, tossed back the covers—maybe sleeps in a silk chemise, maybe not. Kissed somebody good morning, in the hotel. 'Good morning, my beloved,' and out the door, into the street, 5 a.m., down Herengracht—that's goddamned hard to pronounce. Then off for a loaf of cheap bread. But how would I know? I've never been to Amsterdam."

"Well, thank you, anyway, for your detailed police work, Guard Russet," Miss Delbo said. "Now, may I get on with my tour." She did not put it as a question.

Mrs. Lightman stepped up close to the painting, inspecting the bread through a monocle at such close remove I almost had to warn her. Then the monocle touched the bread. "Mrs. Lightman—*please*," I said.

I think I startled her slightly. Taken aback at my impudence, Mrs. Lightman looked at several of her companions, then shoved past me, walked to the coatroom, put on her fox piece, and left the museum.

"Excellent hospitality," Miss Delbo said, glancing from my face to my uncle's, and then to the ladies for affirmation. "Well, I will personally apologize to Mrs. Lightman. Now—let's catch our breath, shall we? Bread is not our emphasis today. So let's move over to the still lifes."

"Or she could've already eaten a Dutch doughnut or hard roll and coffee," my uncle said. "So maybe she wasn't even hungry, which would account for no bites out of the loaf."

"Thank you again," Miss Delbo said. "You're dismissed."

My uncle clicked his heels military-style, as he was wont to do, and went back into the custodian's room. He left the door slightly ajar, turned the radio up—a station that played popular tunes—loud enough to be heard in Room C.

Miss Delbo began to speak about *Still Life with Pears.* I was standing in Room B.

After a moment or two, I went into the custodian's room. Closing the door behind me, I said, "The radio's too loud." I turned it off myself.

"I would've taken her to Halloran's," my uncle said. "I would've paid for everything. The best wine. I would've practiced pronouncing the French label ahead of time."

He was lying on the sofa, shoes off. Brooding.

"How many times did Miss Delbo turn you down?" I said.

"I'd say a dozen. At the least. I haven't kept exact count, DeFoe."

"Well, you've got Natalie, who's fond of you, as you put it."

"Delbo said she wouldn't so much as share a line at an outdoor drinking fountain with me. She's a handsome woman, though, isn't she?"

"Yes, she is."

"What do you mean by that?"

"I mean to agree."

"Can you tell me what she's wearing? Helen Delbo—what's she wearing?"

"A dress."

"Well, that's *always* true now, isn't it? But there it is. You see there? There're many differences between us, DeFoe. You don't take in *details*. You don't take in the details of life. You notice the dress, but do you daydream what's underneath the dress? Things are connected, DeFoe. Things in the world. They're connected."

"What are you going on about? She said no to dinner at Halloran's with you. So how does that make *me* supposed to care what's underneath Miss Delbo's dress?"

He reached under the sofa, took out a bottle of whiskey, and drank a considerable amount.

"Why not call it a day, Uncle Edward. Go to the hotel. Mr. Connaught's not coming in."

"Now I get it. Now I understand. You agree she's a handsome woman. Even though you can't tell me exactly what dress she's got on. Or the way her hair lets her ears show, tucked up along the nape. I hope, DeFoe, you're not afraid of that word 'nape.' Of her neck. That alone should drive any healthy man to distraction. My God, and you've been in the museum with her for *hours* some days. Were you not driven to distraction?"

"Go to the hotel."

He slid the bottle under the sofa. "Her face," he said. "Let's talk about her face. Some might consider it a bit—

what's the correct word?—'dour.' But do you know what? If dour is her natural look, it means—it means, when her face brightens, you *notice.* By comparison, you notice. Do you know why she's turned me down every time?"

"Why's that?"

"Two reasons. One, she thinks she studies perfection when she's here in the museum, and the rest of the time in books. *Thinks* about perfection. In art. Perfection in art. What she's always talking about. The lives of the great *ar-teests.*"

"You just spit."

"So then she meets me. She detects my flaws. She detects that I'm a deeply flawed man. And one night she's tossing and turning in bed. She wakes up in a cold sweat. She can't figure out why, until later that day, when she walks into the museum and takes a good hard look at me. And it unnerves her."

"What unnerves her—exactly?"

"That she's attracted to my flaws. She's with perfection too much; really, she desires the opposite. I'm a temptation. And she's afraid of that in herself. I know people, DeFoe."

"I see. And the second reason, then? Why she turns you down."

"Because the restaurant is wrong. Miss Delbo has no doubt eaten at Halloran's and disapproves of it. But she's too elegant and refined to embarrass me, asking her as I keep doing to eat at Halloran's, figuring it's what I can afford. When naturally she might prefer a candlelit corner table, small portions, sitting with someone who has recently brushed up on his French by living in Paris, say. Delicate hors d'oeuvres, followed by small portions. Not a Halloran's steak."

"That's sure an interesting combination of reasons, Uncle Edward. Your magnetic flaws and the wrong restaurant."

"I've pretty much thought it through."

"I'm sure you have. Please keep the radio off or turned low, okay?"

"Helen Delbo is capable of putting me over the edge. For instance, if I found out—in addition to her looks and smarts—if I found out that she faithfully listened to Ovid Lamartine. And then, if I asked, and she said no to dinner again. That would make me kill myself."

"You've got Natalie."

"Would you discreetly ask her?"

"Ask her what?"

"Ask Helen Delbo if she listens to Ovid Lamartine."

"I will not ask her."

I left the custodian's room. There is plenty of quiet in this museum, I thought, but little true calm.

In Room C, Miss Delbo, wearing a dark green dress with black stockings and black shoes, and her pearl necklace, was talking about *Sunday Flower Market*. However, Imogen was still intensely studying *Jewess on a Street in Amsterdam*.

In a quick, practiced movement, Imogen unfastened her hair from its hairpins; it fell loosely around her shoulders.

". . . notice the complacency in the title *Sunday Flower Market*," Miss Delbo said. "Yet harrowing violence threatens. It lurks just beneath the flower stall, a kind of violation of pastoralism. What else do we see? A child's innocence, surely. What's more, the parents are simply passing the time of day, perhaps imbued with a sense of well-being. A sense that everything is right with the world. It is Sunday. Perhaps they even feel the balm of self-righteousness, as they have just come from church. Look at the dwarf's knife poised to strike. It *is* striking. So we viewers are privileged —privy to the immediate future, are we not? Because the knife of this remarkably grotesque little man is wending its way upward into the startling present. And in advance, we can almost feel it, can't we? And in that sense we are tensed for an experience we shall never have. Time is stopped. And this, dears, is what the Dutch critic L. Van Kellik called 'the infinite passion of expectation.' "

I hated that painting; I loved hearing Miss Delbo explaining it. I went back into the custodian's room, hoping to persuade my uncle not to disrupt the tour again. No need. He had fallen asleep. I stood between Rooms B and C, and listened. As Miss Delbo discussed each of the Dutch, Imogen kept in front of *Jewess on a Street in Amsterdam.* When the tour ended, she walked over to me. "I'm going to come back another day soon," she said. "I like these paintings. Especially the Jewess holding the stale bread."

"I noticed your interest."

"You'd have to be blind not to, DeFoe."

"What about the cinema tonight? Remember?"

"I did promise, didn't I?"

"In fact, you did."

"Yes, but I don't think I'm up to it."

"Why is that?"

"Things to think over."

"Think them over after the cinema. There, that solves it."

Miss Delbo walked over to us.

"Excuse me," she said. "I don't mean to interrupt a lovers' quarrel."

"It wasn't," I said.

"It seems to me not very professional, Mr. Russet, to carry on personal matters while on duty. I never would. But now that my tour is over, Imogen, I was thinking of going to the cinema tonight. The feature is *It Happened One Night*. I've heard good things. Mr. Clark Gable and Miss Claudette Colbert, two American movie stars. My usual Wednesday-night companion isn't available. I thought perhaps, if you were free, we might go together. And perhaps have tea afterward. I have an early class at the university. It occurred to me how silly—all those visits to my mother—the cemetery's been, really, the only place we've talked, hasn't it?"

"I'd love to, but I can't," Imogen said. "I mean, how nice of you to ask. It turns out I promised DeFoe. How's that for coincidence? Though we didn't mention tea afterward, did we, DeFoe?"

"We didn't mention tea."

"In fact, I'm only wanting a hot bath and to think," Imogen said. "But a promise is a promise."

"It is indeed," Miss Delbo said. "Can you fit all those in of an evening?"

"Beg pardon?" Imogen said.

Miss Delbo laughed a little. "I was only putting you

on a bit," she said. "I meant, the cinema, a bath, all that thinking. In a single evening."

"Oh, I see," Imogen said. "I do like to keep busy."

"Well, you both have a pleasant time, then. Perhaps I'll see you there, anyway. Or maybe my friend will ring me up last minute."

We both stood there watching Miss Delbo leave the museum.

"I myself am too busy tonight—sorry for eavesdropping," my uncle said. He was standing in the custodian's doorway. "I'd like to join you for the cinema, but I've got other plans."

"Uncle Edward," I said, "you've never actually been introduced, have you? This is Imogen Linny."

"No, but I feel as if I know you. DeFoe talks about you often. Now's your chance to tell your side of it—," my uncle said. It was supposed to be a joke, but Imogen barely smiled.

My uncle walked over, held out his hand; Imogen took it in hers and began to give a friendly handshake, but my uncle bowed and kissed her hand.

Imogen pulled her hand back sharply. "I didn't like that," she said.

"I'm sorry," my uncle said. "But think it over; maybe later on you'll realize it wasn't so bad. Well, now that we've met, I'll finish my workday on the sofa, while you two get on with your intimate plans, of a sort."

"That'd be a good idea," I said.

"And Mr. Connaught, is he in the museum?"

"Meetings all day."

"Some afternoons are just perfect then, aren't they?" my uncle said.

He went into the custodian's room and shut the door. I sold five postcards, and then the entire Art League was gone. The museum was empty, except for my uncle, Imogen, and me.

"What time is it?" Imogen said.

I looked at my watch. "Four o'clock. One hour till closing."

"I'm going to look at the Dutch paintings for that hour."

"What about tonight?"

"All right. All right. I'll postpone every important thought till much later. But no tea after."

Imogen stood in front of only *Jewess on a Street in Amsterdam.* I must say, it was the longest stretch of time I had seen anyone stand in front of a painting. Unbroken stretch, I mean. No drink of water. A few tilts of her head, a step to either side, getting a slightly different angle, and so forth. Otherwise, she stood directly in front of it. Not too close, either. At about 4:45, Imogen walked over to me. I was sitting on a chair in Room A. "I need some air," she said. "For some reason, suddenly I'm all but choking on anxiousness. I can't say why."

"I'll try and get my uncle awake and out, lock up, then meet you on the porch."

"That painting almost made me faint."

Cupid

We went to Halloran's for dinner and hardly spoke. I paid the bill. "How much should I leave for a tip?" I asked Imogen.

"I wouldn't leave a penny. Our waiter said something nasty about me in French."

"You don't know French, so how'd you understand what he said? It might've been something nice. A compliment. He might've just said it in a snide way."

"He had a look on his face. Leave a dollar, DeFoe. Leave anything. I don't care. Thank you for paying for my dinner."

We walked to the Robie Street Theatre. Out front, we looked at a life-size cutout advertising *It Happened One Night*: Clark Gable and Claudette Colbert stood next to a bus.

"I'm looking forward to this picture," I said.

"It's supposed to be romantic. So don't sit right next

to me, DeFoe. You sometimes get carried away in the cinema."

"Even ten people between us, I still might get carried away. What should I do then?"

"Just sit still. Get carried away, but keep it to yourself."

There was no queuing up. I bought our tickets at the glass booth. Inside, we each separately bought a box of popcorn. There was an even larger, otherwise identical cutout in the lobby. The lobby had a maroon carpet. We found seats in the tenth row from the front—I counted. Imogen sat in an aisle seat, right side of the middle aisle. I sat across the aisle from her. There was only a small scattering of customers. The movie would not start for another fifteen or so minutes. Second row from the front, however, a young couple was already kissing. Imogen took immediate notice of them, as did I. She leaned into the aisle and whispered loudly, "I bet they'll get that over with, then pay perfect attention to the screen. That's probably why they got here so early."

"Why'd we get here so early?"

"Because we were done with dinner."

The theater had 220 seats, each plush maroon like the lobby carpet. I knew how many seats because I had asked the owner, Bertie Witterick, one day when he came into the Glace Museum and the question just popped into my head, no special reason. He was along on a special tour for patrons. I also asked him if "Bertie" was his complete first name, and he said yes. Anyway, it was a big movie house, with two private balcony areas, each with five seats. It reminded me of an Italian opera house I had seen in a magazine.

I finished my popcorn before the lights were dimmed. Then a grainy newsreel came on. Events in Ottawa. Then events in Germany: Adolf Hitler was on a hotel balcony, it looked like, and had his arm stretched out full-length, his trademark salute, in front of an enormous crowd of hysterical well-wishers. The camera caught a few people smiling, as if Hitler himself had given them a benediction, could actually see them close up, even touch them. When really he had to be just a distant blur against the side of the hotel, like a fly on a curtain. A military cavalcade was in progress. A wedge of motorcycles followed by thousands of troops goose-stepping along. Suddenly a little girl ran out and placed a bouquet of flowers in the street. The frontmost soldier on his motorcycle stopped a few feet in front of the bouquet. The soldier dismounted. The little girl, who had stopped the entire parade, ran out again, picked up the bouquet, and fearlessly handed it to the soldier. The soldier picked her up and kissed her on the cheek, and the crowd went absolutely berserk with happiness. The little girl then ran back to her mother, who proudly lavished her with kisses. All the while, the newsreel commentator, with a voice as somber as Ovid Lamartine's, only more baritone, said, "This is the new Germany—," and so on.

In the theater aisle between Imogen and me, a man about forty years old—dressed like anyone else you would see in Halifax—began to goose-step like a German soldier, down the aisle toward the screen. He was tall, and he put his hand up in the air so that it cut into the tunnel of dusty light from the projector and showed on the screen. He poked Hitler in the face, then below the belt. Then he made a fist that opened up into a clacking goose-head shadow on the screen, and he squawked out a goose call. What he did was much to the movie audience's delight, and a few people applauded. He then sat down four rows ahead of me.

I leaned toward Imogen. "My uncle thinks I'm going to be called into the army because of that degenerate—what he calls Hitler," I said, pointing at the screen.

The newsreel ended and the lights dimmed more, and then just the aisle lights were on, plus the EXIT signs. As the music rose and the credits for *It Happened One Night* came on screen, a couple walked past, settled into seats about the fifth row from the front, Imogen's side of the aisle. It was too dark to see their faces. Out of the corner of my eye I could see Imogen studying them, however, so I studied them. The instant they sat down, the man helped the woman off with her coat, which he set on the seat to his left. Imogen immediately stood up, crossed the aisle, and sat down next to me. "That's Miss Delbo," she said. "Her friend must've been available after all."

We could whisper and not bother anyone else, really. The nearest person was the shadow-puppet fellow four rows ahead. "That isn't Miss Delbo," I said. "She's not that tall."

The younger couple in the second row got up and left through a side exit. "See," I said, "*that's* why they got here so early. So they could leave early. They're already romantic—they don't even need to watch a movie. They just need to get right home together."

"Maybe they had a quarrel. Between kissing. You don't know the truth of it."

"Anyway, that's not Miss Delbo, because, look—"

Imogen turned and we both saw that the older couple were themselves now kissing. They did not embrace. It was more a lingering, gentle kiss, silhouetted. "That's not a proper thing," Imogen said. "Not a good response, after such terrible news on the newsreel."

"They came in after the newsreel."

"She *knew* we'd be here. She's a tour guide and a professor. How could she behave like that?"

"Some people act that way only in public. Anyway, it's not Miss Delbo we're looking at."

"DeFoe, go down there and look. I have to know."

"*You* go look. Besides, what difference does it make?"

"Pretty please."

"No."

Staring ahead, Imogen jabbed me with her elbow and said, "Now look." The woman appeared to whisper in the man's ear. He reached over, picked up her coat, and passed it to her. It surprised me, but Imogen now actually half-stood up to observe. I swiveled around; nobody's view was obstructed. Nobody hissed or said, "Down in front!" the way I had seen happen once or twice. "Miss Delbo's put her coat across both their laps," Imogen said, sitting down again.

The couple resumed their kiss, interrupting themselves now and then, so that the woman could look at their laps. Or his lap. They were entirely ignoring the screen.

"It's so stuffy in here," Imogen said. "I'm suffocating from the heat." She pulled her sweater off over her head. She had a flannel work shirt on underneath. "Would you please get me an orange soda?" I got right up and went out to the lobby concession. I bought an orange soda with crushed ice.

At the top of the aisle, as my eyes adjusted to the dark, I could not locate Imogen. Finally, I saw that she had moved to the last row on the right, purposely as far from the couple as possible. I walked back out and crossed over to the other side of the concession, then into the theater. I edged past Imogen and sat next to her. I handed her the soda. She reached into the cup, scooped out some ice, and rubbed it along her forehead and mouth, then pressed some ice to each of her wrists. "That'll stain a shirt," I said. "What's this movie about, anyway?"

"I haven't paid much attention," Imogen said. She took a long drink.

"The soda help?"

"Not really. I'm just very uncomfortable suddenly. Once again, once again, a headache possibly. It's not too bad yet. But I think I'd like to leave."

"All right. Okay. Let's go."

We walked into the lobby. There stood Miss Delbo arm-in-arm with Mr. Connaught. You could have knocked me over with a feather. My curator, her Wednesday companion. They had obviously just arrived. They were each holding a ticket and their faces were flushed from the cold. Miss Delbo was peeling off her gloves. She had on the same black winter coat she had worn earlier to the museum, but when she unbuttoned it, I saw that she had put on a different dress; this was a more casual dress, and she wore more casual shoes as well. Yet she still wore the pearl necklace. "Oh, Imogen, DeFoe," she said.

Mr. Connaught nodded at us and said, "Cold out. Well, we're a bit late, Helen."

"It's my fault, Edgar," Miss Delbo said. "I was certain the picture started at 7:30. But it's always 7:00, isn't it?"

"Well, dear, my meeting went to just after 7:00, anyway. That alone would've got us here late. Let's go inside, shall we?"

"Yes. Yes. How's the picture so far?"

"Can't say," I said.

"You're leaving based on what, then?" Mr. Connaught said. "You are leaving, aren't you?"

"Based on, I'm not feeling perfectly well," Imogen said.

"Poor dear," Miss Delbo said.

Mr. Connaught shifted his coat to his other arm and looked at the clock above the concession. "Well, shall we, then?"

"The theater's just too warm, I think," Imogen said.

"Well, late as we are, we're going to give the picture a try, aren't we, Edgar?"

"Let's."

"You may not want to sit too close to the front," Imogen said. "There's some commotion, a rude couple."

"We like to sit about three-quarters back, don't we, Edgar? Is it crowded?"

"Not at all," I said.

"Well, goodbye, then."

"Goodbye," I said, and we watched Miss Delbo and Mr. Connaught go through the center aisle door.

"You look as if you'd seen a ghost," Imogen said. "What, you don't think they're supposed to have a personal private life?"

"They have worked together for a few years, I guess."

"Now you know why I was so upset."

"Oh, you thought, Here she is, but not with Mr. Connaught."

"Uh-huh."

"Because she wouldn't carry on with Mr. Connaught like that."

"What's their human nature together, who knows?"

Out in front of the theater again, Imogen seemed to just then discover that she was holding her sweater. She took off her coat and I held it and she put her sweater on, the coat over it. We started to walk.

"Well, the museum's changed for me now."

"I bet it has."

"You obviously knew about them being a couple."

"She's always spoken highly of him. When she visits the cemetery his name comes up often. Edgar this, Edgar that, with great affection. It wasn't hard to figure out."

"They only have the briefest conversations in the museum. A few sentences at most."

" 'See you tonight at seven' is one sentence, DeFoe."

"Well, we've walked out of the movie. So where to now?"

"You know what I'd like more than anything? Now that I'm recovered somewhat in the fresh air?"

"Just name it."

"It's not too too cold out, is it? I'd like to stroll to the museum."

"The museum?"

"Yes. The Glace Museum, DeFoe. Where you work. You have a key, don't you?"

"I'm forbidden to use it after museum hours. Unless, say, I'm walking by and see it's on fire. I'd run in and rescue what paintings I could. Barring such an emergency, otherwise no."

"DeFoe—" She slipped her arm under mine, and we walked along like that. "I'd really like very much to look at the Dutch paintings. Don't make a big thing out of this. The museum allows private tours all the time, right? Or do I have to be rich?"

"I've got responsibilities."

"We're out together. You have a responsibility to please me. Look at it that way."

"I'd love to please you. Anywhere but in the museum after hours."

"I'd like to look at the Jewess with the bread again."

"Not tonight. No. Sorry."

"She truly interests me. Aren't you interested, DeFoe, that I'm so interested?"

"You said you almost fainted. What if you fainted? I can't have you fainting."

"I promise I won't."

"And if you break your promise?"

"It wouldn't be on purpose, would it?" She embraced me then and there on the sidewalk; I looked around and realized that the entire time we had been walking toward the museum.

The wind blowing from the harbor made us put our collars up. We were close enough to the wharf to hear the creaking masts of the historical schooners. There were not many people out on the streets. "It feels like snow," I said.

"Actually, I don't know what I mean by that. When my uncle says it, it's like a weather forecast on the radio. He's usually right. He's got a knack for it."

Imogen leaned up against me. "You know what I think?" she said. "I think you think going into the museum is beneath you as a guard. As a guard, your loyalties would be—violated."

"Why ask me to do it, then?"

"Because every now and then one loyalty replaces another, doesn't it? Every now and then a person's got to make a separate world, DeFoe. Just live in a separate world. Even for an hour. Where, say, DeFoe Russet doesn't think like a museum guard. He thinks like whatever the opposite of that is."

"You're philosophical tonight. You must've been doing a lot of thinking lately. The thing is, though, I like being a museum guard."

"That doesn't mean you have to act like one day and night."

Without a word I walked up the steps and unlocked the museum. I went in before Imogen. When we were both inside, I shut the door. The night-light was on in the bookstore. It was enough to see the coatroom by, and Imogen right away hung up her coat. "I might just buy a postcard," she said.

"Imogen, I haven't entirely made up my mind about this yet."

"Is there a flashlight?"

"On the shelf just under the cash register."

Imogen reached down, found the flashlight, and flicked

it on. She held it to her chin, making a fright mask of her face, and walked up to me. "Stop that, please," I said.

She looked hurt, then serious, and said, "Think of that newsreel we saw. All the horrible things in it. Then think of that woman putting her coat the way she did, the one I thought was Miss Delbo. Okay. Okay, we observed both things in a few minutes' time, right? Pretty shocking things to observe, each in their own way, correct? So—wouldn't you agree, taking out your key, going into the museum at night, here, on the safe streets of Halifax, and nobody possibly could be hurt by it, is pretty much, by comparison, a *small* adventure?"

"That is clever, all right. But I'm still a guard, and being in the museum at night is wrong."

"Oh well, then. I should've maybe telephoned Edward to do this. He has his own key, I'm sure. Sometimes an older man knows what really to be afraid of and what not to."

"That's not really fair."

"*Edward the Courageous/Edward the Brave/Edward lay down ghosty weeping same/as any peasant once in his grave./Poor, poor, poor King Edward, poor King Edward, poor.* That's an old English ditty my aunt Maggie taught me, to skip rope by."

Keeping the flashlight beam to the floor like an usher, Imogen walked into Room C. I followed and said, "Maybe this'll be all right."

"So far, so good," Imogen whispered. "Look, there's moonlight in the room. Let's hold hands for a stroll in the museum. Get out of your coat, Guard Russet. You're off duty."

As she helped me off with my coat, I saw the flashlight beam fly across a few paintings. Then she pointed it at the floor again. She put my coat on a corner chair. Then we sat close together on the center viewing bench. She turned off the flashlight and set it upright on the floor. In the moonlit dark, the paintings, chairs, bench, Imogen and I, all cast shadows not shaped like ourselves or like any earthly thing, really. We both looked at *Jewess on a Street in Amsterdam.*

After a few minutes of silence, Imogen said, "Here's what I think. I think she's living a true life and I am not."

"It's a woman in a painting, Imogen. You can't compare you and her. What you just said sounds wrong-headed. It's all wrong."

"No. More exactly, I'm saying, *even* this woman in a painting is living a truer life."

"It's a life you're giving her, then. By losing yourself in her so deeply."

"Now you sound like Miss Delbo."

"It's just that what you're saying is complicated. So I tried to come up with a complicated response."

"My God, look at you. You look nervous. All fidgety."

"Well, I'm not. No more than when we first walked in."

"DeFoe, look at me. Do I frighten you? Do you think you need to guard this painting from me?"

"You've gone crazy."

"I'm not joking. Do you think I'd ever harm it?"

"Of course not."

"All right, then. Leave me alone with it for just a short while."

"I'll be in the custodian's room. Don't use that flashlight, though. I mean, happenstance should a policeman walk by, I don't want to try and explain what we're doing here."

I went into the custodian's room. I turned on the desk lamp, then switched on the radio. A composition for piano, which I kept at low volume. I lay down on the sofa. In ten or so minutes, Imogen came in, closed the door, sat down next to me. She took off her sweater and unbuttoned her shirt. "I'm leaving," I said. "Right now, I'm out the door."

"What's the matter, exactly?"

She switched off the lamp.

"This is the Glace Museum. That's what's wrong."

"This mood doesn't win out too often with me, you've noticed. It's winning out here and now, so we shouldn't ignore that."

"I'm not ignoring it. I'm leaving because of it."

"Come sit closer. Ignore it from closer up."

"There's a hotel nearby, at the wharf. There's your apartment. There's my hotel."

"All three are a walk in the cold. Which would end this."

The evening proceeded then, without interruption, and Imogen did not protest anything we did. And I did not protest. When we finished the first time, I put on my trousers. Imogen did not get dressed at all. Instead, she walked out into the museum and sat on the middle bench, looking at *Jewess on a Street in Amsterdam*. From the custodian's doorway I could see moonlight pooled on the floor. Imogen gazed at the painting without cease. I drank a glass of water and lay back down on the sofa. Imogen stayed with the painting for at least a half hour more. And when she returned to the custodian's room, she did not shut the door. We started right up again. Holding on as if for dear life, is how I remember it.

Later, we sat in the dark. "You know what?" Imogen said, as we sat at opposite ends of the sofa. "Your uncle telephoned me."

"Come on."

"He rang me up last night. I'm telling the absolute truth."

"Why in the world."

"There you go, reaching for your clothes. Upset just at the thought of it, aren't you?"

"You just met him, he rings you up. I don't like it much. I mean, yes, I'm upset."

"The telephone rang. I picked it up. 'This is Edward Russet. How are things?' "

"What 'things' did he mean?"

"Listen to you, all out of sorts. You should be relaxed. After what we just did. You should calmly be able to take any news, good or bad."

"Why'd you mention this? Why here and now?"

"You're right. I apologize. It was thoughtless of me. I take it back. I take back everything I've ever said in my life."

"Now you're mocking me, Imogen. All right, I appreciate your not keeping it from me. Living up to your reputation between us for candor."

"It's not going—if that's what you're worried about. It's not going to lead anywhere, DeFoe."

"My uncle never said a word to me about it."

"He wouldn't, would he."

"Hours with him in the museum."

"Tell him not to telephone me again. It upsets you too much."

"He has a friend, you know. Her name is Natalie."

"I think she was in bed with him while we were on the telephone."

"That sounds about right."

We sat a few more minutes without talking.

"Well, I'm going to look at my new favorite painting again," Imogen said.

"Would you get dressed first, though? I'm going to sit here. But I think we should leave soon."

"I'll look first, DeFoe, then I'll get dressed. I mean, in that order, things won't take a minute longer, will they?"

We left about an hour later.

Late that evening my uncle demeaned me at cards.

I had walked Imogen home. At her door she said, "At least I don't have to pick up after us in my room tonight, as usual." I took it with less humor than I hope she meant it. Then I went directly to the Lord Nelson Hotel, and the second I entered the lobby, my uncle waved me over. "DeFoe, come on, we need a fourth!" Once in a while he asked me to join in like that. My uncle, Jake Kollias, Alfred

Ayers sat at their customary table. Jake and Alfred were each smoking a cigar. The hotel's oldest bellhop, Paul Amundson, was speaking Norwegian into the telephone at the check-in counter. He was at least seventy. Because of arthritis, he worked only the first floor. He had been employed at the hotel since 1915. He seldom played cards. When he did, more often than not the cadence of the game, the repetitious talk interspersed with long, bluffing silences, made him nod off at the table.

I sat down. "I'm pretty tired," I said. "But I'll play for a short while. I've got a little money on me."

My uncle shuffled the cards. "Yes, indeed," he said. "Spending half the night with Imogen, and no luck. I'm just guessing. Now, that can run a man ragged. What do you think, Jake?"

"I think you ought to leave your nephew be."

"Don't run him off," Alfred said. "We need a fourth. Paul there is half asleep on his feet."

My uncle dealt, looking only at the cards. "Two down—five up," he said. "Seven card—"

"After twenty years," Jake said, "we know the goddamn arithmetic."

"Touchy," my uncle said. "Ill humor means bad judgment, be careful with your cards."

My uncle threw down a queen of hearts in front of me. "Ah, Queen of Cupids," he said loudly, almost like a carnival barker calling people inside a tent to see a mysterious creature.

"Cupids?" Jake said.

"I meant hearts," my uncle said. "I must've been think-

ing of something else. I must've been thinking of what I told Imogen Linny—DeFoe's paramour, on the telephone."

"You're wasting your time," I said. "She already told me you rang her up."

"Edward, why not stash that bottle, concentrate on the game," Alfred said. "We don't want to hear family business."

"You're not careful, you boys might miss out on a good story," my uncle said. "Patience is called for here."

Almost at the same instant, Alfred and Jake set down their cards and leaned back. They had seen my uncle display an identical belligerence so often, they knew it was hopeless to try and stop it. I do not think it made them uncomfortable. Maybe it used to, but not anymore. They simply wanted whatever was going to happen between us to be over and done with, and to get back to the cards.

"I'd just listened to Ovid Lamartine," my uncle said, pretending to study his hand of cards. "Natalie and I were extremely friendly for an hour or so. Then Mr. Lamartine's broadcast put me in a depressive state. 'Do you mind if I call a dear friend?' I asked Natalie. 'Dear friend?' she said. 'Someone in need,' I said. And Natalie said she didn't mind at all. So I rang up Imogen Linny. 'How're things?' I said."

There was a bottle and a few empty glasses on the table. I poured myself a glass of whiskey and drank it. "And then you talked for a few minutes," I said.

"Stop right there," Jake said, which surprised me, because he had looked so resigned. "Leave DeFoe and his lady friend alone."

"I'd say we talked more than half an hour, at the least," my uncle said. "You know, the world's funny. What a place the world is. Sometimes you're mysteriously at ease talking with an almost perfect stranger. Of course, I lied, saying 'Dear friend' to Natalie."

"We already figured that out," Alfred said. He pushed back from the table, stood up, and walked to the Men's.

"Sometimes you find yourself saying intimate things. Who knows why, exactly," my uncle said. "I was just so comfortable talking with her. Anyway, lo and behold, I told Imogen about the *Cupid.* The *incident* of the *Cupid.* Mr. Connaught called it an *incident,* didn't he, DeFoe? Lying back on my pillow, the memory just washed over me, I guess. Back in 1930, we had a painting that featured a Cupid. French, I think. Or maybe it was Spanish, from Spain. But I think French."

"And then what?" I said, sweeping all the cards from the table to the floor with my outstretched arm. "And then what, and *then* what happened?" I left the table and stood near the check-in.

Alfred Ayers walked past me and sat down at the table.

"Ah, Alfred," Jake said, "you're just in time for the truth or a lie, one or the other. Keep going, Edward."

Jake and Alfred both bent down to pick up cards, poker chips, dollar bills, and loose change.

". . . I was telling Jake, we got a Cupid painting in the Glace Museum."

And then I left the hotel.

I started walking toward the wharf. I knew I did not want to even be in the same hotel as my uncle. Any proximity in the same hotel was too close. I was feeling deep hatred for him; so deep it made life almost entirely unfamiliar suddenly. That is not a very intellectual way to put it. Does not do justice to the complications of such a sentiment. But at least I did not have to explain it further to myself; feeling deep hatred sufficed. Then I saw the small, elegant Hotel Wyatt a block ahead. I immediately walked into its lobby—what was I thinking? I took out every last dollar in my wallet and secured a room for the night. It all took about five minutes. When I had written *Lord Nelson Hotel, Halifax, Nova Scotia* as place of residence in the registry, the desk clerk gave me a puzzled look and shrugged, none of his business. Then I was in a nicely appointed room on the third floor. Lying on top of the quilted bed, I could look out on the wharf. I telephoned Imogen.

"DeFoe, it's late," she said sleepily.

"Why didn't you tell me that my uncle mentioned the *Cupid*?"

"Let me wake up a minute here. Okay, okay, what? You're right. I forgot to mention that part of our conversation. I forgot to."

"Tell me what he told you."

Imogen did not hesitate at all. "Before you worked at the Glace Museum," she said, "a painting arrived. It was of a Cupid holding a bow. And the Cupid was looking at a couple, all three of them naked, of course. Edward didn't mention which century. And one afternoon Miss Delbo came in for her tour. She was holding forth about this painting. A tour of just four or five people. When Edward walks up and asks, 'Why do the Cupids in all these paintings stick around to *watch*? Why not just do the job—' " Imogen laughed a quick laugh, then stopped herself. " 'Why not just shoot the arrow, then just leave people alone after? These Cupids are little *voyeurs*, that's why! They hide behind trees, or up inside clouds.' Do you know the word 'voyeur,' DeFoe?"

"I don't know a lot of French, Imogen, but I know that word."

"Miss Delbo was furious. She was beside herself is how Edward put it. So then Miss Delbo turns on Edward, and she asks—mind you, this is in front of visitors—she says, 'Mr. Russet, what do you think is the relationship between a man's *private* behavior and the way he interprets a painting, such as this lovely *Cupid*?'

" 'But you didn't answer my question first,' Edward says. And then Miss Delbo slaps him across the face. *Whap!* Miss Delbo slapped your uncle. And that was the answer to his question. And, DeFoe, I don't think your uncle lied to me about this slap."

"It helps explain why he can't bear it that Miss Delbo won't have dinner with him. He can't understand why getting slapped wasn't secretly a sign—"

"—of what? Something that bode well for their future together?"

"I don't know. My uncle doesn't think like other people. I'm sure the slap explains *something*."

"DeFoe, I'm going to hang up now. Ovid Lamartine's earlier broadcast is being replayed, because it was cut off. By across-the-ocean interference of some sort. A technical radio problem. Your uncle telephoned five minutes ago to tell me. From the hotel lobby. He's playing cards, he said. He's going to listen to the broadcast in the lobby."

"Good night, then."

"Things between you and your uncle. I'm sorry—"

"What about them?"

"To me, they feel ill-fated. Maybe not in the long run. I hope not. But in the near-future."

"He's moody is all."

"Well, you know him and I don't."

"You think too much about human situations."

"Maybe so."

"And what do you think accounts for this 'ill fate,' as you call it?"

"What was that sound?"

"It's a knock at the door. It's a bellhop, I think. I asked for an ironing board to be sent up."

"Where are you?"

"The Hotel Wyatt."

"Answer the door, then."

I got up from the bed and spoke through the door: "Just leave it in the hallway."

"Very good, sir," the bellhop said. "Iron and ironing board. Good night."

I sat back on the bed, picked up the telephone. "Imogen?"

"You brought a change of clothes?"

"As a matter of fact, no, I didn't. I suddenly fell into the decision to stay here. I thought I'd iron my present shirt in the morning."

"Do you want to come here? Or me to come there?"

"No, I don't."

"It's peculiar, DeFoe. You live in a hotel; you've obviously paid hard-earned money to sleep in another."

"What do you think accounts for this 'ill-fated' turn?"

"Me."

"Don't flatter yourself."

"This one time only, flattery goes along with the truth."

"You're attracted to my uncle."

"He wants me to be. Any fool can see that."

"I see it now."

"My headache's so bad, I want to die."

"I don't think so."

"You never listen. I've told you how bad it gets."

"You have. I'm sorry."

"Before I hang up—."

"Say whatever you want."

"Then it turns out that Mr. Connaught—this, now, is going back to the *Cupid.* Are you following me?"

"Yes."

"It turns out Mr. Connaught *saw* Miss Delbo slap Edward. And the museum visitors, they were horrified at seeing it. And they complained. They filed a complaint. And Edward, out of his own pocket, had to refund their tour money. He had to apologize profusely. *Profusely.* What's even more, Mr. Connaught took Miss Delbo out for an apology dinner that same night. He felt responsible for what Edward had done. They went to Marcel's, the very expensive bistro. Edward saw them through the window. He claimed he happened to walk by Marcel's on his way to the hotel. That was on a Wednesday."

"What's the day have to do with it?"

"Because from that Wednesday on, every Wednesday —and I don't think less of her, I think she's the most brilliant woman—every Wednesday, after dinner together, Miss Delbo and Mr. Connaught go to the Hotel Wyatt. The very hotel you're in now. Bellhops at the Wyatt told bellhops at the Lord Nelson, who Edward heard it from."

"I don't think less of either of them."

False Alarm

I had slept in my clothes. When I woke, I thought, I've slept in only four rooms over the past nine years. (And not much sleep in Imogen's. Or, come to think of it, in Cary Milne's, either.) It was not much of a thought. It was just a way of realizing how small Halifax had become. Lying in the strange bed, I calculated other things, too. That I ate in the same restaurants: Halloran's, the hotel's—Vizenor's, though rarely. And once in about five years, the Chinese. Basically, I traveled between hotel, museum, cemetery, back to the hotel. I seldom went into a shop. True, I went to the Robie Street Theatre. But for fifteen years I had not sat on a dock at the wharf and gazed out to sea. Just daydreaming, as I loved to do as a child. As regards friends, my uncle was right, I had only two, but now Imogen and my uncle were both dubious. The fact that they had spoken late at night on the telephone felt like a double betrayal, since there were two of them. It did not bode well; it bode whatever the extreme opposite was. I might have a dull intuition, but I could put two and two together. My stomach cramped up. When I got out of bed, I washed my face and, without ironing my shirt, got out of the Hotel Wyatt as fast as I could. But I was late for work. Twenty-five minutes late. Fortunately, Mr. Connaught was attending a seminar at Dalhousie. He was the featured guest. "Tardy!" my uncle shouted as I entered the museum. He had gotten there on time, or close to on time, already enough amazement, I thought, for one day.

But also, he was impeccably dressed; his shoes were shined, his hair combed, he was clean-shaven, and he had a white carnation pinned to his lapel.

Looking me over, he said, "A night of tossing and turning. And you weren't even with Imogen."

"How'd you know that?"

"I telephoned her and asked outright if you were there."

"Did Winston Barnett shine your shoes?"

"Winston did, yes."

"How much did you tip him?"

"Five cents."

"Did he flip the coin in the air? He does that with a small tip, to make it seem special when it's not. He doesn't do that with a bigger tip, I've noticed."

"In fact, he called, 'Heads or tails?' and I said tails; it was tails, and he gave me the nickel back."

"And you accepted it back?"

"I'm a gambler. Winston's a gambler."

"I see."

"You can't tell me anything I don't already know about Winston. He had his shoeshine stand in the lobby of the Lord Nelson before you were born."

"He thinks you're a whoremonger and a hopeless drunk."

"I know that."

"Well, I'm going to work now. First, I'm going to iron these clothes I have on."

I was relieved that no visitors were in the museum. I noticed that Mrs. Boardman still was not in the bookstore, either. I took up my post in Room C.

My uncle walked over. "Now that we're back on speaking terms," he said, "how about we switch rooms? I'll up the usual to seventy-five cents a day."

"No thanks. Not this time."

"I figure you can use the money."

"No thanks."

"It's just that I need to study that Jewess; I need to think about the painting. So as to converse with Imogen Linny. It was her request. That we exchange opinions."

"I'm comfortable in C," I said.

"Imogen has some interesting notions about that painting, you know."

"I never knew her to like talking on the telephone so much."

"I called her right after you phoned her from the Hotel Wyatt," my uncle said. "She told me. I'd phoned her earlier, too, to let her know that Ovid Lamartine's—"

"—broadcast was on later than usual."

"Turns out, we listened to the broadcast together. I mean, at the same time. Her in her room. Me in the lobby, alone, because Jake and Alfred couldn't stand me anymore that night. Telephone to our ear, both of us. Then afterward, we talked over other subjects. This Jewess, for one."

"How cozy."

"It was easy to arrange, really. I had the radio on. She had the radio on. Nothing complicated."

"And what, exactly, were her thoughts about the painting?"

"Well, for one thing, she asked me to steal it for her."

"What a lie."

"And the desire behind her request was genuine. I heard unmistakable genuineness in her voice."

"Desire for what? You just used one of Miss Delbo's words, by the way. Maybe you didn't notice. 'Desire' is one of her words. Ha, ha, ha! That pleases me no end."

"Ask Imogen yourself. I've got nothing to hide. Walk on over to the cemetery right now and ask her. As senior guard, I give you permission. Go on. Go ahead."

"I just might."

"Don't *might.* Just go. I sense this won't be a crowded day. Crowds won't be thronging to the Glace Museum today. Get a breath of fresh air, DeFoe. And, oh, by the way, on your way back from seeing Imogen, pick up some headache powder for me, will you? Last two, three days, I've had the worst headaches of my life. I never used to get them. I lost three straight high-stakes games to Alfred Ayers last night. I don't forgive myself for that. Plus I had a bad headache before and after Ovid Lamartine's broadcast. During, I didn't notice. I put a cold washcloth over my forehead. Imogen's suggestion."

"Get the powder yourself," I said. I left the museum. I walked directly to the Lord Nelson and downstairs to the laundry room, where I asked Mrs. Steig if I could iron some shirts. "Help yourself," she said. "Whatever personal reason in the middle of your workday, I won't ask. But I'll go out for a cigarette, then." She left the laundry room.

I ironed about thirty shirts, stacking them neatly on one of the long wooden tables. It was some of the most efficient ironing I had ever done. I worked at a steady pace, trying not to think, or trying to think only about ironing shirts. Yet my mind was reeling; how my uncle tried to camouflage Imogen's request for him to steal *Jewess on a Street in Amsterdam* within the entire conversation we had at the museum. How he suddenly just interjected that. How he slipped that in, then quickly moved on—or had it been me who had dismissed the subject? How could Imogen have suggested a theft? If my uncle was not lying. How could she suggest such a thing? To my uncle, a guard for fifteen years.

In the middle of ironing a shirt, I unplugged the iron, set it upright on the board, and went to the cemetery.

It was a cold morning. I could see my breath cloud up. Imogen was working around a grave: *Morris Sachs—1840–1927.* She was dabbing some sort of medicinal pitch on the bark of a shrub. When she saw me, she deflected my intention to confront her by saying right away, "What, playing hooky? Would you be a dear and get me some hot tea at the corner?"

Without a word, I turned and walked to the sandwich shop on the corner of South and Robie. In my gloved hands, I carried a paper cup of steaming tea back to the cemetery. Taking it from me, Imogen leaned back against Mr. Sachs's gravestone, legs outstretched, and sipped the tea. "Thank you, DeFoe," she said. "I didn't mean to make you run an errand."

"You're welcome."

"To what do I owe the honor of this visit?"

"Why'd you ask my uncle to steal a painting?"

"Oh, *that.* Oh boy, uncle and nephew in those small rooms sure don't keep any secrets, do you?"

"My uncle keeps telephoning you, Imogen, and you're not hanging up on him. When at first you asked me to ask him not to call you. Don't you find anything wrong in that?"

She calmly sipped the tea. "Boy oh boy, no secrets at all."

Imogen reached into her coat pocket, took out a cube of sugar, unwrapped it, and dropped it into her cup, stirred with her finger, licked her finger, and dried it on her coat. "One thing is perfectly clear to me, DeFoe," she said. "Your uncle—and I hardly know him, but already I know this much—he'd be willing to steal a painting for me. Not just because I *asked.* But because he's enticed by bold acts of the imagination. That's Miss Delbo's phrase, but who cares, I used it how I meant to. Edward would steal it. And you, my paramour for two years now, would not. But even that's not my point. My actual *request*—" She finished her tea, crushed up the cup, and threw it at me, striking me hard in the face. "The *point* is, I did not ask Edward to steal the painting. I simply said that if I ever met a man who would make such a romantic gesture as to steal a painting for me, I could imagine running off to, say, Amsterdam with him."

"To my uncle, that's the same as asking."

"I didn't say I'd sleep with the same man in Amsterdam, by the way."

"What'd he say back?"

"He said, 'Would you consider Tahiti?' Because Amsterdam was soon to be in peril. According to Ovid Lamartine."

"And that was it?"

"Not quite. I said that Amsterdam was the only place in the world I wanted to go. I said I wanted to walk along the Herengracht canal and stay in the Hotel Ambassade."

"He knew you meant from the painting, then?"

"He knew. He said, 'Take DeFoe. DeFoe's never been out of Halifax.' "

"Oh, my uncle's full of generous contradictions these days, isn't he?"

"Another *point* is, it should be interesting to you, DeFoe, why I am so desperate to be alone with that painting. So, because I'm your friend, I'll tell you why. Because I am estranged from my soul. And a single sleepless night of studying *Jewess on a Street in Amsterdam* in the privacy of my home, I am convinced, would help me reconcile."

"Miss Delbo has brainwashed you out of your former self. Just with that one phrase, 'Soul. Estranged.' And all the rest. You can use her words all you want, Imogen. But it will never persuade me that you actually think like her."

"That's yet another point," Imogen said. "Miss Delbo knows how I think—you don't."

"Do you have a headache now? Is that why you're talking this way?"

"Oddly enough, I don't."

"So, these are supposed to be clearheaded ideas?"

"Very, very thought out and clear."

"To have a painting stolen for you?"

"The very clear idea of it occurred to me last night, right while talking with Edward. Our conversation inspired it, you might say. And the idea immediately appealed to me. It stuck like glue."

"This is crazy. Crazy talk."

"You're angry because I slept with Edward."

"No, you didn't."

"He didn't tell you? Your secret clubhouse in the museum there? He didn't tell you?"

"You're lying. Because when? Where?"

"Think about it. There were give or take approximately six or seven hours between the end of Ovid Lamartine's broadcast and when Edward had to be at work."

"Imogen, you were with me earlier in the custodian's room last night. Clothes entirely off both of us. If what you say is true, how could you?"

"Nights between bad headaches, my appetites are out of control, it seems. On the phone, Edward said, 'Shall I drop by?' So I said, 'Well, it's the middle of the night, but fine.' "

I sat down. I leaned against the opposite gravestone. I

knew what I was going to say moments before I said it. Then I said it: "I'd steal the painting for you."

Imogen picked right up on this. "I'd really just want it for a night. You could have it back at the museum before it opened. Before Mr. Connaught got there. Does he ever get there early?"

"Only when a new exhibition goes up."

"DeFoe darling, I'm sorry. I'm sorry I didn't ask you first, before hinting at it to your uncle. But of course, the actual thought hadn't got into my head yet, had it? Until I spoke with Edward."

"You didn't sleep with him."

"Us in the museum last night was very nice."

"What about you and my uncle?"

"He spent the night, but he couldn't *do* anything, he gets so agitated over Ovid Lamartine's broadcast."

I refrained from saying, "But otherwise you would have." I stared at Imogen; she stared at the ground.

"I just don't feel like going back to work," I finally said.

"You mean you want to shriek at Edward but wouldn't in the museum. Visitors or no visitors about."

"Maybe so."

"You're welcome to stay here."

I leaned against the shed and watched Imogen clip around two more gravestones, then rake around a third.

"I'm leaving now," I said. "Are you available for dinner?"

"Not tonight. And I don't have plans with Edward."

"I wasn't going to ask."

"Of course you were."

I left the cemetery and walked all over Halifax. Up Oxford Street, down Cunard along the North Common, over to Sackville, South Park past the Lord Nelson, Iglis, Barrington, down to Lower Water Street. At least fifty blocks. I did not eat lunch. My truancy from the museum lasted until 3:45.

When I got back to the museum, I realized that I had left the door unlocked. My uncle was not there. No curator, no guards. No visitors. No one in the bookstore. And when I walked into Room C, I saw that *Jewess on a Street in Amsterdam* was not on the wall.

I felt a terrible panic, which, almost immediately, was replaced by: *I'll turn my uncle in to the police.* My uncle, who had raised me since age eight.

My uncle Edward walked in. "I smoked a cigarette across the street," he said. "I saw you get here."

He hung his coat in the coatroom. He stood about ten yards from me, held out his hands as if framing a picture. "Still life with pissed-off nephew," he said.

"Where's the painting?"

"And which painting is that?"

"You know which painting. I can bring the law down on you."

"Where'd you ever hear such language? Some American gangster movie?"

"I'm going to the police. You're a museum guard. How could you let Imogen Linny persuade you? It's one of the Ten Commandments. It's one of Mr. Connaught's courtesies."

My uncle walked into Room C and looked at the empty place where *Jewess on a Street in Amsterdam* had been. Then he stared out the window.

"It's funny," he said. "On my way here, I didn't notice it was about to snow. But just now, out the window, it's graying up in that unmistakable way. It's going to snow, all right. The first snow of the year, really. Except for a few dustings last week."

"You stole it, didn't you?"

"Nope."

"You stole it to please Imogen. To go to Amsterdam with her."

"Wrong."

"I'm going to the police."

When I got to the front door, my uncle called out, "DeFoe!"

I turned and looked at him.

"I ironed this uniform myself. Shirt, trousers, tie," he said, tapping his lapel. "And then I did four of her blouses. I think she appreciated a man around the house, even if only for a night."

I walked to the police station. It is at Raintree and Gottingen Streets. From the outside, it looked welcoming, like a library. Inside the station, I hung my coat on the coatrack. I had never set foot in this building before. I noticed that the dome ceiling was flaking paint. Spits, then hisses of water near the round black handle of the radiator. It would drive me crazy, I thought, if I had to listen to that sound all day. The radiator made a few dungeon clanks, voices echoed down the wooden stairs. To the left of the elevated desk, a secretary was typing. I stepped up to the desk. The nameplate read: *Sgt. Pinnie Oler.*

"Sergeant Oler," I said. "Excuse me."

He looked up from his book. He was about fifty. His narrow face was pale, his lips cracked; he looked as if he had just gotten over a bout of flu or had something worse he was not getting over. He was reading a mystery. On its cover was a cloaked man in an alley, a human shadow following him along a brick wall. On the sergeant's desk a radio was playing "Across the Alley from the Alamo," a popular American song. Next to the radio was a chipped-beef sandwich, half-eaten, set out on a piece of wax paper. It was the first year wax paper was in neighborhood stores. Anyway, he looked annoyed at my interruption, and at first did not even look at me. He tore off a strip of the wax paper and used it as a bookmark, shut the book, sighed. He tapped the book's cover with a pencil. Looking at me, he said, "I'd hoped to get to the murder part before my shift ended. What can I do for you?"

"I'd like to report a crime," I said.

"You're in the right place. Your name?"

"DeFoe Russet." He wrote that down.

"And—"

"I'm a guard at the Glace Museum."

"What's the crime, exactly?"

"A painting's been stolen."

"On your shift?"

"I work six days a week, all day. Not Mondays."

"Well, today's not a Monday. Was it stolen last night?"

"It wasn't there this afternoon, when I got to work."

"A serious thing for a guard, isn't it?"

"Very serious. My uncle stole it."

"You know this for a fact, eh? His name?"

"Edward Russet. He's also a guard."

"Same museum?"

"Yes. And I believe that I know where the painting is."

"Where's your uncle?"

"He's at work."

"Does he know you're here?"

"Yes, he does."

"So, then. He's at the museum, waiting to be arrested."

"As we speak. The painting's called *Jewess on a Street in Amsterdam.* In case you need to know that."

"Where might this painting be, then?"

"In his hotel room, at the Lord Nelson. Or at the apartment of a Miss Imogen Linny. She's caretaker of the Jewish cemetery on Windsor Street."

"Jews off the street in Halifax."

At first I did not get it, then I did.

"It's a little joke," he said.

"Well, it's where she works."

He handed me an official form. "Write down Miss Linny's home address, please. If you know it."

I wrote it down.

"What's your relationship to Miss Linny?"

"How do you mean?"

"Well, you know her address apparently."

"That's complicated."

"Never mind. I couldn't care less. If it matters, it'll matter later on."

"Okay."

"I'll send an officer back with you to the museum, Mr. Russet. Wait on that bench over there."

I sat down on the wooden bench between steam radiators. They both needed adjustment; each dripped too much water for them to be in good repair. "Mr. Tremain, the museum's custodian, could fix these radiators," I said.

"We have our own man," Sergeant Oler said.

In a few minutes Sergeant Oler went to confer with a young policeman in a side room. Sergeant Oler went back to his desk. Then the officer walked out and stood in front of me. "I'm Officer Kellen," he said. He was about my age, give or take a year. He had a strong bearing, very upright. He had an almost comically square jaw and dark brown eyes, neatly trimmed black hair. "I'm assigned to this alleged theft."

I stood up and we shook hands. "DeFoe Russet," I said.

"I read your name tag."

We both put on our coats and scarves, then walked out of the station house and toward the museum.

When we got to Agricola Street, a few blocks from the museum, Officer Kellen said, "Important assignment coming up for me," matter-of-factly.

"What assignment is that?"

"Guarding a big celebrity in a few weeks. Ovid Lamartine. The radio personality. He's coming to Halifax. Ever heard a broadcast of his?"

"A few times, yes."

"I never have. But I'm going to start. It'll be like doing my homework. Brush up on the man, absorb myself in the assignment before he arrives. By the way, it's not exactly secret, but keep his visit under your cap. Between us two in law enforcement, eh?"

"Lamartine says Canada's going to be in a war with Germany down the line. He says no chance it won't happen. You and I are about the same age. We may be called up."

"I'd be willing to serve, right off first thing."

When we walked into the museum, I saw that my uncle was talking with Mr. Connaught in the middle of Room C. Mr. Connaught looked over, squinted his eyes, put on his eyeglasses, then walked over to us. "What's this, then?" he said.

"You are?" Officer Kellen said, taking out a notebook and pencil.

"Edgar Connaught. Curator of this museum. How may I be of service?"

Checking his notes, Officer Kellen said, "It's an Edward Russet I'm concerned with."

"I'm Edward Russet," my uncle said. He stepped up alongside Mr. Connaught.

"Your nephew, I believe it is. Your nephew here claims you've stolen a painting." He referred to his notes again. "Called *Jewess on a Street in Amsterdam.*"

"In point of fact," Mr. Connaught said, "the painting wasn't here when DeFoe Russet came back to work. It was on loan, as it were. At the private residence of Mr. van der Waals, the Dutch attaché. He had an important luncheon of some official sort and requested that I bring the painting—his favorite of the group—to his house quite early this afternoon. Which I was more than willing to do. And is under my jurisdiction to do. The government of Holland, you see, partly sponsored this exhibition."

"I'm writing all of this down," Officer Kellen said. "This little family quarrel."

"I'm sorry you've wasted the city's time," Mr. Connaught said. "It's an unusual misunderstanding is all. We've never had a theft. I personally delivered the painting to Mr. van der Waal's and, not a half hour ago, back to the museum."

"So the painting in question is here?" Officer Kellen said.

"Follow me, please," Mr. Connaught said.

In a moment, all four of us stood in front of *Jewess on a Street in Amsterdam.*

"False alarm," my uncle said.

"The Dutch attaché telephoned me at home last night," Mr. Connaught said. "Normally, I'd keep my guards apprised of such a situation. I take full responsibility for the mix-up."

"Look, Officer," my uncle said. He threw his arm around my shoulder. "You'll have to forgive my nephew. I raised him from a boy. His parents were killed in that terrible zeppelin crash, 1916. Your own parents—were you born and raised here?—they might've told you about it. One of Halifax's biggest tragedies. Anyway, my nephew's given to overpowering daydreams. Peculiar daydreams. People suddenly taken away, you see. Disappearing. Real people.

People in paintings—he stands with paintings all day, you understand. Don't get me wrong, he's a very competent guard. Pristine record. Though he was a bit tardy this morning. As you've seen for yourself, he worries over our paintings. Which, all in all, is a professionally good thing, of course."

"I don't know about any of that," Officer Kellen said. "I'll file my report."

"Yes, of course," Mr. Connaught said, at once shaking Officer Kellen's hand and gently turning him toward the door.

When Officer Kellen had gone, Mr. Connaught said, "Well, that's enough excitement for today, don't you agree? Let's see, DeFoe, you're in Room C, correct?"

"Room C, yes," I said.

"From now on, please try to work out your suspicions of your uncle outside the museum."

"I'm sorry. The painting was gone, and—"

Mr. Connaught actually clapped his hands over his ears. "I don't want to hear it," he said. He lowered his hands. "Keep an eye on *all* the Dutch paintings, will you, DeFoe? Don't play favorites. Should a thief reveal himself." He winked at my uncle, which infuriated me no end. My uncle went to Room A. Considering my false alarm, however, the serious nature of my accusation, the humiliation of it all, I could only bite my tongue and stare at the floor.

"Sorry again," I said.

When Mr. Connaught went into his office and shut the door, my uncle took the immediate opportunity to stand between Rooms B and C. "The thing I found interesting," he said, "was how Imogen needs a lot of ice water before slipping into bed. In all of my experience, I've never encountered that before. In and out of bed, she drank I'd guess ten full glasses."

He went back to Room A.

Dinner with Miss Delbo

"Imogen is no longer Imogen," Miss Delbo said. "Not the Imogen you knew. Or thought you knew."

"I hate riddles. Every riddle I ever heard since I was a boy confounded me."

We were sitting in Halloran's. It was November 29. It had been weeks since I had seen or spoken with Imogen. That afternoon, Miss Delbo had conducted a tour for Dalhousie's visiting professors. When the professors left, she took me aside. "I think it may be time for us to have dinner together," she said. "It may be useful to you, DeFoe. I prefer Halloran's. But I'm not set on it."

We met at seven o'clock. Halloran's was not crowded. Miss Delbo wore a gray woolen suit. I was in my guard uniform but had removed the name tag. We made small talk until the waiter brought our meal. I had a steak, and a potato with a dollop of sour cream. Miss Delbo ordered potato-and-leek soup, salad, and, oddly enough for dinner, a scrambled egg. I had requested the same bottle of wine my uncle most often ordered, Beaujolais. I tried to pronounce it correctly. The waiter poured me a sip for my approval. "Very nice," I said, because it was a familiar good taste. He poured us each a full glass, then left our table. We each drank a little. An awkward moment, because there seemed nothing in common to which to propose a toast, so we did not.

"Imogen's been living with you all this time, hasn't she?" I said.

"At her request. I installed her in the guest room. She brought only a few changes of clothes, toiletries, and little else. I suspect she's given up her apartment."

"She has. I asked the superintendent of her building."

"Friends told me you also inquired at the synagogue."

"They were polite. But they said they weren't at liberty to give out information about employees. And she hasn't been at the cemetery, either."

"There's a replacement caretaker. Imogen's quit her job. She no longer draws a salary. She's been relying on small savings. I ask very little for my tutoring. I ask nothing for room and board. Now and then she pitches in for groceries. I don't mind the arrangement."

"Tutoring?"

"I'm tutoring Imogen in Art History. Something she's always dreamed of studying."

"She never told me that."

"Well, it's rather a crash course, but nonetheless. We're

keeping to the Dutch. Sixteenth, seventeenth, eighteenth, nineteenth centuries. Right up to the present."

"Right up to Joop Heijman."

"He's not in the literature, DeFoe. He's merely in the Glace Museum."

"And what's Imogen going to do with all this new education, do you think?"

"She'll carry it around in her head. When she's in Amsterdam."

"Amsterdam?"

"She'll be going."

"Right into the monster's jaw. What Ovid Lamartine calls Europe."

"I told her as much. I said to be a student of art, she had to be a student of history along with it."

"What'd she say to that?"

"She said she couldn't take on both."

"You have such lofty conversations in your house."

"DeFoe, this isn't easy to describe; our Imogen is no longer who she was."

"You said that already."

"You know, it's quite a surprise. She and I, living in the same house. I only knew her from the cemetery, really. Yet slowly, week after week, we've built up our acquaintance. Now we take three meals a day together, except if I lunch with colleagues. Except Wednesdays, when I have dinner with Edgar. We're like two old maids. We've even laughed about that. She's quite good company. And quite dedicated to her studies. I'd risk the word 'obsessed' here.

Making up for lost time is how she sees it. She stays up till all hours."

"Doing what? Oh, studying—"

"The second night she was in my house I'd gotten up for a hot chocolate and I saw her lamp was still on. I was at the top of the stairs. The guest room is on the first floor, just off the dining room. Then I saw her come out of her room. I all but gasped. She was dressed *exactly* like the Jewess in the painting. You know, the thick dark clothes. And then Imogen walked out the front door. Later—the next day, actually—Edward told me she'd come to see him at the hotel. They speak by telephone nightly, news that might upset you, but there it is. After seeing Edward, she went to sit with *Jewess on a Street in Amsterdam.* To study it. The next morning at breakfast she was very matter-of-fact about all of this. About how she'd dressed—utterly without embarrassment. 'I was inside the museum last night,' she said."

"She has a key to the museum?"

"Edward had a copy made for her."

"That's not legal."

"Oh, come now, DeFoe."

Miss Delbo and I ate in silence for a few minutes. She poured herself a second glass of wine and did not offer one to me.

"Imogen said she'd asked you to steal the painting," Miss Delbo said.

"No secrets in your house, eh?"

"Fewer and fewer, it seems."

"How often does she go to see the painting? Study it."

"Nightly. Every night."

Miss Delbo looked at me a moment, then put her hand over mine, which I quickly withdrew. "You have a look of pity on your face," I said. "Why would that be?"

Miss Delbo sat straight up. She looked remorseful, caught in the act of revealing her true opinion of me, and now one truth tumbled headlong into another. She could not stop. "Imogen is lost to you, DeFoe," she said. "I may as well state it now as later. You aren't—forgive my bluntness—you aren't a man who recognizes his own nature."

"I recognize a lot of it. I just don't know what to do with what I recognize."

"You've all along thought that, with Imogen, persistence was the trick. You thought sheer doggedness would win out. *I will keep ironing Imogen's blouses, until sooner or later, eventually, Imogen will appreciate my ironing her blouses and come to rely on it.* Such blind nonsense."

"No subject's been left unspoken between you two, I guess."

"I only know what she's chosen to tell me."

"Fair enough."

"Given your nature, how could you not see any and all of Imogen's attentions to you—even her stingy attentions—as encouragement? You've deceived yourself, DeFoe. You might think of this as 'woman's talk,' but I'm making it between *us* now. You think that love need only be comprised of all sorts of hard-won reliances. And perhaps with some people that's true. But I guarantee you, it's not so with Imogen Linny."

"Thank you for telling me what I think."

"Angry with me or not, hear me out, DeFoe. Rest assured, Imogen and I have shared many confidences. She in fact *does* admire your persistence. Two years' worth now, is it? And she is quite humored by it."

"I see."

"But mostly she's endured it. Endured it like a headache that comes and goes. 'Endured' is a word I've carefully chosen. It can't be easy to hear. Or to acknowledge."

"Ah, but now that she's got you and my uncle to confide in, she won't have to endure me, right? That's what you're saying, isn't it?"

The waiter came near our table, and Miss Delbo frowned and dismissed him with a flick of her hand.

"One evening over dinner," she said, "Imogen told me how you were with each other. In the bedroom."

"I'm leaving."

I stood up from the table, but Miss Delbo clutched my wrist and said, "Please. I asked you to dinner because I'm trying to inform you about Imogen. Not to coddle you. You deserve as much."

I shifted to another chair, moved my place setting and napkin over in front of me. "You have no business knowing such things," I said.

"Truth is truth, DeFoe. All I'm saying is that from the start, Imogen and I fell into a kind of desperate honesty with each other. I spoke of my life, she spoke of hers. Her choice of details has been quite startling. Often."

I poured my second glass of wine and drank it too quickly.

"Look, I didn't intend to become a schoolgirl tattletale. Not at all. I only want to tell you facts straightaway. That Imogen goes to the Lord Nelson Hotel every night. And when she visits your uncle, she doesn't go as Imogen Linny. She goes as the Jewess in the painting. I could never have imagined such a thing. But it's God's truth."

Miss Delbo now began almost gasping for air, as if she had, for the first time, fathomed the strangeness of what she had just said. I handed her a glass of water. She drank it, put her hand on her chest, and calmed down.

"Excuse me," she said. "Something caught in my throat."

"Imogen's had a mental collapse, hasn't she? Gone off her rocker. Headaches lined up too closely in a row."

"Not in my opinion. No, it's more— How to say it? Ever since I've known her, first at the cemetery, now in my house, she's been on the verge of two things in combination. Two things. I believe these two things have taken control now. She's *embodied* them."

"My God, Miss Delbo, will you *please* use plain language? Which two things?"

"First, there's the disgust with her own life. She feels a deep-seated ignorance of the world. Never have I seen so bold or excruciating an example of this. Or even read about one. 'I deserve my worst headaches' is one thing she often says. Poor darling.

"And, you know, perhaps I represent the opposite of ignorance to her. She thinks I'm knowledgeable beyond what I truly am. She thinks I'm wise. When all I really am is highly educated by her standards. I don't try to talk her out of these opinions. I'd be loath to do that. Because what would be the point? Imogen needs to see me in a certain light. I allow that, because I believe it has provided her with notions of what is possible in her own life. This has progressed to such an extent—the hours upon hours we've spent at her lessons—that to say, 'No, you're quite wrong about me, dear,' would be shattering. Just cruel."

"I still don't get how she is day-to-day. How is she day-to-day?"

"Day-to-day. Well—I can tell you something about every *night*. That I can tell you about. At table, she insists we discuss that phrase 'the soul's estrangement and reconciliation.' I think I might go mad."

"I know that phrase."

"One day, weeks and weeks ago at the cemetery, I was visiting my mother's grave. Imogen and I got to talking. We often did that. Anyway, that morning I'd been writing a lecture about how certain artists were tormented by their themes. And how torment was what both freed them to paint tormentedly and was in turn their limitation. I had found certain good examples. I was thinking my lecture through.

"Imogen noticed me deep in thought, waited, then asked what I was thinking about. And off the top of my head, I quoted a somewhat obscure Jewish philosopher, whose name escapes me just now. But he'd written about art. I'd come upon his writings during my doctoral studies in London. There wasn't much of his I could use, really. Here and there, flashes of brilliance. But—and I can't for the life of me remember which painting he was referring to—he used the phrase 'dramas of the soul's estrangement and reconciliation.' I loved the sound of it. It felt important. And all these years later, I uttered it in the Jewish cemetery in Halifax, Nova Scotia.

"The odd thing was, the very instant those words came out of my mouth, I could see that Imogen latched on to them. With immediate dedication. Rather like a trapeze artist I once saw, gripping the trapeze sent across to her by her partner. Yes, and I mean just that. Imogen's face held a certain determination. As if her life depended on holding tight to those words."

"Everything you've told me, I feel as if I'm on the moon with it."

"Then let me state it clearly as possible, DeFoe. Imogen feels estranged from her very soul. See how those words work together? She believes that becoming the Jewess in the painting and going to Amsterdam—to stand on the exact street, in front of the exact hotel, the Hotel Ambassade—is her only chance to reconcile. This is fixed in her mind. I, too, at first was 'on the moon' with this. How could it really be? If I had been a stranger to Imogen, and had by chance observed her from across the street—in her costume—how could I have thought anything but 'She must be advertising a new theater production of some sort'? Or, 'I think I've just seen my first Gypsy.' Or some such oddity for Halifax. But that's not it at all."

"Better off if it were."

"She's *chosen* this for herself."

"Why—let me ask you this. Why couldn't she just sit

next to you in your church. Synagogue. Why couldn't she—I don't know the right word—*become* a Jew. If that's what she wants. Why would she want that? To be like you? I can't make any sense of this. It's terrible. What are you saying?"

"The word you're looking for is 'convert.' To *convert* to the Jewish religion. To Judaism. But you see, DeFoe, that's not necessary. Our tradition is, if your mother is Jewish, *you* are considered Jewish. Imogen knows that much, I'm sure. No, Imogen needs to be *this* woman in the painting. *This* Jewess."

"I know nothing about your religion, Miss Delbo. Except for the gravestones. I've looked pretty carefully at those. And I know what I've heard Ovid Lamartine say."

Miss Delbo stared at the tablecloth. She cleared her throat, then drank more wine. She fidgeted with her napkin, shaking her head back and forth slowly, but said nothing.

"You know," she finally said, "a certain kind of man, when he realizes that the woman he's in love with is about to leave him for good, decides to propose marriage. For your sake, and Imogen's, don't do that."

"She'd laugh in my face."

"Would that make you ask again?"

"You think you understand my 'nature' that well, eh?"

"I apologize."

"Maybe I've heard enough."

"Our Imogen—mind you, she had a seamstress go to the museum, look at *Jewess on a Street in Amsterdam*, and fashion clothes in exact replica. Imogen of course told me all this. It cost her forty dollars. She could scarcely afford that. All that money; it further convinced me she could not be stopped from crossing over into this new life."

"That's what you call it, a new life? And she actually now wears these clothes in public?"

"The average night goes like this. She studies Dutch paintings for hours. She fills notebooks with jottings. I haven't pried. She puts on the clothes. Midnight, often later, she walks out the door."

"The bellhops haven't mentioned seeing this—"

"This *apparition*? This young woman in her funny costume?"

"However you choose to say it."

"Have the bellhops actually ever met Imogen?"

"No, I don't think so. But my uncle is close friends, he would have bragged—"

"Still, they wouldn't have known to make the connection between you and Imogen."

"The night clerk and whatever bellhop's on duty are often asleep in the lobby. Depends on how late Imogen gets to the hotel. Whoever goes upstairs, they wouldn't ask. If the person looked as if she knew what she was doing. Besides, the hotel gets a lot of foreign visitors. Come to visit other foreigners staying at the hotel. Lots of foreigners come and go; the night clerk might take Imogen for that. If he noticed at all."

"There's one more thing to tell you."

"I don't want to hear it."

"They—your uncle and Imogen—they don't do what you might think they do together."

"I find that hard to believe."

"That was a direct confession from Imogen. A direct answer to my direct question, that is. Imogen even said that sometimes, *often,* in fact, when she visits Edward he's not alone. He's got a woman friend with him."

"What's this 'friend's' name?"

"Natalie."

"That's her name, all right."

"And that some nights Natalie is not in Edward's room. Though from the perfume in the air, Imogen knows she's been there earlier. No matter if Natalie's there or not, they only talk. Edward goes over Ovid Lamartine's broadcasts. He apparently warns her against going to Amsterdam. Imogen, you should know, has for weeks now spoken as if she is the Jewess in the painting. She'll hardly—even at breakfast, pass the tea, pass the scones—she'll hardly answer to the name Imogen anymore. Edward's said the same is true in his room. I am not all that shocked."

"What name does she prefer now?"

"Mrs. Heijman. She insists that I call her Mrs. Heijman."

"Oh my God."

"Insists."

"She thinks that the Jewess is Joop Heijman's wife, then."

"She's convinced of it."

"My uncle hates your tours."

"He hates that I wouldn't have dinner with him. I'm sorry. He's your uncle. He's your professional colleague." Miss Delbo closed her eyes and sighed heavily, then opened her eyes again. She rubbed both sides of her head. "Obviously, I've had too much wine. I've had too loose a tongue. Emotions are flying every which way, aren't they?"

She pointed to her plate with her fork. "Look at this," she said. "I've hardly taken a bite, I've done so much talking. Everything's cold. The soup is cold. *If there's to be no soup tomorrow, cold soup today is a godsend.*"

"What?"

"Oh, just thinking out loud. It's a Jewish proverb. Certain scholars have interpreted it to verify that we Jews have no real belief in the afterlife. And that the life we're given is hard."

"It just sounds as if it's about soup to me."

"DeFoe, I like you. I do like you. I've put some thought into you. You know, people can't help whom they love. In your case, that has two meanings. You can't help that you love Imogen. And you can't *help* Imogen. She's heading into God knows what. In a sense, she's no longer here in Halifax. In a sense, she's already in Amsterdam."

"What if that goddamned painting had never arrived? What if it had never come to the museum? If Imogen had never seen it?"

"It's too late for that, isn't it? You really only need know this. The delusion that Imogen is under—that she's the Jewess—it's the very air she breathes."

"She put you up to this, didn't she?"

"No. What do you mean?"

"She asked you to convince me, didn't she? So she didn't have to face me."

"That simply is not true. My deepest, deepest conviction, DeFoe, is that Imogen is a perfectly sane young woman doing a perfectly sane thing. In light of how she has for so long considered her life a confinement."

"And I'm just in the way. But my uncle isn't."

"I don't know how she sees Edward in the scheme of things. I really can't say. He listens to her. There's that, I suppose. She knocks, he opens his door. She stands there in those clothes. He doesn't shut the door in her face. They share Ovid Lamartine."

"What's in all of this tolerance and understanding for you, Miss Delbo? All these attentions paid Imogen."

"Partly, it's selfishness. I'm afraid it's that I feel covetous. I feel taken over by the boldness of what Imogen's doing. Perhaps I'm envious. Of her trying to determine her own fate. I step back and watch this delusion of hers unfold into a practical thing, a thing she must do to survive, because there's nothing more practical than that, is there? To survive. And believe me, she will not be dissuaded. No opposing logic will work. Imogen Linny will go to Amsterdam. Come hell or high water, she will go."

"You're right. I can't help that I love her. But maybe you're wrong about not being able to help her."

"I knew that if our conversation lasted more than five minutes, it might lead to this."

"How so?"

"Painful as it's been, I've tried to be direct with you. Do me the same courtesy, please. Imogen's asked you to steal the painting, has she not?"

"And I said I would steal it. But I don't know if I could actually do such a thing."

"You must."

"I beg your pardon?"

"I said, you must steal it for her."

"Miss Delbo, you should stop this kind of talk here and now. Before you say something you'll regret."

Miss Delbo clutched both my wrists tightly. "Do it," she said. "Not for your own reasons. Not to please Imogen. Not as part of your hopeless persistence. But because it will finally send her on her way."

"And I'm the one to do that for her. Whom she's humored by. Whom she endures. The museum guard who'd steal a painting."

"DeFoe, listen to me." She let go of my wrists. "You're ignorant of certain things. Everyone in Canada is. I go to synagogue every Friday night. I hear terrible rumors from Europe. People's relatives suddenly gone. No word from them. You've heard Ovid Lamartine speak of this. His broadcasts. Of deathly forebodings. Adolf Hitler. All of it. Well, they aren't rumors.

"Untold horrors, DeFoe. The Jewish community here, even here in the Maritimes, we hear things. We know things. We have relatives in Poland, Germany, all over. Yes, in Amsterdam, too. Though Adolf Hitler is not there yet. Nightmares, DeFoe, I can't begin to—" Now tears filled her eyes.

"Yet you're asking me to help Imogen go there."

"No—well, in a way, *yes.* Moreover, I'm already convinced she's going. There's no turning back, as I've said. What we hear—what we know—is that Hitler wants every last Jew dead. Dead and gone. Erased. But he isn't in Holland yet. He isn't in Amsterdam. But it's clear he wants Germany to swallow all of Europe. What we did—what Edgar has done— Now listen. Edgar wired Joop Heijman in Amsterdam. Indeed, Mr. Heijman lives at the Hotel Ambassade. At my request—*my* insistence. Edgar has told Joop Heijman about Imogen's intent to come to Amsterdam. He's spared Mr. Heijman certain details. He's begged that Mr. Heijman give Imogen a slap in the face, as it were. To try and shake her back to reality."

"Does he know Imogen thinks she's his wife?"

"Not that. Not yet."

"You can't possibly trust such a thing. What if Joop Heijman falls over dead in the meantime? Has he answered the wire?"

"I'm afraid not."

"Does he even have a wife? What do you know about him?"

"We know he lives in Amsterdam. We know his hotel."

"The best thing is to send Imogen to her aunt Maggie's, in Vancouver. For a rest. Somehow force her to go there. I'll sit next to her on the train to Vancouver myself. Did you even know she had an aunt Maggie? I did. I knew that."

"Have you been listening? You haven't understood a thing. Imogen is no longer Imogen. So this Aunt Maggie you speak of is no longer her aunt."

"I can't eat. I don't have an appetite."

"No doubt," Miss Delbo said, "there's a simple way to take the painting. My God, my God, listen to me. A professor of Art History, a guide—listen to what I'm saying.

I'm to be an accomplice. No matter. No matter, really. Because there's an emotion to all of this bigger and more important than who participates in it. There's a simple way to take the painting from the Glace Museum. And in the end, everyone might be better off if it's stolen, who can tell? Who can predict? You go to the museum after it closes. You take the painting. You bring it to my house. You leave. You come back for it early in the morning. You return the painting. You hang it back on the wall. Imogen will have spent the night with it."

"But she's already been alone with the painting all night—in the museum."

"Edward's provided that. You haven't."

"And whatever happens next—should Imogen get swallowed up in Amsterdam—whatever happens next will just happen. And we just step back and wait for news. Or don't hear from her ever again. And chalk it up to fate. Fate set in motion by a half-baked plan. I can't do it."

"You must."

We sat for at least a full ten minutes in silence. Our waiter did not know what to do. Finally, he placed a check on the table.

"You never said what the second thing was," I said. "The second thing Imogen was on the 'verge' of. Second, after coming to despise her life so much that she's had to become someone else."

Miss Delbo looked up from the table and stared out the window. "She was on the verge of— I can't bear to say it."

It was not a riddle; I caught her meaning right away.

"Has she actually tried that? I can't believe she would. She wouldn't do that."

"Such a child."

"Has she actually tried that? Answer me. Has she?" I had raised my voice, so that the waiter whispered something to another waiter, pointing at me. I waved some dollar bills in the air and our waiter hurried over, took the money and check, went to the cash register. We stood up to leave.

"She hasn't tried to kill herself, no," Miss Delbo said. "Not in my house. But she's spoken of it. She spoke of it in regard to some artists she's studied who'd done themselves in— And the wives of some artists. But I knew she was referring to herself."

Miss Delbo put on her coat and left the restaurant two or three minutes before I did. As the waiter returned with my change, I sat watching her through the window. She put her collar up and slowly walked down the street.

Imogen's Tour

Noon the next day, Wednesday, November 30. My uncle had not yet come in for work. I held the clicker: so far, nineteen visitors. One young couple spoke German, I thought at first. But I was wrong. It was Dutch. I am not at all worldly with languages. Especially when people speak in near-whispers, as they had. Many people get reverent around paintings, as if they are in church. The woman walked up to me. "Excuse me, Mr. —" She looked at my name tag. "Mr. Roo-sit," she said. "My new husband—this is Uwe. U-w-e. We are on our honeymoon. We're from Rotterdam. Hello, and thank you for having this painting exhibition."

"I'll tell my curator. He's not here now. I'll say you enjoyed it."

"Yes, tell him, please, hello from us. We, my husband and I, have seen three of these paintings before. Not the *Jewess*, though. Not the pears."

The couple drifted through Room B, only glancing at the permanent collection. They spent fifteen or so minutes in Room A, perused the postcards, decided no, then strolled out the front door.

In the museum, it was a normal morning. My uncle had not shown up. Mr. Connaught was off lecturing. I was alone with the paintings.

Often employees from neighboring shops and business offices came in during their lunch breaks. In summer, people would eat lunch on the squares of grass on either side of the steps, drop in for a brief visit. Colder months, their visits were briefer yet. Sometimes just five minutes. But it was nice they fit paintings into a busy life. Over the years, I had come to recognize our regular lunchtime visitors. We were cordial.

While I kept my eye on things, I went over my dinner conversation with Miss Delbo. I took it apart, put it back together, isolating a sentence here, a sentence there. "She is lost to you." Mulling it over. (Middle of the night, having not slept a wink, of course, I got up to make tea. I said out loud, "Endure—of course, that's right." Yes, I had often felt merely endured.) I thought back on my visits to the cemetery, our walks through the city, vigils in her apartment as headaches racked her. Hour upon hour upon hour spent with Imogen. Now, of course, I felt pathetic. It struck me that Imogen, Miss Delbo, my uncle, even Mr. Connaught, in his own way—certainly Ovid Lamartine—were all somehow beckoned by the world. Whereas I seemed only to be day-to-day enduring it. I felt locked out in the cold. The particular cold of my narrow life; I had not even philosophically ever thought of it as a life, only days lined up behind and in front of me. The narrow alley of cold, of having been born and raised in Halifax, a place I could never, not for the life of me, figure out how to leave.

I shifted to the other side of Room C from *Jewess on a Street in Amsterdam.*

"Imogen heading toward God knows what—" I turned to the voice saying this. But no one was there.

My uncle and I were scarcely on speaking terms. What was odd, however, was that each day he would bring me an object from my childhood. He obviously had been ransacking the hotel's basement storeroom for items I had not seen since I was eight. Each one sent a little jolt of memory through me. He would call me into the custodian's room. "Remember this?" he would say. I would say, "Yes, I do," or, "No, I don't," and often that would be all we said for the remainder of the day. It took me a full work week—six objects—to figure out that with these objects my uncle was really saying, *No matter what or who's come between us, we can't slam shut the door. We have a past. Don't forget that.* In a way, he was using these objects to resurrect my affections. Or at least not allow them to entirely die out. And truth be told, even after all that I took as terrible betrayals, I still loved him.

The first object was a model ship inside a bottle. "Your father and I made this together," he said. I turned the bottle in my hands, inspecting it from all angles. "We made it when you were five. You used to wear this American cowboy shirt. You wouldn't take it off. You slept in it." He was laughing and crying, making a little scene in the custodian's room. I put the ship-in-a-bottle on the shelf; I did not take it home.

However, the object that forced me to say "Enough!" was a Canadian library desk. One night, in mid-November, my uncle had lugged it up the hotel steps, into the electric lift, then down the hall to my room. I found it there when I returned from dinner alone at the train station.

My mother had bought the desk for me when I was seven, just after the Gilbert May Primary School I attended had burned to the ground. School furniture spared by the fire was sold at auction. I remember walking among desks, tables, file cabinets. I remember that the table cost a dollar. A lot of money for us back then, and my mother had outbid another woman by a quarter. We carried the table home from the schoolyard, which took us over an hour on a sweltering day. On the way, we stopped for lemonade at the Lord Nelson, our mid-journey reward. Serving as doorman that day was Paul Amundson—the bellhops took turns at this job. Paul made us leave the table on the sidewalk in front of the hotel. My uncle was already living there, but we did not see him that day. He would have been working at the train station.

My father carried the desk into my upstairs bedroom. That very night, I got up well after midnight to sit at the table. I slid open the drawer, traced my fingers over the gouged swear words, hearts with lovers' initials inside them, TILL DEATH DO US PART, and other such promises. I pried up the top of the metal inkwell, rubbed my finger along the pencil gulley. There was the strong, unmistakable smell of smoke. I worried all night that in some secret place, a knothole, the fire was still smoldering; it could combust and burn down our house. My worry built up, until I slipped downstairs to the kitchen, filled two glasses with water, went back to my room, and doused the desk, inside and out. I dried it with a shirt. But if memory serves, the smell of smoke could not be got rid of.

Emotionally speaking, my uncle kept upping the ante. Because even after I had said "Enough!" he brought in a photograph of my mother, father, me, him together, taken in front of the Lord Nelson Hotel, the day my uncle moved there. He brought in this photograph the afternoon after my dinner with Miss Delbo; my uncle got to the museum at 2:30. I had not yet had any lunch. When I looked at the photograph, I said, "From now on, if I want something from when I was a kid, I'll go down to the basement and get it myself."

He did not look wounded, or even surprised; he gave me a blank stare, grabbed the photograph back, and went into Room A. He sat in a chair, staring at the photograph. I could not stand it. I went in, grabbed the photograph from him, said, "Once you give it, you can't take it back. I've got that fucking school desk in my room for good now. I'm not leaving it to anyone in my will, either."

Mr. Connaught walked in.

"Either of you take lunch yet?" Mr. Connaught said.

"I've had a bite," my uncle said.

"And you, DeFoe?"

"Not yet," I said.

"Well," Mr. Connaught said, "grab a quick lunch, then. Because there's a tour, half hour from now. It's the wives of visiting Members of Parliament, of all things." He went into his office.

I ate lunch indoors at the Lord Nelson. I purposely took an hour. When I got back to the Glace, I fully expected to see Miss Delbo holding forth. I hung up my coat, walked into Room C, and was met by an astonishing sight. Imogen was leading the tour. My first impulse was to get Mr. Connaught, have him toss Imogen out; quickly, though, I realized that he had to know of Imogen's being in the museum. This was between him, Imogen, and Miss Delbo. My uncle came over, took me by the arm, led me to the wall opposite Imogen and the three wives of Parliament. "DeFoe," he said, "this is once-in-a-lifetime museum behavior."

Imogen was standing in front of *Jewess on a Street in Amsterdam*, dressed like the Jewess. It was all just as Miss Delbo had described.

I was a breath away from shouting, "Imogen, what in hell are you doing?" But my uncle whispered, "You think you know a person—"

We both leaned against the wall.

The women each were in their late fifties, I would guess. They each wore a woolen suit; the two with brown hair wore brown suits, the one with black hair wore a suit of coarse blue material. They spoke in pronounced British accents and seemed quite upset that, as one was now complaining, "a Miss Helen Delbo" was not leading the tour.

"Very well, then," the woman in the blue suit said. "If this is to be it, carry on."

Imogen took no notice whatsoever of my uncle and me. "Please join me in front of my portrait here," she said. From their expressions, I thought that the women looked slightly amused that such a small, quaint museum would go to such lengths for authenticity on their behalf. They each shrugged, nodded, even looked curious as to what was about to take place.

"Let me begin"—Imogen said, her voice a bit nervous, but she was enunciating clearly. Though with a sort of poorly done accent. Dutch was what I suppose she was attempting—"by telling you how the artist Joop Heijman came to portray me standing in front of the Hotel Ambassade. In Amsterdam.

"You see, I'd been walking all night, street after street. Because I'd just learned of my parents' deaths. They were in Germany. They were swallowed up by untold horrors there."

"Filthy bastards," the woman in the blue suit blurted. She caught herself up short, pressing her fist to her mouth.

"Miriam!" another woman said. She was the most haughty-looking of the three, to my eyes. Pursed lips, rapidly shaking her head in disapproval, she said, "What can she know of such things?" She turned to Imogen. "What are you, dear, an actress?" She then pushed past her companions, went to the coatroom, put on her coat, and left the museum.

"Stay through it with me, won't you, Eleanor," Miriam said.

"Yes, yes. Of course I will," Eleanor said.

"Go on, then, dear," Miriam said to Imogen.

"And I was just about to go on past," Imogen said,

"when out walked Joop Heijman. He'd just taken breakfast at the hotel. 'Excuse me,' he said, 'but haven't I seen you at the Jewish cemetery?' You see, I was caretaker of the Jewish cemetery in Amsterdam at the time. 'Why, yes, you possibly could have,' I said. Joop told me he walked all over the city. He often stopped at the cemetery, and now recognized me. He brought me inside and we had tea. He realized that I had not had breakfast. He bought me breakfast. He watched me eat. We talked for hours—I did not go to work, even. He had brilliant, clear thoughts, and suddenly he said, 'May I do a painting of you?' He offered me money, which I desperately needed but refused. Because, you see, everyone knew of his genius. I myself had seen a number of his paintings. I thought it would be an honor to be painted by Joop Heijman."

"When you get back to the hotel," my uncle said to me, "take out the Gideon's, page through it till you find *She became what she beheld*, or something like that."

"—and he did many paintings of me. I accepted only meals. He painted me working at the cemetery. He painted me—as you see before you now—in front of the Hotel Ambassade. And while he painted me, we fell in love. Just weeks before, with my parents' death, I had become estranged from my very soul. My marriage to Joop Heijman helped me to reconcile. And now you know my deepest secrets."

Eleanor applauded briefly; Imogen frowned.

"But then tragedy struck. For, just two months after our wedding, my beloved Joop was stricken by a heart seizure and now is bedridden. He no longer paints. His recovery is slow, very, very slow. Naturally, I quit my job to take care of Joop. How would I make ends meet? So when the curator of this museum, Mr. Edgar Connaught, wrote to my husband, asking for a painting, I informed him of our circumstances. I accepted his kind, kind offer to speak to visitors here, in Halifax, about my husband's paintings, about our life in Amsterdam. I must earn money. I send Joop money, of course, but I don't know when I can return to him. You see, I am a Jew. And considering the horrors befalling Europe and mankind—"

"That's directly from Ovid Lamartine," my uncle said. "She got that directly from his broadcast: 'befalling.' We were sitting on the same goddamn bed, me, her, Natalie, when Ovid said that."

He said it loudly again: "befalling." Imogen and the two women turned toward my uncle.

Then to me my uncle said, "I've seen enough," and went into the custodian's room.

"And tell us," Miriam said to Imogen, "where do you reside now? Here in Halifax, I mean."

"I am allowed to sleep in the custodian's room of the museum."

"That won't do," Miriam said. "We'll look into a proper room."

"Impeccable research," Eleanor said. "You've very much inspired me to see all of Mr. Joop Heijman's paintings. What a lovely, lovely innovation, a *gift* really, your performance. And I'm going to have my husband write to your curator as much. But might I make a tiny suggestion? Your accent, while quite fetching, is hardly Dutch. Unless, of course, you weren't in fact supposed to be born in the Netherlands. You didn't mention your country of birth."

Jaw clenched tight, eyes squinted nearly shut, Imogen tried to look untouched by Eleanor's heartfelt remarks. Yet when the two women moved over to *Still Life with Pears* on their own, the tour guide Imogen choked back sobs and hurried from the room. She went into the Ladies', came out in a few minutes. I could tell she had washed her face. Imogen left the museum.

My uncle, who had just come out of the Men's, was zipping up his fly. "Not bad," he said. "Imogen was not bad at all, first time out in public as a Dutch woman."

In front of *Still Life with Pears*, Eleanor said, "I know you believed it was really the wife, Miriam. But come now. Come now."

I stayed in Room C. My uncle went to Room A.

When Miriam and Eleanor left (no postcards), my uncle walked into Room C. "DeFoe, you've no doubt heard by now. Ovid Lamartine's coming to speak, right here in Halifax. In the flesh. It was announced in the newspaper. Why not go with me to see him? We'll go together, uncle and nephew, what say? Just like old times. Because in the future, after all these present estrangements, we'll want to look back and remember this special evening together, eh? This historical event."

"I'll think about it," I said.

"That's all I ask."

"How'd Imogen's tour come about? She's been working

on that little speech of hers for some time, don't you think? How'd it come about, Uncle Edward?"

"Life in Halifax used to be so simple, didn't it, DeFoe?"

I ate dinner alone at Halloran's. I knew that my uncle was eating at the train station. I wanted to avoid him. In fact, later I went in through the hotel's delivery entrance, in case he was playing cards in the lobby. I went straight up to my room. I had brought a book with me, *A Short History of Dutch Painting*, borrowed from the museum shop. I dozed off after reading the introduction. When I woke, it was 11:15. I lay there thinking. I suspected that Miss Delbo had not only allowed Imogen to do the tour but no doubt had rehearsed the lies with her. And Mr. Connaught, he must have been in on it, too. The tour was supposed to show—to whom? Imogen herself?—how Imogen had "crossed over." I sat in my chair. The incident of the tour had become yet another part of a jigsaw puzzle I could not work out. I changed my shirt, threw on my coat, and walked out of my room and down the back stairs. Leaving through the delivery entrance, I set out directly for the Hotel Wyatt.

At the front desk, I said to the gawky, half-awake clerk, "Would you please ring up Edgar Connaught? *Connaught*. Or it might be under *Delbo*. If it's under either name."

"I'm new—second night," the clerk said. He ran his finger along the guest register. "Okay, okay, here it is, Delbo."

He lifted the house telephone and rang the number.

"Yes," he said, "this is Mr. Hanover, at the front desk. There's a Mr.—" He looked at me.

"DeFoe Russet."

"A Mr. DeFoe Russet downstairs to see you," the clerk said into the telephone. "Very good, then." He hung up the phone. "You can go up now."

"Mind telling me which room?"

"Yes, yes. That would be—Room 205. One flight up. Stairs to your left. Or there's the lift."

I started toward the stairwell. "Excuse me, Mr. Russet," the clerk called out. I stopped and looked at him. "There's a packet came earlier for a Miss Helen Delbo. The clerk before I came on didn't deliver it. Would you mind?"

He was not following proper hotel etiquette. I knew, from living at the Lord Nelson, that any personal item should be delivered by one of the hotel staff. Well, the clerk was almost brand-new to the job.

I took the packet and started up the stairs. On the first-floor landing I stopped, looked at the thick envelope. It had the words WORLDWIDE TRAVEL AGENCY, with a logo, a silhouette of a luxury liner, waves lapping against the hull. I said to myself, "Don't open this," then took out my penknife, carefully slid it along under the flap. I took out the contents. It was a pair of third-class ocean liner tickets. One made out to Imogen Linny; the other made out to Edgar Connaught, c/o The Hotel Wyatt. But the envelope indeed was addressed to Miss Helen Delbo, c/o The Hotel Wyatt.

I held on to the railing. Finally, I gained composure enough to walk to Room 205 and knock on the door. Mr.

Connaught opened the door. "I'd never have taken you for Sherlock Holmes," he said. He turned away, leaving the door open. I walked in and shut it behind me. A tray of biscuits and tea was on a small table, at which sat Miss Delbo.

I threw the tickets down on the table.

"Sit down, won't you, DeFoe," Miss Delbo said, looking at the tickets. "I imagine you've had quite a start."

I sat down opposite her. "I looked in the packet, if that's what you mean."

"That desk clerk should be sacked," Mr. Connaught said.

It was the first time I had seen Mr. Connaught in clothes other than a suit. He had on black trousers, a dark blue shirt, black shoes.

"What difference does it make, Edgar?" Miss Delbo said. "DeFoe understands that Imogen is going to Amsterdam, don't you, DeFoe? He just didn't know you'd be accompanying her." She poured me a cup of tea. "When I left Imogen at home, about five o'clock, she was weeping like a widow her first night on the widow's watch. I assume her tour went badly."

"Not so badly," I said. "She convinced one person."

"She was frustrated the British women didn't all utterly believe she was who she said she was. *Knows* herself to be, that is."

I looked over and saw that the bedsheets, blankets, quilt were disheveled; the sight put me more ill at ease.

"I'm happy to have a new room to visit," I said. "You know, I pretty much keep to my own hotel, the museum, Imogen's apartment formerly. My little sheltered life. I've never been on the open seas, for instance. I've stared out at them."

"You're uninvited here," Mr. Connaught said. "And you've torn open very private property."

"It's remarkable, isn't it," Miss Delbo said, "just how much time each of us has spent thinking about Imogen Linny. Remarkable how much we've been willing to do on her behalf. For the moment, I wish I'd studied philosophy, not art. All we've done on behalf of her desires. What, then, do we all have in common? You, DeFoe—Edgar, myself? I wonder. Perhaps it's envy."

"The three of us in this hotel room live with paintings too much," Mr. Connaught said.

"Oh, Edgar, not your longing for the 'real world' again! Spare us," Miss Delbo said.

"Did it ever occur to you both, you might be sending Imogen to her *real* death?" I said.

"Think what you're saying," Mr. Connaught said. "Did you look at the tickets? Of course you did. One for Imogen. One for me. Whatever your dealings with Imogen Linny, I couldn't care less, really. But I know Helen cares for her dearly. Helen feels, don't you, dear, that while perhaps a desperate strategy, still, this gamble with Mr. Heijman could save Imogen in the end. Your Imogen, DeFoe, *is* going to Amsterdam. She's to be a Jewess in Amsterdam. You, I understand, listen to Ovid Lamartine on occasion. You know that Helen is Jewish. Helen herself wanted to escort Imogen to Europe—I would not have it. No. 'You are a Jew,' I said. Simple as that. Mr. Russet, I would rather die than allow Helen to go."

"In this, you might consider Edgar a brave man. A chivalrous man."

"Stupid may be more to the point," Mr. Connaught said. He turned to me. "But no one's put a gun to my head. I do this of my own volition. I've a wire from Mr. Heijman. I've told him to expect us. I didn't go into details. He has wired to me, 'There are others of us here,' meaning painters whose work should be *protected.* I will make that a reason for going, as well. I will attempt to bring back more of Mr. Heijman's work. I will see what I can do, on all accounts."

I looked at Miss Delbo. "Please don't do this," I said.

"You can't help whom you love," she said.

I left the Hotel Wyatt.

One-thirty a.m., I sat in the lobby of the Lord Nelson, just trying to think. To think things through. The night clerk, Ferris Adler, was asleep in his chair in front of the telephone switchboard, with its plugs and wires, headphone. Paul Amundson was in a corner chair at the back of the lobby, asleep, head down on the newspaper. He might read, nod off, wake up like this all night, I knew. I sat on the sofa, far left of the front door, partially blocked from view by tall potted plants to anyone entering or leaving.

It was snowing out when Imogen walked into the lobby about 2:00 a.m. Dressed, of course, as the Jewess. No coat on. No hat. I watched her cross the lobby, go past the front desk and over to the lift. She pulled open the cage gate, stepped in, slid the gate shut, pressed the button. The door closed.

Forget sleep, I said out loud. I sat in the lobby till 4:15 a.m. The door of the electric lift creaked open. Imogen slid wide the cage, stepped out, slid the gate shut. Glancing neither right nor left, she walked directly across the lobby and out the front door. No doubt on her way to study herself in the museum. In that last, solitary crossing of the lobby, I was finally convinced.

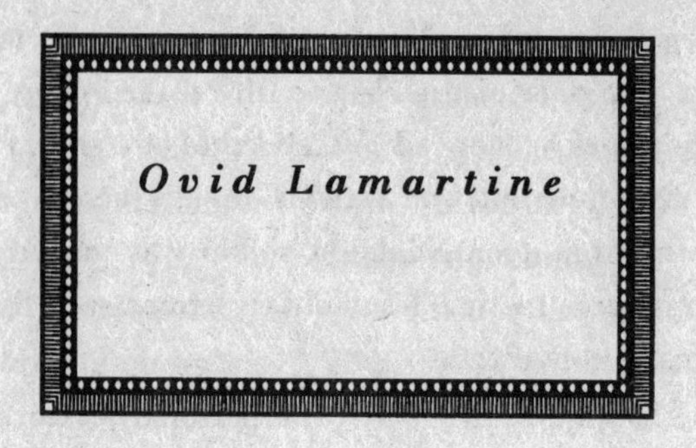

Ovid Lamartine

On December 4, just after I had returned from lunch, Ovid Lamartine walked into the Glace Museum.

That Ovid Lamartine was in Halifax had been front-page news. The newspapers said he was going to meet with local and foreign dignitaries. And he would give a public speech, 8:00 p.m., in the ballroom of the Lord Nelson Hotel. Tickets cost one dollar. In fact, he had broadcast from Halifax the night before. "Hitler is said to love many Dutch paintings," Lamartine said. "*Never* have I heard a more terrifying revelation to the civilized world, in any language, and I speak five." I had agreed to meet my uncle for Lamartine's speech.

It turns out, Mr. Connaught had been informed that morning of Ovid Lamartine's request to broadcast from the Glace Museum. My uncle was only fifteen minutes late for work. At 1:30 Mr. Connaught fixed the CLOSED sign to the inside of the front-door window. Then he called my uncle and me into his office. He got right to the point. "Mr. Ovid Lamartine is to broadcast today, this very afternoon, from right here in the Glace Museum," he said.

"I need to sit down," my uncle said. He sat in the chair opposite Mr. Connaught's desk.

"Let me tell you the whys and wherefores," Mr. Connaught said. "First, we're to receive a group of paintings by Mr. Joop Heijman. Mr. Lamartine personally escorted them from Amsterdam."

"We're putting up a new exhibition, then?" I said.

"Not at all," Mr. Connaught said. "What's happened is actually more complicated. More urgent, you might say. It seems that Mr. Adolf Hitler intends to ransack the great museums and private collections of Germany. And he has authorized monies not be sent to support exhibitions of certain kinds of paintings, to which Germany had previously committed. He is making such judgments. It seems he has, shall we say, narrow tolerances for some kinds of art, a lust for others. Now, as Hitler's armies build—well, no need to go into all that here, just now. More to the point, the paintings that Joop Heijman has sent are mostly on Jewish themes, you see. To my great surprise, the Glace Museum is the only museum in Canada or America to ever have shown Heijman's work. Now we'll have the honor of having ten of them for safekeeping. Plus, of course, the one we already have.

"While I haven't been privy to everything surrounding this circumstance, I do know Ovid Lamartine was introduced to Joop Heijman in Amsterdam. They met a number of times. Consequently, Mr. Lamartine brought the paintings to Halifax, with Mr. Heijman's full consent. This Mr. Lamartine accomplished admirably.

"When he arrives today, he'll have an assistant who will help unload the paintings. You'll help as well. I'm told that Mr. Lamartine has a letter from Joop Heijman, and he'll read that letter as part of his broadcast. That is the extent of my knowledge. Except that Mr. Lamartine is said not to suffer fools gladly."

Mr. Connaught had a few more instructions. As we listened, I could tell that my uncle was flabbergasted by this good luck. He barely nodded or said a word. When Mr. Connaught dismissed us, my uncle went into the custodian's room and changed into a freshly laundered shirt.

In Room C, guarding the Dutch from no one, I kept nervously checking my watch. And at 2:10 there was a loud knocking at the door. Mr. Connaught stepped from his office. My uncle was in Room A. "That would be Ovid Lamartine," Mr. Connaught said. He opened the front door and Ovid Lamartine stepped inside. He took off his overcoat and handed it to Mr. Connaught. He was wearing a brown suit, white shirt, bow tie, brown shoes. My uncle walked up next to me. "From his radio voice," he said, "I would have expected him to be younger." Lamartine looked to be about sixty. He was a tall man, and yet slightly stooped. He had an absolutely haggard face, a grid of wrinkles scoring his forehead. Deep crow's-feet around his eyes. A sagging chin. All in all, a face that seemed to have registered every grave situation he had broadcast about. But that might have been a convenient way to think about his face just then, since on the radio he spoke only about somber events.

"Let me hang up your coat," Mr. Connaught said. "A pleasure and honor to have you here."

"Thank you, sir," Ovid Lamartine said. And there was the familiar voice.

Mr. Connaught gestured to my uncle, who took the coat from Mr. Connaught and hung it in the coatroom.

"I'm Edgar Connaught, curator. We spoke briefly by telephone."

"Ah yes, Connaught," Ovid Lamartine said. They shook hands. "Good to meet you." He looked over at my uncle and me. "And these must be your trustworthy gendarmes."

"DeFoe Russet on the left. And Edward Russet."

"Fellows," Ovid Lamartine said, giving us a military salute, "would you kindly help my assistant. He's outside right now unloading some paintings from a truck. His name is Gertjan Vincent. He's come all the way from Amsterdam. He was my translator there."

Now three people came into the museum, each lugging some kind of reel-to-reel tape-recording device, microphone, other radio equipment. Two men and a woman. They breezed past us and started to set up shop in Room C as if they owned the place.

"They're my Canadian crew," Ovid Lamartine said. "Very professional. They'll set up. We'll do the broadcast. It'll be over in an hour or so. Then, kind sirs, you can open your museum to the public again. Simple as that. We've done this all over the world. Your museum is a piece of cake compared to, shall we say, hit-and-miss situations in Europe."

"I've listened nightly," my uncle said.

"I thank you," Ovid Lamartine said, studying my uncle's face a moment. "My assistant—" He gestured toward the front door.

"Of course," my uncle said.

Ovid Lamartine was all business. My uncle and I went out into the street. We saw a man about my age, short and thin, wearing a woolen sweater, dark trousers, new work shoes. He was unloading a crate. He had already leaned two crates against the flatbed truck. He looked over and said, "Museum guards, not Canadian customs police. Ah, that's good," and flashed a big grin, as if he had said something clever and worldly. The assistant laughed, and my uncle climbed onto the flatbed, maneuvered a crate to the edge, lowered it to me. He then jumped down, and together we carried the crate up the steps and into the museum. My uncle had propped open the door. When we returned to the truck, the assistant had two more paintings waiting for us. He leaned against the truck. "Gertjan meets—?" he said, holding out his hand.

My uncle and I each gave our names and shook Gertjan's hand, and went right back to work. The three of us unloaded the ten crates in short order.

"Mr. Lamartine wishes me to pick him up in one and one half hours, exactly," Gertjan said. "Coffee where, then?"

"Four blocks up Agricola Street," my uncle said. "This street. Toward the park. Or you might find a vendor in the park."

Gertjan turned and walked down Agricola.

"Let's watch the broadcast," my uncle said, as if it would be a dream come true.

As the crew set up with great efficiency, we joined Mr. Connaught and Ovid Lamartine in the office. "Fellows," Mr. Lamartine said. He was sitting in the chair across from Mr. Connaught's desk. Mr. Connaught sat in his own chair. My uncle and I stood to either side of the desk. "You got them all nicely lined up. Thanks a million. I sailed, second class, with these paintings crammed in all around me. Immigrant stowaways we were. Exquisite paintings. In my opinion, Joop Heijman's an artist of the first rank. True, brave artist. In Amsterdam I was staying at the Hotel Ambassade, the same as depicted, I see, in your *Jewess* in the museum here. Edgar's just shown her to me.

"That's Joop's wife in the painting, by the way. Anne Meijer—she's dead. Killed two days after Kristallnacht. Know what that is, by any chance? Kristal nacht—'Crystal Night'?"

"I heard it on your broadcast," my uncle said.

"Indeed. November 9, a few weeks before I sailed to Canada, there was a brutal assault on Jewish-owned businesses, synagogues, Jewish homes. Throughout Germany. Beatings. Murders. Broken windows all over the streets. Broken glass. There's no turning back now."

Ovid Lamartine had obviously given us a shorthand version of the horrors he knew about firsthand. He looked lost in thought a moment, then snapped back.

"I saw a photograph of Anne Meijer, plus she's in all the paintings I brought. Beautiful woman. Joop is devastated. Anne was in Germany, trying hope against hope to get her mother and father out. She was murdered in the street. Joop will stay in Amsterdam. I begged him to come with me. But he'll stay there. He's not a Jew. I'm convinced he'll stay."

"The newspapers have been headlining Hitler's march into Vienna—last spring, correct?" Mr. Connaught said. "And everything else. But we're still in the dark about a lot of it, obviously. Less so because of your broadcasts, naturally."

"Untold horrors," I offered, because it was Miss Delbo's phrase.

"For every one told, ten thousand not told," Ovid Lamartine said dismissively. "You can't possibly—"

"Well, then," Mr. Connaught said.

"Anne Meijer was shot down in the street. Joop Heijman will never know where her body was taken. He's gone into nervous shock. He's assured me he'll never paint again."

"Mr. Lamartine," Mr. Connaught said, "I understand that your broadcast today is to be largely about Joop Heijman."

"Entirely about," Ovid Lamartine said. "I'll be reading from his own words." He reached into his worn leather grip. He took out pages of stationery and showed us the top page. It was printed in English on Hotel Ambassade stationery. "His English is broken but perfectly fine for our purposes. I didn't need my translator with him."

He held up the first page and read: *"Dear Curator Mr. Connaught—*

"I am trusting that my ten paintings from here, Amsterdam, will reach your Glace Museum in good brave hands of Ovid Lamartine, your fellow citizen Canadian. He is leaving shipboard with my work. And he has the knowledge of the murder of my wife, Anne Meijer, in Berlin. The terrible news of such was told me at breakfast here in the Hotel Ambassade where I reside. And where I met Ovid Lamartine. He agreed to bring my paintings to you. Because, where else to send them? You have been keeping on your wall Jewess on a Street in Amsterdam, *and Ovid Lamartine will inform you that the painting is of my wife.*

"Now, let me tell you of each painting."

At this point Ovid Lamartine choked up and could not go on. "I'd better save my voice for the broadcast," he said, glancing away.

"Yes, of course," Mr. Connaught said. Ovid Lamartine went into Room C to join his crew.

My uncle went out to watch. In the office, Mr. Connaught said, "Imogen Linny is not to know about these new paintings, of course. If at all possible. Knowing so many of Joop Heijman's works are here, and what their subjects are, might possibly have an untoward effect."

"She might listen to the broadcast," I said. "It'll be broadcast when?"

"I don't know. Not tonight, I think. What with the public speech."

I was a breath away from saying, "Anything to keep her here." Instead, I went out and stood next to my uncle.

The crew had set up a makeshift studio. Ovid Lamartine sat on a swivel chair at a desk and leaned close to a microphone. "Testing," he said, "testing, testing." The sound checker, one of the men, was adjusting a gauge, calibrating the reel-to-reel. "That's good," he said.

"Right," Ovid Lamartine said. "All set to go?"

The chief engineer, if that is what he was called, said, "Recording—*now*," and snapped his fingers.

First, Ovid Lamartine gave a brief biography of Joop Heijman. He told how they had met. When. Where. He told of their many conversations in the Hotel Ambassade, his visits to Heijman's studio. He told of Anne Meijer; he read the opening passage from Heijman's letter to Mr. Connaught. His voice remained professional and steady, cracking just once, when he said, "Anne Meijer." He paused, took a deep breath, not on purpose dramatic. "The complete letter I will now read connects one man, one artist, Mr. Joop Heijman, in Amsterdam—and his resplendent, murdered wife, Anne Meijer—connects them to *history*. And now we can no longer say, 'We Canadians didn't know. We didn't know such things could happen.' "

Ovid Lamartine gestured to the engineer, who stopped recording. Ovid drank a glass of water. He nodded to the engineer.

"Now," he said, "I shall read the rest of the letter—in Joop Heijman's own words. Mr. Heijman's descriptions and reminiscences of his paintings of his wife, Anne Meijer:

"The first painting is titled Anne Meijer Waking. *The hotel where we lived together, Hotel Ambassade, is on the Herengracht Canal. There, a double light sometimes flew up,*

reflected up to our windows, that of direct sun and the sun off the water. I could say this better in the Dutch language, but so be it.

"Anne woke every morning at 5:00 to prepare her school lessons. She taught small children. And she rose to make breakfast and coffee five mornings weekdays each the same. I might be already in my studio working, or not. If I was in the kitchen before her, it was sometimes I who made the breakfast.

"But as for the painting, two, three mornings in a row I stood in the bedroom doorway to watch Anne Meijer waking. So I saw her actually waking. I felt that was somehow important, you see. I do not think like an opera, the always big emotions of an opera, but of smaller incidents within an apartment or hotel room. So, waking those three mornings on purpose early enough to see Anne Meijer wake up, and she did not say, 'Good morning, darling,' like in American movies about rich people in New York. She said, 'What time is it? Did I sleep too late? The children have been tiring.' How she would say it in English? Exhausting, *I think. Exhausting, as to be worn out."*

The woman assistant opened a thermos, poured tea into a cup, set it in front of Ovid Lamartine, who smiled at her. He leaned away from the microphone to take a sip, then continued with Joop Heijman's letter.

"The next painting I want to tell about is Anne Meijer and the Rabbi of Amsterdam. *You see him and Anne sitting in a café, here, in the painting. This elderly man was Anne Meijer's rabbi since she was a child, all through childhood and up to when she died. This rabbi is a very learned man*

—he is still alive. A very serious man, who was known, Anne told me, to have just one cup of coffee a year. This was true, Anne told me. And because it happened only once a year and nobody could predict when exactly, because it was that way since she was a little girl, she always considered it 'historical' to her Jewish life. The rabbi is having a cup of coffee! How we would laugh. I very much wanted to capture such a moment. But Anne forbade me to see it only in my mind, she demanded I see it with my own two eyes first, then to paint it, and I said, 'But how can this possibly happen?' And somehow—a miracle of good thinking—Anne simply went to her childhood rabbi and asked him did he have his cup of coffee yet this year, he said no he had not yet, and she asked would he have it with her? He said yes! And when the morning arrived, I sat across the canal, inside a restaurant looking out through a window, to watch them talking. Anne did not feel bad or guilty or worried about this, no, because she said, 'Well, he's going to have the cup eventually so why not with me, whom he has known so many years?' And so I saw them talking. I saw them having coffee. A lovely nice warm summer's day like any other, except for all of what I've described.

"And I remember, just now, as I write this, what Anne's father had explained to her, why the rabbi had such a wild big beard flowing down, which she had asked why. Her father had explained that the rabbi had a lot of ancient arguments and opinions, sacred books, sermons, ideas, too many of all of these to keep in his head, so he had to store some in his beard. He told her this when she was very small, when all wild logic made good sense whenever it originated from her father. Later, she knew it wasn't true, naturally, naturally, but still

it pleased her that her father could invent such a reason for the rabbi's beard. So when the day of the cup of coffee arrived, I made sketches. They talked, drank coffee, Anne did not look across the canal even once. Not once. She was a very—disciplined. Very very disciplined person, my Anne. This rabbi knew the sacred books and talked of them—and even I, a doubter about God, and certainly not a Jew, would go hear him speak now and then at the German synagogue.

"And do you know, in the end, they each had two cups of coffee. Anne at home said, 'Well, maybe he won't have one next year, then.'

"And of course it was fated to me to tell him about Anne's death in the streets of Berlin."

Ovid Lamartine finished his tea.

"*Next is called* Anne in the Café du Tambourin," Ovid Lamartine said, turning a page. "*It is a painting come from Anne's request, 'Paint something that each time I look at it I laugh,' which was her one ever request for a painting. Understand, her request came after a terribly hard month of work at her school, another teacher was ill, Anne had to take on extra. Well, as you will see, it is really a copy of Van Gogh's* Woman at a Table in the Café du Tambourin, *but I hope a good painting anyway! Anne was never in Paris, not that she told me about. Though one day she did receive at the hotel a postal card, as you say. From Paris, 'from a friend,' she said. She said, 'Oh, it's all right, some people become a friend once they are no longer something else to you.' I manufactured a jealous temper and tore it up, this card. You see the pieces if you examine closely of the postal card on the floor of the café, under her table! In the painting, I have made her just having torn up the card, as she sits in Paris. I have shown to myself that she no longer cares, and tore up the card. But otherwise here is Anne Meijer, like in Van Gogh's, which is the painting in which he really discovered bright colors. He—Van Gogh, forgive my lecture—was living in Paris, then went to live in the South of France, where he found more and different bright colors. But notice Anne sitting exactly like the woman in the Van Gogh, arms folded across the table. Small round café table. This painting succeeded in making Anne laugh. We simply had put out a table in front of the Hotel Ambassade. I made the sketches. We brought the table back inside."*

Now Ovid Lamartine stood up. He walked directly out of the museum, without so much as a nod to his crew or to my uncle or me. The young woman assistant said, "I'm told he does this. He walks. He thinks. He comes back."

We all stood around, waiting for Ovid Lamartine's return. Mr. Connaught came out of his office, and the young woman said to him, "Mr. Lamartine asked that I offer you complimentary tickets to his lecture tonight." She handed him two tickets.

"I'm afraid I won't be able to attend," Mr. Connaught said. "But my guards here perhaps would like the tickets." He held out the tickets, and my uncle snapped them right up and put them into his back pocket.

"Thank you, thank you, thank you," my uncle said.

Coatless, Ovid Lamartine walked into the museum, sat down, took up the next page of Joop Heijman's letter. The reel-to-reel whirred. "*Next is* Anne Meijer at the Bicycle

Repair," Ovid Lamartine read. *"Paul Van Eerden owns a repair shop, at Keizersgracht 108. It is a crowded, cluttering shop. His good reputation makes certain there are customers always, from when the shop opens to the day's end. We had Paul Van Eerden for dinner just three times during our marriage, all three times within two weeks! Nobody knew why, really. Good feelings were between us always. I remember, a week before she left for Berlin, I said to Anne, 'I would like very much to paint you in front of Paul's shop, all right?' The very next afternoon, a Saturday, I made forty-one sketches. She rode her bicycle there, stood with it out front. Anne rode the bicycle home. I spoke with Paul awhile, a short while, then slowly walked home.*

"And here, the next painting: Twelve Steps, *it is called. In our hotel apartment we have a row of wooden pegs on the wall, in the hallway corridor. On one peg there hangs a smock from Anne's childhood, it has a beautiful pattern of birds. It was—when she was a child—what she wore at meals to keep her dress clean. So, as you see, I have painted Anne as a child—she stands in the rabbi's library in the synagogue. And naturally the smock she has on is again to keep her dress clean, which is a nice summer dress. She is about to visit the rabbi for the first time in her life alone. It is a big moment. An important moment. She is wearing the smock because she wants to keep the dress clean up to the last possible moment. My wife explained all of this, her memories of it. How she waited in the library—you can see the spines of many books. The shelves and shelves of books. Waiting there, she paced off the number of steps to the rabbi's door, from the library to the door, and back. Over and over she counted, one, two, three,*

four, five, six, seven, eight, nine, ten, eleven, twelve. Twelve steps. She paced, and she was at the rabbi's door—and suddenly it opened! She looked up, and there he was. She took off the smock, ran back, and put it on a chair."

Ovid Lamartine went on without a break to read the rest of Joop Heijman's biographies of five more paintings. Gertjan had come back; he and the crew stood by, silent, patient, attending to Ovid Lamartine's every whim. Now, almost done with the broadcast, he signaled to the engineer, who, once again, switched off the reel-to-reel. Ovid Lamartine then stood up and walked to *Jewess on a Street in Amsterdam*, and looked at it for three or four minutes. When he sat at the table again, he looked distraught. He took out a cigarette, lit it, and smoked it while staring at the floor. Each gesture seemed to have such dramatic purpose, more even than a movie actor in a movie. And it was remarkable to me: here we all were, curator, two guards, witnessing a violation of museum rules, smoking a cigarette, but Mr. Connaught did not protest. We just watched. Finally, Mr. Connaught said, "His profession must take its toll. It can't be easy." It took Ovid Lamartine the entire cigarette and a glass of water to be able to read the rest of Joop Heijman's letter.

He read: *"The painting* Jewess on a Street in Amsterdam *shows Anne Meijer in front of the Hotel Ambassade. Let me explain. It is an explanation only I could give, nothing is apparent in the painting itself, except what you see, a woman holding bread. But Anne had been awake all night, no sleep at all, because, why? Because a student of hers—name of Johanna—had suddenly appeared at our door. 'I don't want to go home. I want to stay here with you, teacher' is what she said. Anne took this little girl Johanna in. I went off directly to the girl's house. There I found out she had a big quarrel with her mother and father. The girl Johanna ran off. Ran away. She came to adopt Anne, or wanted Anne to adopt her. For a while I let the girl paint in my studio. I put her in front of a canvas and let her paint. In my studio, where I never allow anybody. Anne made us lunch. Soup. The young student filled the canvas with colors. Nothing you could say, 'Oh, what a nice horse!' or 'Is that your house?' but just colors. A cigar brown. A red. A gray. The girl said nothing, and then Anne took her home. Talking, talking, talking with her all the way down the stairs.*

"This all upset Anne terribly. That night she tossed and turned in our bed, all night for hours, until finally she got up and got dressed and went out. In Dutch it is something clearer, makes more sense, you see—but she said, 'Let me think it out,' and I believe she walked much of the night. I think she walked along many streets. Early in the morning, 6:00, I went downstairs, and there was my wife, Anne, standing in front of the hotel. The loaf of bread was bought at the bakery, Herengracht 109. The bakery opens at 5:00. Anne knew every baker. She knew everyone in the bakery. They have on the wall a painting of mine, a still life with biscuits on a plate. New bread comes out at 5:00, and all through the morning, more comes out. And you see, I never eventually heard more about the student Johanna. Were Anne not gone I would ask. It went perhaps so deep into my memory because we had no children and I believe that was part of what upset Anne so much, that the student Johanna had chosen her."

After a moment's pause, Ovid Lamartine said, "It has been an honor and a privilege to share with you the words of the artist Joop Heijman, who survives in Amsterdam. And let me say this directly—Mr. Adolf Hitler murdered his wife, the Anne Meijer of the letter you have just heard. This is Ovid Lamartine, within twelve steps of the painting *Jewess on a Street in Amsterdam*, broadcasting from the Glace Museum in Halifax, Nova Scotia. Remember: if you wish to make God laugh, make plans. This is *Dateline: Europe*."

Gertjan helped Ovid Lamartine on with his coat. Ovid Lamartine shook hands with Mr. Connaught, then with my uncle and me. "Thanks for the use of your fine museum," he said. "And your personal hospitality." He walked out the front door. Fifteen or so minutes later, the crew had packed up all the equipment and themselves were gone.

"Let's open right up," Mr. Connaught said. He took the CLOSED sign down and went into his office.

"I'm worn out from all the excitement," my uncle said. "I'm going to the hotel. If he asks, tell Edgar anything you want. Use your imagination."

On his way out, he passed an elderly man and woman who had just come into the museum. They kept their coats on. They each had white hair and had scarves around their necks. The man had so many liver spots on his hands, they were like two maps of islands. The woman sneezed hard into a handkerchief. She unbuttoned her coat, locked her arm through her husband's, and they walked to *Still Life with Pears*. They stood well back. But I said, "Not too close, please." They both looked at me. I was hovering no more than five feet away. They moved over to *Sunday Flower Market.*

"See that dwarf," I said. "He's just about to do in that goat. Then maybe the boy in the cart. What do you think?"

The couple just stared at me. They moved again, facing away from me, in front of *Jewess on a Street in Amsterdam.*

"And what's your educated opinion about this painting?" the man said. I suppose he figured I would offer a comment anyway, so why not get it over with. Even turn it into a friendly conversation.

"I think she's the most beautiful woman I've ever seen. Sometimes, and I'm in the room with her a lot, I imagine her with her clothes off. Museum guards are only human. Don't think we aren't."

"I don't think about you at all," the man said.

The woman looked at my name tag, took a pen and piece of paper from her purse, and wrote down my name. She then led her husband into Room B. On their way out, she turned to me and said, "We've really only come to see the Canadian works."

At five o'clock I said to Mr. Connaught, "Good evening, then," walked to the Lord Nelson, and fell into a deep sleep. I woke at 6:45, and ten minutes later met my uncle in the lobby. There was already much activity. Journalists and photographers were milling about. The bellhops kept to a corner table. Finally, Alfred, Jake, and Paul went upstairs to Paul's room to play cards. In the lobby, a sign inside a metal frame read:

OVID LAMARTINE
TONIGHT 8 P.M. FIRST FLOOR BALLROOM
LECTURE
"WHAT CANADIANS SHOULD KNOW ABOUT
HITLER'S GERMANY"
ADMISSION: $1.00

Underneath the lettering was an enlarged photograph of Ovid Lamartine sitting at a desk, speaking into a microphone. On the desk was a file folder with a flaming swastika, the symbol of Hitler's Third Reich, on the cover. The folder was marked TOP SECRET.

My uncle and I met at the check-in desk. He was dressed to the nines. He had on what looked like a new suit. At least it was one I had not seen before. He had on a freshly starched white shirt, buttoned to the top. His shoes were shined. He had gotten a haircut. He looked very dapper. I was in my guard uniform.

"I've already been in the ballroom," my uncle said. "I put my coat across two seats, front row." He awkwardly embraced me.

"Let's go in," I said.

We sat front-row center. Slatted fold-up seats had been set up in neat rows. Already people were lining the side and back walls. There was a cordoned-off section for newspapermen. There were five chairs onstage, each with a RESERVED sign, which struck me as obvious. When we sat down, my uncle discreetly produced a flask and offered me a drink. I declined. Looking around the ballroom, he said, "Amazing. Absolutely once-in-a-lifetime remarkable."

"Bet you thought you'd never actually meet your hero."

"I'm surprised they didn't hold this event in a bigger place."

"Believe it or not, there're probably people in Halifax who've never heard of Ovid Lamartine. They'd say, 'Who?' "

"Idiots. Deaf, dumb, and blind. Close their eyes and ears to history like that. Fools."

"Nice clothes you're wearing. You look as if it's your first day of school."

"I'm showing a little respect. Unlike you, still in your same suit. You could've at least changed your shirt."

"No time. I worked all day, until I went home and took a nap, and when I woke up, time to meet you."

"How long does it take to change a shirt, thirty seconds?"

"If it's already ironed."

"This is goddamned small talk between us."

"I prefer it."

"The big subjects, DeFoe. You never—"

"Uncle Edward—shut up a minute, stop talking a minute, will you? Do you know, when my parents died, what I thought about night after night? For maybe a year. I thought, *What was the last thing I said to them?* I mean, that morning, right before the zeppelin. Before you and I sat down for lunch. You see, for the longest time I couldn't remember, and then suddenly it came back to me. I'd said, 'The sky's too big today.' Mother and father immediately—didn't hesitate a second—looked up at the sky, and my father said, 'No question about it. You're right.' "

"Why're you telling me this? Here and now."

"Because I remember it every goddamned day of my life is what I'm telling you. What I'm saying is some things are *my* big subjects. Not yours. I don't necessarily want yours. I have my own. They might be smaller, but they fit my life. So leave me alone about it. Imogen Linny was my big subject; then she became yours, too. I've got some subjects I don't even tell you about. I regret ever telling you about Imogen in the first place. I regret the day you two met. It was the biggest mistake in my life, just even to introduce you."

"You lost your parents. Now you're about to lose Imogen—that's what connects them. Imogen told me she's going to Amsterdam. It's a fact of life. She's going, DeFoe. She'll be *gone*. So—maybe in a year, say. I mean, time passes. So maybe in a year we can talk to each other like human beings. I can wait. What else am I going to do? Imogen's a passing fancy."

"Not to me."

"Well, you think that *now*."

I turned away from my uncle. I noticed that scattered throughout the ballroom were no less than thirty policemen.

My uncle took a swig from his flask. Local dignitaries filed onstage, along with Ovid Lamartine, who was carrying the loose-leaf pages of his speech. The moment he appeared, a number of people rushed the stage, holding out autograph books or pieces of paper, pens, calling out, "Mr. Lamartine, would you?" and so on. Two policemen crouched at the edge of the stage, scanning the crowd. Ovid Lamartine nodded in a weary, resigned way, walked to the front, bent down, took a woman's pen, and signed her autograph book. Every step he took, Officer Kellen was right there next to him, acting as Ovid Lamartine's bodyguard. I knew it was a big day for Kellen, too. He studied each autograph seeker, all but placing himself between Lamartine and anyone else. "Please, one at a time, please," he said. "Step back now. Step back now." But Ovid Lamartine said something to Officer Kellen, who himself then stepped back five or so feet. Officer Kellen's face was stern, his holster was unsnapped. He moved a few steps closer to Ovid Lamartine.

I wanted to see my uncle's reaction to all this excitement, so I turned to him, and in that instant, a look of terror overtook his face; he said, "No!—" and pushed hard past me toward the stage. Mind you, this all happened in a matter of blurred seconds. I turned with my uncle. To the right of a cluster of autograph seekers, a short man dressed in a brown suit and bow tie lunged forward, holding a pistol. A shot was fired—Ovid Lamartine raised his hand to his cheek, drew it away, and looked at the blood. He took a step forward, then fell back against Officer Kellen. The shooter pushed in among the autograph seekers, there was a second shot—the woman who had been first to get an autograph suddenly looked dumbfounded, then fell in a swoon, and no one caught her, and she slid sideways off a man. I heard her head hit the hardwood, I was that close. All was panic now; my uncle launched himself at the shooter. I said, "Don't—he's got a gun!" Which of course was why my uncle went for him. Now a third shot pierced my eardrums, smell of gunpowder, I almost tasted it. Officer Kellen brought his hand to his chest, then collapsed to the floor. Glazed look on his face. He had lifted his revolver but could not risk shooting into the crowd—

My uncle was now on the man. And then my uncle was flat on his back. And I had heard no gunshot. I can only assume now that his body muffled it.

I think that my uncle Edward was dead by the time he hit the floor. I think he was already gone. Two or three people—I do not know, maybe a dozen—stepped over him while fleeing. I leaned down next to my uncle. I was vaguely aware of the pandemonium taking place: shouting, crying, pushing, chairs knocked over.

A fourth, then immediately a fifth shot rang out. A dignitary onstage fell, and a police officer fell. Suddenly the murderer was out in the open, next to the stage. And two policemen slammed him to the floor from behind; a third came up and started to pummel him about the face and the back of his head. Two more officers caught his arm midair and threw him off. "Ambulance! Now—ambulance! Ambulance!" a voice shouted.

A strong hand on my shoulder, and I looked up to see a kind, distraught face, a man in his sixties. He said loudly next to my ear, "I'm a doctor! Please. Let me look." I stood up. My heart was pounding. *Pounding*, and I did not know what to do at all. I raged then toward the murderer, pressed to the floor. I kicked him in the head. I saw blood at his ear, and then a police officer slugged me square in the jaw and I reeled backward into the front row of seats. I had not been knocked out, just dazed, and I sat up in a chair. The officer who had struck me sat down next to me. He held my arms. "Son, son, hold on," he said. "Hold on now. Are you related to this man?" He nodded toward my uncle. The doctor had opened his blood-soaked shirt and was inspecting a stomach wound. Then he closed the shirt. The doctor took off his own suit coat and laid it over my uncle's face. "Oh —no," I said. "No, no, no, no." The officer said, "Are you related?"

"He's my uncle," I said.

"Stay here," the officer said.

I hid my face in my hands, but could hear the absolute stampede out of the ballroom. There were screams and shouting, and at one point someone yelled, "It's over! It's over!" But who could believe that? I looked up. There were at least ten officers holding down the murderer, who was moving his head with great difficulty back and forth, as if gasping for air. "Fucking son-of-a-bitch," he said, over and over.

"He's a foreigner?" an officer said to his sergeant. I recognized the sergeant as Pinnie Oler. Sergeant Oler was riffling through the murderer's wallet. He examined a card or license of some sort. "He's a Canadian citizen," Sergeant Oler said. "Lives here in Halifax." He looked over and recognized me, I think. He sat down in the chair next to mine.

My head was pounding, as if the noise had suddenly entered it, and I felt all cramped up and clutched over in the chair. "The guard from the museum, right?" Sergeant Oler said. "You going to be sick?" I shook my head no. "Okay, okay now, son. I'm going to ask you to stay right here, understand? Because we need you as a witness. Understand? I've just been told this is your uncle lying dead right here, and I know you want to kill the bastard who did this, but try and stay in the seat, understand?"

"I've already kicked him."

"I saw that. And nobody's going to care about that. You aren't responsible for that. Jesus, what a bloody mess—look at this, will you?" That last sentence he said more under his breath. He squeezed my shoulder. "Wait here now."

The doctor was summoned onstage, and I watched him examine both Ovid Lamartine and Officer Kellen; each time he shook his head grimly. Police officers had formed a circle around the bodies, keeping away the photographers. "Back off!" Pinnie Oler said to one as he approached the stage. "I'll kick your goddamned face in!" The photographer backed off a few yards, snapped a picture, turned, and Sergeant Oler kicked him in the backside; then two other policemen yanked him by the collar and pushed him down the aisle a ways and let him stumble off.

The air was filled with gunpowder burn; my uncle's blood had pooled out and was running in a stream up between my shoes. I held perfectly still. The blood moved around either side of my left shoe. For some reason, I heard the hotel shoeshine man Winston Barnett's voice just then: "I'll have to use two different brushes on this—" But, of course, Winston was not there.

The last thing I remember before Sergeant Oler escorted me from the ballroom was his saying to another officer, "We've got four dead, officially. Keep the newspaper hacks out of the station as long as you can. This Lamartine's no small potatoes."

After I gave a statement at the police station, I had to identify my uncle's body at the morgue, on Broyton Street. A police officer, whose name I never caught, drove me over there. I told him I wanted to walk home. He said fine. I stopped in an apothecary's and telephoned Miss Delbo at home, told her the news, and asked her to call Mr. Connaught. I hardly registered her response. I just said what I had to say and hung up. And then I did not know what else to do, so went to the hotel and directly up to my room. But word about my uncle must have spread fast among the bellhops and the rest of the hotel staff, because some decision had been made, and my telephone rang. It was Mrs. Steig, from down in the laundry. "If you want, I'll leave a few baskets of shirts down here," she said. "I'm going home, DeFoe. My condolences. Natalie fainted from the news, in the second-floor hallway. She was sent to hospital, and I'm going over to see her now." I heard her break into a sob. "Edward was always a gentleman to me," she said. She set the telephone down on its cradle.

Taking the back stairs so as to avoid the bellhops, I went down to the laundry. Mrs. Steig had lined up five wicker baskets full of shirts. Somebody, one of the bellhops no doubt, had left a bottle of whiskey on the ironing board. Taped to it was a note: *When you've had enough of this, don't forget to unplug the iron. We don't want a fire, do we?* It was signed, *Ever practical, Edna Steig.*

I did drink some whiskey. I kept a clear enough head

to iron, though. I went through the first basket, concentrating harder and harder on each consecutive shirt. And then I realized, much to my shocked surprise, that I was still wearing my guard suit coat, which was stained with my uncle's blood, and so was my shirt, from when I had embraced him, lifted the doctor's suit coat and kissed my uncle once on the forehead. I took the suit coat off, then my shirt, and threw them into a hamper and put on a newly ironed white shirt, I do not have any idea whose shirt. I pressed the iron down on yet another white shirt—the sounds of the ballroom set up a racket in my head. I could not shake the sounds. Nor the sight of my uncle. Laid out in the morgue. A tag on his big toe. I went on to the second basket. It was warm and humid in the laundry room.

I ironed for an hour, maybe two, I do not know.

Quite silently, except for the light rustle of her dress and the slightest clearing of her throat, Imogen Linny stepped into the laundry room and sat down in a wooden chair in the corner nearest the door. She did not walk up to embrace me; I did not embrace her. I looked at her for a moment. She was dressed as I had seen her in the museum when she had led her tour, dressed as she was that night when she walked through the hotel lobby, into the electric lift, up to see my uncle. Dressed as the woman in *Jewess on a Street in Amsterdam.* Her face was swollen from crying. "The worst news" is all she managed to say. She was looking directly at me when she said it. Her face held a certain defiance, childlike; she was beautiful, I thought, and in no common way pitiful. I stood at the ironing board, she sat in the chair. She simply sat there watching me iron shirts. No conversation whatsoever. No jolt of further estrangement; certainly no sense of reconciliation. We were locked in the immediate present is what sensation I felt. In front of Imogen I worked my way through the next two baskets of shirts. I was taking five, six minutes with each; *Work carefully around the buttons*—an entirely different voice, Altoon Markham's, came back to me. The hundred mindless decisions of ironing a shirt.

When the folded shirts were all neatly stacked in baskets, I glanced over at Imogen; her head was bowed. I then walked past her and up the back stairs to my room. Standing at my streetside window, I saw Imogen leave the hotel—now the desk clerk, maybe the bellhops, would see her—and wander across the street, into the park. I did not even beg the question should I sleep? Forget sleep. Forget ever sleeping.

The next morning, a tower of newspaper headlines:

FOUR KILLED BY ASSASSIN
AT LORD NELSON BALLROOM

RADIO "VOICE OF CONSCIENCE"
OVID LAMARTINE STRUCK DOWN

MURDER WITNESSED BY HUNDREDS

Museum Guard's Attempt at Heroics Fails

Murderer Briggs Roland, 53,
offers reason for brutal attack:
"Ovid Lamartine gave us too much bad news."

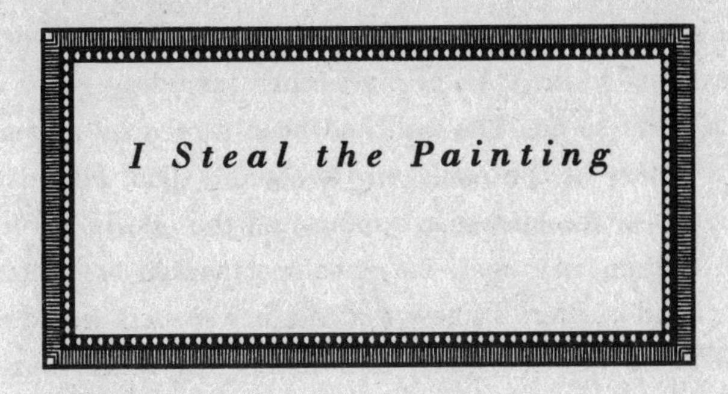

I Steal the Painting

The morning after the murders at the Lord Nelson Hotel, I went into my uncle's room. I simply had asked the desk clerk, Warren Kastner, for the key. He did not hesitate. In the room I went directly to the small safe in the bedroom closet. I had kept the combination taped to the back of my bureau mirror: 16, CLOCKWISE TO 5, LEFT TO 19. I took out all the contents and laid them on the bed. The bed had not been made; maid service—it was not Natalie's floor—must have felt a little spooked to come in. I understood that. There was fifty-five dollars in cash. There was an envelope full of newspaper clippings about the zeppelin crash, my mother's and father's obituaries. In a larger envelope, my uncle's Last Will and Testament. The will itself was sealed with wax. I opened it. It was brief. I was disappointed that it was so out-of-character; I mean, no opinions, no ramblings. Of course, I should not have had such personal expectations of language for a will, even my uncle's. No instructions for his gravestone. It left all "worldly possessions" to me. "All of my clothes, including guard uniforms," and so on. The will had been signed by my uncle and a notary at the bank, on October 1, 1935. He left me the radio in the custodian's room and the one in his hotel room. I then tore open the envelope marked MY OBITUARY, hand-written. I knew that the newspapers would continue to be full of articles mentioning my uncle. But the obituary kept in his safe was to be the official document for the obit page. Attached was a note: *Please bring to newspaper.*

Here is how the obituary read:

> Edward Russet (age), of Halifax, Nova Scotia, died (date). His beloved brother, Cowley, and sister-in-law, Elizabeth, died in the zeppelin accident of 1916. He is survived (if true) by his beloved nephew, DeFoe Russet, also of Halifax, and his wife, Altoon Markham, of Regina, Saskatchewan. Edward Russet was a museum guard at the Glace Museum for (number of years).

There was a second note attached:

> *DeFoe, if it's you reading this, please send a copy of the obituary to: Altoon Markham*
> *c/o the Todd Hotel*
> *45 Cliffe St.*
> *Regina, Saskatchewan.*
>
> *PLEASE—NO FUNERAL.*

I broke down then. I could not help myself. I sat on my uncle's bed, exhausted from no sleep. I looked around the room. He had owned so little. No chance ever of his room being cluttered. I looked in the closet; his clothes were neatly arranged. At my uncle's table I filled in the blanks of his obituary. He died at age forty-eight; he had been a museum guard for fifteen years.

Locking the door behind me, I returned the key to Warren Kastner. "Warren, my uncle's room needs to be tidied up," I said. "And please have Jake—or somebody—bring his personal belongings to my room, okay?" Warren nodded. "You got it," he said. I walked across the lobby and said hello to Jake Kollias and Winston Barnett, who were talking near Winston's stand. "Are you all right?" Jake said to me. "Anything you need?" I just shrugged. "Come on, then," Winston said. "I'll give you a free shine."

After my shine, I walked to the newspaper office and delivered the obituary. It cost me two dollars for the next day's edition.

I then walked to the Wiggins Funeral Home, where my uncle now resided. It was the funeral home I had requested, because it was the only one whose name came to mind. The director, Mr. Peter Wiggins, met me in the reception room. He was a stout, mustached man, with thick black hair swooped back in tight waves on either side of his head. We shook hands. "My heartfelt condolences, Mr. Russet," he said.

"Thanks."

"Would you like to sit down?"

"I prefer to stand, thanks."

"If I may ask, where is your uncle to be buried?"

"I don't know."

"Generally there're prior arrangements, you see."

"He didn't make any."

"I see."

"What do you suggest?"

"Well, in my opinion he should have a hero's funeral, trying to save Ovid Lamartine like that."

"My uncle didn't want a funeral. In his will it says, 'No funeral.' "

"All right then. There's the cemetery plot. There's the casket, the undertaker's general tasks. Cemetery crew. A minister, priest, whatever the preference."

"I have forty or so dollars saved. Plus a fifty-five-dollar inheritance."

"Can you somehow raise another hundred? I could work it out, cut corners here and there. That would, mind you, not allow for certain more extravagant services. But your uncle, from what I read, was a working man, was he not? A museum guard. A modest burial would be in keeping. We could see it in that light."

"I think it's the light I can afford to see it in."

"Then it works out conveniently."

"Okay."

"There's no shame in any of this, Mr. Russet."

"Thank you."

"All the articles about your uncle's bravery. Perhaps someone would come forth. A benefactor."

"That would be wrong, a total stranger. I couldn't accept that."

"I understand. Of course."

"I'll need a little time."

"Of course."

"Thanks."

"How much time, do you suppose?"

"A day or two."

"That's fine. Fine, then. He was a brave man cut down in his prime, your uncle. The world is falling apart, Mr. Russet. A museum guard, a gentleman, murdered like that. In the service of mankind. Just like Ovid Lamartine. Always serving mankind."

"I guess today's papers—I haven't looked—are full of my uncle and Mr. Lamartine."

"Quite prominent. To my mind, your uncle's a hero. I hope they hang the son-of-a-bitch who did this."

"Me too. That's how I feel."

"If I were you, I'd want to be the hangman. Personally."

"To be honest, it hasn't all sunk in yet."

"I see that a lot in my business. It often takes a few days, and even then. I'm sorry for your loss, Mr. Russet. I hope they hang the son-of-a-bitch. I realize I'm outside of funeral home etiquette, saying as much. But I've said it and meant it."

"I don't forgive him."

"I wouldn't. 'Gave us too much bad news.' There's *only* bad news out of Europe these days. What'd Briggs Roland expect, sweetness and light? You hang him. I'll refuse the body. How's that? We'll work together on that."

"Okay, Mr. Wiggins. I'm going now. I'll speak with you soon."

"Did your uncle have a religion? If you don't mind me asking. Because that's useful information in my business. Because I can make inquiries for a gravesite. Some churches are more charitable. But I'd have to be aware of a religious preference, if there was one."

"No, I can't say there was."

"For instance, did your uncle go to a particular church, even as a child?"

"He never said."

"No preference, then."

"He pretty much disliked them all equally."

"He was a philosophical man, then, I take it."

"In his own way, yes. Yes, he was."

"He acted in good faith. Last night."

"I'll remember you said so."

"Mr. Russet, I'm obligated to ask. Do you want to view the body? I've made him look peaceful."

"I trust you did, Mr. Wiggins. But I think I won't view my uncle."

"That's your privilege. Goodbye, then, Mr. Russet."

We shook hands, and I left the funeral home.

Because I did not know where else to go, I went to the museum. Mr. Connaught had left his office door open. He could see visitors come and go. When he noticed me, he hurried right out. He stopped a few feet away from me. "There's absolutely no need for you to be here today,

DeFoe," he said. He had genuine concern in his voice. "Go home. Take care of family business. We're fine here. I meant, I'm fine, that is. I've hired a temporary guard, beginning tomorrow. And I'm taking a sudden leave, for 'personal reasons' is what I've told the Board. They don't need to know anything else. My seniority speaks for itself."

"I read the tickets closely, Mr. Connaught. I know when the SS *Hagersforse* leaves Halifax. Tomorrow, isn't it?"

"Precisely, DeFoe. I wish—and don't wish—it were elsewise."

"I've got nobody else. I need some advice. Is why I'm here. I didn't know it till just now."

We went into his office, sat down opposite each other.

"My uncle left me fifty-five dollars," I said.

"You need funds for a proper funeral, is that what's front and center on your mind? I imagine it might be."

"That, and where to bury my uncle. I don't know which church cemetery, since he didn't practice a religion."

Despite himself, Mr. Connaught burst into laughter, just for a moment. "I'm sorry, DeFoe," he said. "But *never* has there been a greater understatement."

"No, I guess not," I said. I laughed a little, too. "There's public cemeteries, of course."

"Edward's a hero, Ovid Lamartine—now, this just occurred to me. Lamartine said one of the things most intolerable about life is that you can't control where the truth comes from, let alone what the truth is. You've gotten a lifetime's worth of truths these past few weeks, haven't you? What with Imogen Linny's decision. And now Edward's untimely death. The spectacle of it. I can hardly believe it myself. I can hardly believe we won't be seeing Edward in the museum anymore. I don't see how you can even remain standing up, DeFoe, let alone come in here today. I should fairly collapse, if it were me. The grief and confusion, what to do, what to do. Everything and whatnot. Perhaps your being an orphan from so early on—Edward apprised me of all of this, of course—perhaps your being an orphan provided you with some familiarity with sudden absence. Gave you some inner resource to call on at such moments. I of course can't say."

"I've got to bury my uncle is my main problem just now, Mr. Connaught."

"We're down to the most practical business, then, aren't we?"

"Yes, sir. We are."

"I've made a decision just now. Just this very moment. I've decided to— How much do you need?"

"One hundred dollars."

"I will personally provide that amount."

"I'd need it to be a loan. I can't accept it otherwise. But since I have nowhere else to go, I accept."

"Accept it on your own terms, then."

"I'll take a little out of my weekly pay."

"That's fine."

"I appreciate it."

"I know. In fact, I'll give you the money right now, from the museum safe. I'll replace it from my personal account."

Mr. Connaught got up from his chair. "DeFoe," he

said, "let's have this clear between us. I know that Edward would not approve of our little transaction here. Of my assisting."

He opened the museum safe, which was part of the desk. I looked away as he worked the combination, even though I could not even see the spin lock. He took out five twenty-dollar bills, closed the safe, spun the lock. He handed me the money.

"There now. That's done, isn't it."

"Please write out an IOU."

"Come now, DeFoe. Is that necessary?"

"There's still the question of where to bury my uncle. I'll go back to my room and think it over. Maybe ask the bellhops."

"You'll have Edward buried in my plot."

"What—"

"I have a plot. Actually, I've had it for years now. It's in the cemetery just off Connaught Road, no relation. Except, you see, I always thought it was a frightening irony. *Connaught Road*, the cemetery there. It always made me a bit uncomfortable, truth be told. I have no ancestors in Halifax—nor anywhere in Canada. I was born and raised outside London. Well, up to the age of fourteen, that is. Then I came to Canada. So—last year, actually—I decided that I didn't want to be buried in Halifax at all. I wanted to be returned to England. My sister, well, she's all but senile now. But long ago she told me that she, too, wanted to be buried in England. I've arranged for that. In fact, she's never owned a plot here. There it is, then, DeFoe. How's that for wrapping it up nice and neatly? And already paid for. Edward can move right in. I'll take the necessary steps. A matter of a telephone call, I imagine. Perhaps a small amount of paperwork. Here, let me write out a letter to that effect; you deliver it to the funeral director, right?"

Mr. Connaught slid a sheet of museum stationery out of his top drawer, wrote two paragraphs, signed the letter, folded it into an envelope, handed it to me.

"Whether or not it's for generous reasons, your doing all this is very generous," I said.

"It's all decided, then. I'll keep my reasons to myself. We'll just let sleeping dogs lie."

"You've been a good employer, Mr. Connaught. No matter what happens now, that's been true. I've always thought it. I've got no complaints."

"Your uncle will be provided a decent burial, DeFoe. These are the bargains with the Devil, aren't they? Of sorts. Let's not forgive each other our trespasses, and just get on with the business at hand, shall we?"

"My uncle didn't want people standing around a hole in the ground. That's how he put it. He said that, sober, more than once."

"Honor his wishes, then. Who would have come to a funeral? If there was one."

"The bellhops at the Lord Nelson. You, I imagine. Miss Delbo, I imagine. I think she would have. A few other museum guards—a fellow from over in Dartmouth. Natalie, who works at the hotel. And I'll face up to this: Imogen Linny. For the short time they knew each other, she'd have been there. They had a separate kind of friendship is the best way to put it, I think."

"This morning an officer named Pinnie Oler—apparently you've met. He came into the museum with a request. He called your uncle a hero. He'd just come from putting Ovid Lamartine's body on a train to Toronto, where his brother resides. This officer, Pinnie Oler, suggested we name a room after Edward. Here in the museum. He, Sergeant Oler, said he'd petition the Glace family. He said he himself could get a thousand signatures from citizens of Halifax. He was enthusiastic, in a somber way. He suggested that we memorialize Edward on behalf of the city of Halifax, for a job well done. For acting as a responsible citizen, without cowardice. I told Sergeant Oler, and meant it, that I'd take his request to the Board of Directors. He thanked me for that. I, of course, will not be at our next meeting. But I hope to bring it up at a future one, DeFoe. I promise you, as well."

"Mr. Connaught, you and my uncle—you never—"

"We had a *truce*, DeFoe. In my experience that's much better than one has with most people in the world. I won't have a moment's hesitation or feeling of hypocrisy speaking on behalf of a permanent commemoration."

I stared at the desk a moment.

"He wasn't a bad museum guard," I said.

"He despised the job. For the most part."

"Which room would you think? To name after him."

"Room A. He much preferred Room A; it was the quickest to leave from. Close to the custodian's room, too. His radio."

"I'll be taking the radio, eventually."

"I think that Mr. Tremain would have attended the funeral. He and Edward got along well."

I stood up and turned toward the door.

"You're a successful museum guard, DeFoe," Mr. Connaught said.

I left the museum.

That evening just after dark I stood in front of Miss Delbo's house, 404 Albemarl Street, staring in through the dining-room window. It was a dark green, two-floor, wooden house with a chimney, black shutters, a small porch. There were patches of snow on the roof. It was a quiet neighborhood. Imogen sat at the table, shuffling through books, feverishly writing in a notebook or journal of some sort. Every so often Miss Delbo walked past, stopped at the table, looked over Imogen's shoulder, pointed to a page in a book. I saw both their mouths move, and then Miss Delbo would disappear into another room. It was quite cold out. It had snowed a little that day, and now it was again. I found myself mumbling as if to Imogen, "Maybe in a day you'll actually be gone." Testing out that possibility. I felt both shattered and hopeful. Hopeful, because deep in my heart I could no longer bear her presence in Halifax without seeing or talking with her. Shattered, because even after the betrayals, mind-boggling confusions, I still felt I could help who I loved. And I loved her.

At wit's end, I went back to the hotel. Usually Winston Barnett went home at six o'clock, but there he was in the lobby. His stand was dismantled and placed in the corner.

"I've been waiting for you, DeFoe," he said. "Some of us are holding a little memorial service in the kitchen." He had his Sunday suit on.

I followed Winston into the hotel kitchen. The long table, where baker Francis Voigt shaped and pounded bread dough, made his loaves, biscuits, scones each day by 7:00 a.m., had been cleared. Chairs were set all around. Jake Kollias, Paul Amundson, Alfred Ayers, each dressed in a suit, were already sitting down. A few bellhops who had long ago retired, and whom I had not seen in years—Peter Aldrich, Ignatius Stamp, Stanley Lane, among them—were standing near the table.

"Here's DeFoe, then," Alfred said.

The bellhops crowded around me, each giving me a pat on the back or shaking my hand, condolences all around. Good clear things were said. Awkward, painful things were said. All well-meaning. "I've already wiped the slate clean," Jake Kollias said. "One hundred eighty dollars owed me for poker debts, over the last two, three months, gone up in smoke, eh? Out the goddamn window. DeFoe, it's nobody's worry now."

"Best thing to do, my advice?" Alfred said. "Drink till you think you're mayor of Halifax."

"That's the ticket," Jake said. "Give DeFoe here a stiff drink, will you, Paul. Norwegians don't scrimp when they pour, do they now."

"I never have personally," Paul said. He poured me a whiskey.

I threw it back. The whiskey burned my throat and spread a warmth in my chest. Paul said, "I drink this stuff to forget my family in Norway. Then I always drink too much of it, and my family in Norway's all I can think of."

"Can't win for losing," Jake said.

There was subdued good cheer for an hour or so. Stories about my uncle all around. Mr. William Tecosky, my old boss at the train station, was in the kitchen with us, reminiscing back twenty years. "Other than Edward commenting about a passenger's choice of a suitcase now and then, or some other such snobbery, he was one of the best men I ever worked with," Mr. Tecosky said. We ate part of a ham that was supposed to be served for the next day's lunch in the hotel and some potato-and-leek soup. But mostly we drank whiskey, and in fact ransacked the wine cellar without fear of the consequences. At about ten o'clock, all the present and former bellhops, plus Mr. Tecosky and I, were slumped at the table. Paul Amundson was asleep on the floor; he had gathered a pile of chef's aprons and hats into a makeshift bed. Twice during the evening he had gone on and on about something in Norwegian. It seemed to wear him out. Earlier, too, Warren Kastner had looked in on us, but finally gave up any hope that a bellhop would actually help an arrivant or somebody about to leave the hotel with their luggage. In fact, at one point, when I had gone to the Men's, I saw a man standing next to three suitcases and a trunk, in front of the check-in counter. He was smashing his fist down on the counter bell. I do not know where Warren Kastner had gone; the bellhops were weeping and laughing in the kitchen. The man, dressed in an expensive overcoat with a fur collar, looked at me. I went behind the counter, surveyed the wooden hive of keys, took out the key for Room 38, handed it to him, and said, "The bellhops are indisposed just now. Why not take your bags up, the paper-work can wait." He looked badly affronted. He put the key on the counter, turned as if to leave, saw it was snowing and that his cab was gone, then picked up two suitcases and walked to the electric lift.

Back in the kitchen, I sat between Jake Kollias and William Tecosky and drifted off to sleep. I did not sleep for long. I woke with my face close to Jake's. I had drunk more than I ever had, and guilt tore through me. The dull pain of guilt, because I had come to despise my uncle for his time with Imogen, and now he was dead. Despised him for shov-ing the ineptness of my life in my face so often. For saying, "She drank so much ice water—." That kind of thing, which had been my intimate knowledge about Imogen before it was his. I could not figure out why my uncle had so fiercely added to my woes with Imogen, is how I thought of it. But maybe he was only doing what he had always done, living tenfold what I could, and the most recent part of that simply included Imogen. I was dizzy with opposing logics (Miss Delbo's phrase). I said out loud, "You had Natalie. You should've left Imogen alone." Jake lifted his head slightly, his eyes barely squinted open. "What?" he said. "What'd you say—you should've what with Natalie?" He tried to focus his eyes on me, then said, "Oh, fuck it, I'm nodding back off," and laid his head down on the white table-cloth.

I stepped out into the lobby. The three suitcases were gone; the trunk was still there.

I went back into the kitchen, got my coat. I more or

less navigated my way out the front door. The cold night air snapped in my nostrils, slapped my face, sobered me a little. I slowly walked down South Park to Agricola Street. In front of the Glace Museum, I fumbled for my key. Finding it, I walked up the stairs, unlocked the door, stepped inside, shut and locked the door behind me. I stamped snow from my shoes. I took off my coat and hung it in the coatroom. I do not know why, but suddenly I spun the postcard rack hard, postcards flew off, landing all over the floor of Room A. I bent down and spent the next few minutes picking them up, returning them to the rack.

The museum was cold. I took the flashlight from under the bookstore counter and walked into Room C. I sat on the viewing bench in front of *Jewess on a Street in Amsterdam.* By the light of the streetlamp I could see snow drifting down past the windows.

There are any number of ways a painting can be ruined for a museum guard. Ways a guard can come to hate a painting; come to beg another guard to switch rooms. Beholden, until he asks you in turn to switch. Yet how could I ever have imagined the sequence of events that had so terribly ruined *Jewess on a Street in Amsterdam* for me? I could scarcely breathe the same air as this painting.

I went into the storage room. I was searching for an empty crate to put *Jewess on a Street in Amsterdam* in. Instead, I found only the newly arrived crates. They were stacked against two walls. Each was marked HEIJMAN, followed by the title in painted black letters. Mr. Connaught must have lined them up this way.

In the custodian's room I found a screwdriver. I unplugged the radio, carried it and the screwdriver into the storage room, plugged in the radio there. I turned it on, fiddled with the dial, then caught a serious radio voice. A voice new to me: ". . . and so, friends, tonight in honor of that great Canadian citizen and hero Ovid Lamartine, we will broadcast his last public words to us. This was recorded on the afternoon of his tragic death, at the Glace Museum, here in Halifax. We shall all pray for his soul. And now, Mr. Ovid Lamartine."

As the broadcast went on, I unpacked the crates. Crates filled with the very paintings about to be described, minute by minute, in Joop Heijman's letter on the radio. Read in Ovid Lamartine's ghost-voice. I could still hear him shuffling the pages. Now when he said, "*The first painting is titled* Anne Meijer Waking . . ." I located that very painting, worked loose the crate's screws, pried it open. I set the painting against the wall in Room A, close to the storage-room door.

I did the same with each of Joop Heijman's paintings; *Anne Meijer and the Rabbi of Amsterdam*, *Anne in the Café du Tambourin*, *Twelve Steps*—my favorite of the paintings, my favorite of Joop Heijman's explanations. Then *Anne Meijer at the Bicycle Repair*, followed by the other five. When Ovid Lamartine got to *Jewess on a Street in Amsterdam*, I turned up the volume. His voice carried well out into the museum. I went to Room C, took down *Jewess on a Street in Amsterdam*, and carried it into the storage room.

Finally, the broadcast ended. "And that was heroic

Ovid Lamartine," the new voice said. "Recorded yesterday. We shall miss his brave voice, the news of the world he brought us—" I turned off the radio.

For a fleeting moment I thought to replace the permanent collection in Room B with Joop Heijman's paintings. Then I did so. I had never much enjoyed Room B.

It took me roughly an hour to hang the paintings. They were too close together. But even by flashlight, I could see that it was a beautiful exhibit. I took pride in it.

I chose *Anne Meijer at the Bicycle Repair* to put in place of *Jewess on a Street in Amsterdam.* Somehow I did not want her place empty, even if I should get the painting back before the museum opened. I squared *Anne Meijer at the Bicycle Repair* on the wall. I stepped back and studied it. Standing in his shop doorway was Paul Van Eerden. He was tall and heavy and had brushy sideburns, his gray hair seemed to be flying out from under his black cap. He filled the doorway. His window and the shop itself were crammed with bicycles.

I fit *Jewess on a Street in Amsterdam* in the crate. I did not linger in the museum then. But before I left, I lined up the empty crates neatly. I then carried *Jewess on a Street in Amsterdam* out the door, leaned it against the porch railing, locked the door behind me, then hefted the crate down to the street. We had, I remembered, a painting of a criminal in the museum once—whether a thief, a murderer, or both, no one knew. He was slipping from a country house. During Miss Delbo's tour, she said, "In the dark of night, undetected by anyone or anything, except, perhaps, his conscience—" The gusty wind made *Jewess on a Street in*

Amsterdam somewhat tough going. The crate was rough-hewn, splintery, ungainly to carry, heavier than I had at first thought. I had to stop every block and rest, just for a moment. I would set the crate atop my shoes, so as not to let snow seep in. I worked my way across the city. And then, once again, I stood in front of Miss Delbo's house. I looked at my watch: 3:10. Imogen was still awake. I had a sudden thought: Had Imogen been to the museum earlier that night? Fate could have had it that she walked in on me as I was crating up *Jewess on a Street in Amsterdam.* She might have seen the rest of Joop Heijman's paintings then.

Through the window I saw an array of headache medicines on the table. And a big, oblong suitcase, very old-fashioned-looking. Maybe it had belonged to Miss Delbo's mother. Imogen put one book in the suitcase, then took it out. Could not decide. Could not decide, then put it back in. Took it out. Set the book down on the table.

Holding the Dutch painting, standing like a cinema waif in front of a house in the snow, I admonished myself: *You can turn around, bring the painting back—now! Just do it. Only two people other than yourself will know that you did not steal it, Imogen and Miss Delbo. Imogen will either leave for Amsterdam or she won't, and life will go on. You will bury your uncle and life will go on.* I knocked on the door.

Imogen opened the door and all but shouted, "My God, you've brought it!"

At the bottom of the stairs, Miss Delbo appeared in her nightgown, robe, and slippers. "I'll put on tea," she said. She went into the kitchen.

I kicked the hallway rug with the tip of each shoe, wiped my feet the way I was taught to by my parents, carried the crate into the dining room, and leaned it against the table. Imogen stood back from me, staring at the crate. "It's already what? Two, three in the morning, isn't it? Just a few precious hours with it, then. But that will suffice."

"Suffice," I said.

"It's the exact word I meant to say."

"Would you have gone to Amsterdam without these precious hours?"

"What a question. What a question, isn't it? Because it doesn't *apply* now, does it? The painting *has* arrived. I *am* going."

I sat at the table. Besides all the books, papers, medicines, there was a map of Amsterdam; I noticed that Herengracht was circled in black ink.

"I'm just going to stay a few minutes," I said, forcing calm into my voice. I could not look directly at Imogen. "But while I'm here, I'm going to call you Anne Meijer."

The kettle whistled. "Anne Meijer?" Imogen said.

"I know more about who you've become than you do."

Miss Delbo came in with a tray: cups, napkins, the teapot, a small bowl of sugar, a sliced lemon, saucers, spoons. I pushed aside some books and she set down the tray. She poured each of us a cup of tea. Imogen sat down. Miss Delbo sat down.

"You see," I said, "yesterday, in walks Ovid Lamartine into the museum. He did his last broadcast from the Glace Museum."

"But who's Anne Meijer?" Imogen said.

"I take it you didn't hear Mr. Lamartine's last broadcast earlier tonight, then? You of all people, going to Amsterdam, should've been goddamned transfixed by it. Because he told all of Canada, except for you, that Anne Meijer is Joop Heijman's real wife."

Imogen threw her hands up to her mouth, gasped slightly, but immediately a calm look crossed her face. "All you've really done," she said, "is remind me of my name, which, because of my recent tragedies, I'd forgotten. It's normal—when life knocks you on the head, the way it has me—to forget a thing or two. You'd know that if you were worldly."

That set me off, the manner in which I was still the predictable suitor, a lackey delivering a package in the snow, along with a little extra useful information. I would be given tea and then dismissed, so that important things could get done. Important places could be got off to. I was endured. I felt a sudden exhaustion, a desire to crawl into the old-fashioned suitcase, curl up and sleep for the first two days and nights of the Atlantic crossing, and wake having absorbed all the knowledge in the books and able to talk expertly with Imogen for the rest of the journey to Amsterdam. Lying next to her, third-class passage. And maybe desire is the opposite of the scattering of desire. Mine was utterly and completely focused on Imogen, there in Miss Delbo's dining room, no matter how estranged from her life I actually was.

But my one recourse was to get set off. I pushed back

from the table. I picked up a heavy book on Dutch painting and flung it at the front window; great ostrich plumes spread across the glass, but the window did not break. Right away Miss Delbo grabbed Imogen by the arm and pulled her to the stairs, at the same time shouting, "DeFoe—stop this! You've gone out of your mind, stop it!" I picked up book after book, hurling them at every window I could see. One book I threw down the hallway, smashing a mirror. I swept my arm along the mantelpiece, scattering family portraits, Old Country, Canada, and the brass many-candled Jewish candelabrum with Hebrew writing at the base, vases—all on the floor. I kicked in the front-door window. Imogen and Miss Delbo backed up the stairs. They were clutched together, Miss Delbo shouting, "Stop! Stop!" I had already succeeded in smashing no less than five or six windows—cold air was in the house. "DeFoe, it's over now," Miss Delbo said. "It's over now." I threw an armful of books into the fireplace grate. There had been no fire burning, but ashes burst up into a cloud, filling that part of the room. Ashes drifted down onto the table, the furniture, into my hair, my eyes. I overturned the dining-room table. I saw the next-door neighbor's lights go on. I went to the front door. "DeFoe, get out! Get out now!" Miss Delbo screamed.

I heard broken glass underfoot. Ashes in my mouth. I opened the door, a jagged piece of glass fell onto the floor. A man dressed in a nightshirt, overcoat, and slippers was on the porch. "What's this?" he uttered—but I did not even see his face. I pushed past him hard. He almost fell from the porch. "Helen?" I heard him call out. But by then I was running down the street.

I went to the museum. I turned up the radiators, tried to sleep in the custodian's room, but could not. I sat with the Dutch paintings. The SS *Hagersford* was departing, 8:15. At 7:00 a.m., I set out for Miss Delbo's house. I pounded on her door, and Miss Delbo answered. She was wearing an overcoat; there was a fire in the grate. Books were stacked on the table again. "I'll get a window repairman out this morning, I hope," she said. She turned away.

I followed her inside. "Where's the painting?" I said.

"Here. Just as promised." She pointed to the crate, now in the living room, propped against the sofa. "When Edgar arrived here, Imogen pointed to the painting and said, 'DeFoe stole it and brought it to me, because I asked him to.' "

"And what'd Mr. Connaught say to that?"

" 'My God—to think a museum guard is responsible for our first theft.' "

"At least Imogen had her precious hours with it. Her precious goddamn hours. Free her soul, whatever else you schemed out."

"You did a lot of damage here, DeFoe. Look around you. My neighbor wanted to call the police. I asked him not to."

She stood against the living-room wall, pulled up her coat collar tightly against her neck. She looked out the window. "Drear day to be at sea, don't you think? My Edgar chaperoning someone not his own daughter. Nor even a beloved niece—"

"You talk as if it's a *dance* they're off to, Miss Delbo. Or 'My first trip to Europe'—postcards and snapshots. *Chaperoning.* Maybe you're the one's gone mad."

"I only meant—"

"You only *meant.* Nothing I care to know about, what you *meant.* I didn't sleep. I'm taking the painting now."

Without another word spoken, I took *Jewess on a Street in Amsterdam* from Miss Delbo's house.

And why did I not return *Jewess on a Street in Amsterdam* to the museum? Because, and I'll say this straight out, I sent it away. I sent it to Altoon Markham, c/o The Todd Hotel, 45 Cliffe St., Regina, Saskatchewan. I had my reasons.

I went to the Lord Nelson Hotel and sat on the porch. I had my guard uniform on, of course. I had my own electric heater, and in a short while it was warm enough so that I could open my coat and be comfortable. The crate holding *Jewess on a Street in Amsterdam* was on top of the next table over. There was no one else on the porch. Jake Kollias happened out. "Hey, DeFoe," he said, "I've been knocking on your door half the night. Where've you been? I've been—we've all been—a bit worried, eh? You okay out here? Radio predicts sleet later on. Did you notice, Christmas tree's not up in the lobby this year. Nobody felt like it. All the boys and I agreed. We just couldn't stand the good cheer, what with Edward. Management complained, said, 'Got to have a tree. For the patrons. For the full-time residents.' Et cetera. But the boys and I made a fuss, no tree. Besides which, who's got to be in the lobby more than bellhops?"

"My uncle would've appreciated what you did."

"DeFoe, pal. When's the funeral? We were all wondering."

"He didn't want one, Jake. It was specified 'No funeral' in his will. I made other arrangements."

"None of us were told. Or else I wouldn't even have asked."

"I know that."

"He's going to at least have a stone, isn't he?"

"In the Connaught Road cemetery. I'm working out the details."

"Because, over the years, you can then keep saying goodbye to a person. If they have a stone. I mean, you can stand there and talk to them. I do that with my mother—not my father, though. He's buried in the Old Country. My mother's here in Halifax."

"I'll let you know exactly where. Maybe we can visit together, okay?"

"Can I get you something? Tea—anything? I know you sometimes like coffee."

"Tea would be fine. But you don't have to. I can get it."

"Take it easy. Sit. I'll get your tea."

"While you're in there, could you bring me out some hotel stationery and a pen?"

"You got it."

Jake went into the lobby and soon was back with a pot of tea, a cup, napkin, spoon, sugar. And a stack of hotel stationery. A pen. "Got a letter to write?" he said.

"One letter," I said. "And one other thing."

Jake saluted me. "Stay all morning," he said. "Nobody

else's going to frequent the porch on a day like this, is my guess." He went inside.

Now and then I looked up from my writing to see someone walk in or out of the hotel. Or walk past the hotel along South Park. The morning carriages. Automobile traffic was light. People were walking to work. But mostly I kept my head bent to the paper. After a few false starts, I wrote:

> *Dear Altoon Markham,*
>
> *My uncle—and still legally your husband, I believe—died two days ago, here in Halifax. I bet that the newspaper and radio in Regina, Saskatchewan, carried the story.*

I went on for eleven pages. I told her the exact circumstances of my uncle's murder, filled her in on some of his life. Of course, I did not mention Natalie, or anyone else, really, except the bellhops. She had been friendly with some of them. About my uncle's Last Will and Testament, I lied.

> *In my uncle's Last Will and Testament he listed his possessions. There were very few, actually. His clothes, of course, and my inheritance, which was $55. There was very little else. However, he did own a painting, called* Jewess on a Street in Amsterdam. *You are of the Jewish faith, aren't you? If I remember right. Anyway, as I have earlier written here, I became a museum guard, and so I worked with my uncle, and I heard his opinions often enough. Few paintings escaped his harsh judgment.*

However, he liked Jewess on a Street in Amsterdam *very much. So much that he personally bought it from the artist, whose name is Joop Heijman, as you will readily see, since he has legally left the painting to you. (I do not know his reasons.) So I have sent it herewith. My uncle paid for it little by little out of his museum guard salary. It is entirely paid for, too. You do not have to worry.*

I will always remember your kindness on the day that my mother and father died.

Yours,
DeFoe Russet

I easily forgave myself, then and there on the porch of the Lord Nelson Hotel, for my lie. And otherwise for using *Jewess on a Street in Amsterdam* as a token of repayment for Altoon Markham's kindness so many years before. And I thought maybe the painting would provide some small happiness, as a painting, in and of itself. My uncle *had* mentioned her name, in the note attached to his will; Altoon still must have been in his thoughts. And to this day I often try and imagine her, in her room at the Todd Hotel. Though I have never been to Regina, Saskatchewan, and do not know what the Todd Hotel looks like. I imagine *Jewess on a Street in Amsterdam* on her wall. I imagine her liking the painting very much.

Next, I wrote out my confession. It took me a long time. It was past ten o'clock; I knew that the museum was supposed to have opened. Who would unlock the doors, the new temporary guard? Had Mr. Connaught given him a key? It was no longer my business. I was no longer a museum guard.

I had crumpled up at least twenty pieces of hotel stationery. In fact, Jake had come out, seen the stack was nearly depleted, and brought me more. In the end, my confession was two sentences. My signature was at the bottom. Plus the date: December 6, 1938. I gathered up the rejected pages, tossed them into the wastebasket near the waiter's station, though the waiters were all inside. I sat down again. I finished my tea. I then got a shoeshine from Winston Barnett. I tipped him an extravagant 15¢. "Come into an inheritance," he said, trying for a joke. "I always thought my friend Edward had a million stashed away in his mattress."

I went back out onto the porch, slid the letter and confession into my coat pocket. I took up the crate and set out for the train station, nine city blocks away. At the station, I did not see Mr. Tecosky. I arranged for the crate to be sent to Altoon Markham by train. Letter tucked inside. It cost me twelve dollars, fifty cents.

Then I walked to the Halifax police station.

I stepped up to the elevated desk. "Sergeant Oler," I said.

He looked up from his paperback mystery. "Jesus," he said, "DeFoe Russet. It's you. The nephew. How're you holding up?"

I handed him the piece of hotel stationery. He read it slowly, then said, "*Jewess on a Street in Amsterdam* again, eh? You sure keep her dance card filled, don't you? Last time, you blamed your uncle—may he rest in peace. You blamed a national hero museum guard for stealing a painting. Blamed him for the exact same crime, as you say you yourself have now committed. Interesting family you come from, DeFoe."

"The painting is gone from the museum this time for certain," I said. "I took it. It's gone from Halifax."

I thought, *Finally, I've owned up to something.*

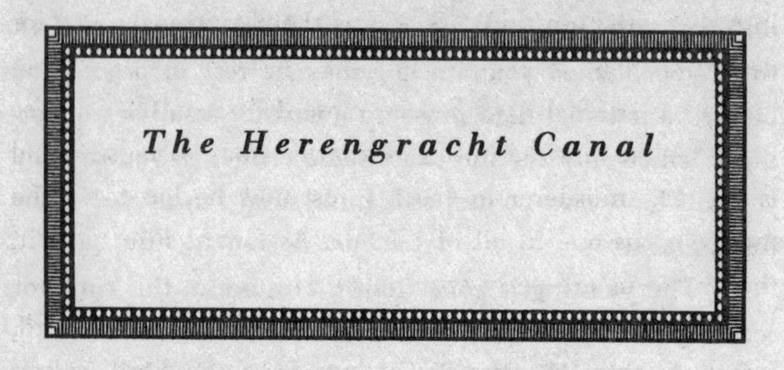

The Herengracht Canal

I have looked at Citadel Prison on the hill in Citadel Park, in the middle of Halifax, since I was a child. And now I am inside.

Briggs Roland is four cells down the gray corridor. I have been here forty-three nights. My sentence is six months. On at least ten nights I have heard Briggs Roland getting beat up, by either the guard Michael Hartog or the guard Everett Finn, Finn being the largest of the two. One night Finn shouted, "I had to throw my radio out, you son-of-a-bitch, because I can't get the truth on it anymore. Your being in my prison, I take very very personally. I resent that I have to breathe the same air as you. I take that very personally." I heard Briggs Roland say, "Get on with it, then." And he was slammed against the wall. I heard the thud of fists.

Voices carry loud and clear, though sometimes it is hard to tell from which cells. Just last night, between beatings, Everett Finn said, "That was the main meal. Now for dessert!"

I have seen Briggs Roland close up, out in the exercise yard. We are allowed in the yard twice a day. Briggs Roland is the only murderer in Citadel; just now he has to be the most famous one in all of Canada. As Guard Finn puts it, the rest of us are petty criminals.

The first time I saw Briggs Roland in the exercise yard, I realized that my memory of him from the Lord Nelson ballroom was correct. He is a puny man, no more than five feet six inches tall, with narrow shoulders, no match for Everett Finn. And actually, I have seen him closer up than I had ever wanted to again. Because Guard Finn likes to parade him past me early in the morning, on their way to breakfast, where Guard Finn sits directly next to Briggs Roland every single bite of eggs and toast. Anyway, Guard Finn does not speak to me, he just pushes Briggs Roland's face against my bars and I see the bruises and bloodshot eyes. I suppose Guard Finn thinks it does my heart good.

Last week Briggs Roland handed me a note. I waited until I was back inside to read it. *I hope Ovid Lamartine rots in hell, but I killed your uncle by mistake.*

My one visitor has been Miss Delbo. I never expected her to come, but she has, twice a week. All the visits allowed. She has not asked me where *Jewess on a Street in Amsterdam* is. "All I know or need to know is that Imogen Linny had her necessary vigil with the painting—. Whatever else, DeFoe, you tried to help someone you loved, even though not in a way you approved of but in a way she assigned you. Actually, I don't care where the painting is, not that you'd tell me anyway. You were a good, conscientious museum guard. I know you'd never harm a painting."

Each Thursday and Sunday, then, Miss Delbo brings me the previous few days' newspapers. She marks any and all mention of events in Europe. Hitler and so forth. She underlines the word "Amsterdam" whenever it appears. I suppose that is our private way of referring to Imogen Linny. "How can we know if these horrible events in Europe actually weigh on Imogen's mind at all, DeFoe?" she once asked, but did not expect an answer, and I had none. I had the terrible curiosity but not the gumption to ask if she had heard at all from Mr. Connaught.

From my small window I have a view of Halifax Harbour and can see the topmost masts of the historical schooners. Hour after hour, that is my framed view. It has got me to thinking about Simon Glace's oil painting *The Glace Museum*. I still think of it at best as a nice painting, even with the scale of it being askew. But what I finally realized was that there are no seagulls in it. It definitely is a realistic painting, so having no seagulls is inaccurate. I am not saying it is wrong. No seagulls was Mr. Glace's artistic choice. However, he should have known better. I was raised near the wharf. I have been down there hundreds of times. I have looked at it from the museum window for two years. There are always seagulls whirling above the docks. Rain, shine, in the average storm, it does not matter—there are seagulls. All right, maybe not when the worstmost gales batter the wharf; that would be an obvious exception. Or during an ice storm. But on any cloudless day as in *The Glace Museum*, gulls would be in the sky. That should have been a given.

Yet I remember that during a tour Miss Delbo said, "It is simpleminded arrogance to think, *I wish she or he would have*— You have only what is right in front of you to judge. Every brushstroke is the artist's opinion about existence." I knew right then and there that Miss Delbo had said something important, though I could not completely make heads or tails of it. Maybe I had trouble thinking of Mr. Simon Glace as an artist in the first place.

Truth be told, I do not miss guarding *The Glace Museum*. But I miss being a museum guard. I have to consider my future without it. I was thinking that I might write to my old employer, Mr. Tecosky, and ask for a job at the train station. No doubt he has read in the newspaper of my present address. In a letter to him I would own up to my theft of *Jewess on a Street in Amsterdam* and give him full opportunity to judge me on my merits and demerits, as my uncle used to say. I can ask Everett Finn for pen and paper, an envelope and postage. That is allowed. He can take it out of the $2.50 per week salary I receive for working in the Citadel laundry. I am down there ironing five, six hours a day. The plain blue trousers, blue shirts, white socks. I work the day shift. A man named Fordy Unterberg irons at night. I have seen baskets of shirts he has ironed; he does very good work.

Two days ago, Sunday, Miss Delbo said, "I'm sure that you remember Sergeant Pinnie Oler. His brother, Frank, has been approved of by the museum's Board of Directors and by the acting curator, Professor Leonardi, from my department at Dalhousie—so Frank Oler will be the new guard. Sergeant Oler, of course, knew that there were vacancies.

Frank Oler is a retired policeman. He's quite qualified, in that respect. I met him. As far as his knowledge of or interest in paintings, he is a lummox. He told me he used to paint houses. But what with Edgar in Europe— Well, it was entirely out of my hands. It would have been nice to have a guard I could actually converse with."

Today is February 22, 1939. Miss Delbo visited. As usual, we sat across the table in the visitors' room, watched over by the day guard there, Madison Alt. She showed me a newspaper article about a Montreal millionaire, born and raised in Halifax, though, who had created the Ovid Lamartine Scholarship in Journalism at Dalhousie University.

Then Miss Delbo reached into her purse and set a stack of letters on the desk. They were held together by string. "And, DeFoe," she said, "I've brought these—" She slid the letters over to me. Guard Alt noticed and walked over. Miss Delbo said, "These are *personal*—"

"So's a knife or sawblade, ma'am," he said. "But I don't suppose you've hidden either of those, eh?"

"Letters from Europe," she said.

"Oh, letters from Europe," Guard Alt said. He shrugged and went back to his post.

"From Mr. Connaught," I said.

"From Edgar, yes."

"Imogen's dead, isn't she?"

"The letters concern her. You read them and draw your own conclusions, DeFoe."

"What conclusions? Either she is or isn't."

"Edgar doesn't have knowledge of that."

Miss Delbo looked exhausted; never unkept, no, never that. But she did appear awfully worn out. She must have suddenly felt how I was sizing this up, because she said, "My teaching—well, my life at university is going badly. Students have complained of my being distracted. I hope you don't mind my telling you my little woes."

"I don't mind at all. I appreciate your coming to see me so often. I guess you already know that."

"I'll want these letters back, naturally. And Edgar wouldn't suppose I'd share them. With anyone."

"I'd never let on. If I ever see Mr. Connaught again."

"I have to be going now."

She held my hands a moment in hers, then left the Citadel.

December 21, 1938

Dear Helen,

As you can see from the stationery, I am living in the American Hotel, Leidseplein, a few blocks from the Hotel Ambassade.

Imogen Linny was sullen much of our passage. She stared out to sea from a deck chair, huddled under blankets like an invalid. She refused conversation equally about the past or future. If I as much as suggested a scone or tea, she responded only with a nod or shake of her head. It was as though I were nursing someone back from a long despondency, or illness, or someone still very much in the throes of one. For the most part her meals consisted of dry toast, tea, headache powder. Our rooms in third class were across a narrow corridor from each other, C3 and C9. As sole sponsor of our passage—financially, I mean—I had to scrupulously divvy out our shipboard funds, remembering by the hour that I did not know how long, exactly, we might remain in Amsterdam. Nor did I have any idea of what even the basic things cost there. Did I tell you that I took out monies from my sister's account? Well, I did, and no matter; she is hardly aware of the day and weather anymore, and I am her one living relative. I did not take out a large amount, really. A sufficient amount. Nothing unscrupulous, I want you to know.

Sometimes when I knocked on Imogen's door, she called back, "Not now," meaning that she did not wish to stroll on deck, or that she was racked with seasickness, which somehow spared me. I implored her not to continually wear the clothes of the Jewess—that could wait until Amsterdam, I tried to reason with her. But to no avail. Our rooms were either overheated to sweltering or else the walls were cold to the touch, little in between. One got the impression that Imogen required the delusion that those were all the clothes she had packed, which was nearly true. When she did venture out on deck, she cut a decidedly eccentric figure. I noticed many sidelong glances and stares, and on occasion, the rude pointing of children. That is, someone to be avoided. On our fifth day at sea, she told me, "I've had a lovely bath," but it was not said in normal, casual passing, but with emphasis, as though to assure me she was in control of her practical habits. At table, the few times we had dinner together, she persisted in introducing herself to other passengers either as Mrs. Joop Heijman (at which point she clarified, too, that I was not her husband) or as Anne Meijer.

Even given these few details, Helen, you must try and understand that there was no possible way I could have foreseen how utterly peculiar an experience this all would prove —and we had not yet set foot in Europe! As she herself stated to perfect strangers, without so much as a hint of doubt and with a voice full of hopefulness and adoration, "I am returning to my husband." And at breakfast one morning—the first morning she was able to come to breakfast, actually—a rather haughty, nonetheless perceptive, perhaps even intelligent woman of late age, said, "Surely you are the only Jew aboard ship. The only Jew choosing to go into *Europe, young lady." And Imogen seemed pleased to be recognized as such. The woman was a Canadian citizen "on my last holiday, obviously, to my ancestral Netherlands, for who can predict how long?" as she put it. Imogen evidently warmed toward this woman. To my astonishment, their central topic of discussion was none other than Ovid Lamartine and Mr. Lamartine's tragic murder—the elder woman had been in attendance at the Lord Nelson Hotel that night, sitting toward the back of the room with her husband, both of them great admirers of Mr. Lamartine. What was even more astonishing was that this woman had at one time actually employed notorious Briggs Roland! Apparently she and her husband own Carriage & Cabby, the transportation service in Halifax and Dartmouth, and at one point—she thinks it may have been their traditional employees' Christmas party—had Briggs Roland, at the time a carriage driver, in their house. As the conversation went on apace, Imogen, now more succinctly affecting a peculiar sort of accent, proceeded to regale this woman (her name, I forgot to mention, was Mrs. Morley Holthausen) with her life story. That is, her life with Joop Heijman. A "very fulfilling life, a very ennobling life," she said. At one point Imogen referred to me as "my husband's Canadian benefactor." Mrs. Holthausen knew the Glace Museum, though she had seldom visited (I have never seen her there, to my recollection), once or twice perhaps. "I've not been a patron," she said. "But if your museum exhibits this fine and unusual woman's husband's works, then by all means I will write out a check here and now." Which she indeed did. And which, to my shame or lack thereof, I accepted. When Imogen spent time with anyone shipboard but me, it was with Mrs. Holthausen. On one occasion, the latter descended from first class to seek out Imogen in her room, and they took tea together on deck.*

I had any number of conversations. The SS Hagersford *was full of people going to fetch relatives, gather personal items of sentimental and other value, close up houses, and then flee Europe as soon as possible. Talk of Mr. Hitler dominated, as you might well have expected, Helen, most opinions raging against. Though a Mr. Stephen Schenone offered that "history is often comprised of purges of this or that sort," with an optimistic smirk and a shrug of resignation. The sort of expression that tries to indict all listeners: "Oh, you are such children." Quite menacing, really. I only saw him once afterward; he was utterly inebriated, sitting amidst other slurring German drunkards, and when I walked past, he said, "What goes on down there in the Jewish whorehouse, third class, Edgar? Come, come, you are among birds of a feather here, each of us with certain experiences, eh?" Lastly, at breakfast the morning before our arrival in Amsterdam, Imogen sat with Mrs. Holthausen and myself. Imogen had toast and jam and tea. Mrs. Holthausen, now truly and affectionately concerned about Imogen, said, "My dear, considering the drear future, with Adolf Hitler run amok, ask your good husband to come to Canada, won't you? You mentioned that you have no children. You could live in a cottage at our country estate, along the Cape Breton seashore. It's lovely there. My husband has little affection for nature, but I think it's heaven. I could look in on you, see to your peace and quiet and your financial well-being until your husband established a Canadian reputation. We could promote that among our friends, of course. An offer of refuge like this doesn't come along but once in a lifetime, I assure you." And, Helen, I report to you fully that Imogen's response was, "As for the future, kind Mrs. Holthausen, I can only look forward to the smell of paint mixed with the aroma of Dutch coffee." That, Helen, you may well recall, is the very sentence you provided for the text of the Glace Museum's catalogue for "Eight New Paintings from Holland"; more specifically, in describing* Self-portrait in Artist's Studio, *by Cees Rietveld.*

However, don't let my letter so far imply that Imogen was congenial. Except for striking up an acquaintanceship with Mrs. Holthausen, sullen reclusiveness defined her. And yet when we actually stepped off the gangplank and onto the soil of Amsterdam, Imogen became so animated in expression and spirit, to say the very least, it was as if she had now allowed herself to take in oxygen and open wide her eyes, and put one foot in front of the other with assurance. In fact, she insisted that we immediately go to the Hotel Ambassade (we had no rooms set aside for us anywhere in Amsterdam), at Herengracht 341, an exact address I had provided her from my correspondence with Joop Heijman. Imogen had just the one old suitcase; I had two small ones. Using Imogen's map, we set out along the quite narrow streets filled with bicyclists. We walked with misdirection, though—until we were stopped by a Dutchman, who simply said, "Lost?" We admitted to it. He carried Imogen's suitcase and led us to the Hotel Ambassade, then waved over his shoulder, not waiting for thanks, as if helping us had been an annoying but nonetheless obligatory task.

The hotel, I should mention, is quite accurately depicted in Jewess on a Street in Amsterdam. *Indeed, the entire section of Herengracht, shops, canal, et cetera, was immediately recognizable.*

At which point, having stood not more than two minutes in front of the Hotel Ambassade, Imogen fainted. And I've since come to believe that her fainting was the result of an uncanny combination of things. First, she was, generally speaking, famished; she had eaten sparingly at best for many days. Then there were the ravages of seasickness. Her too-heavy clothing (although Amsterdam is cold now). And, far more elusive, and far more difficult to describe, but nonetheless a decisive contribution, is the mental nervous shock of her passage from one existence, as it were, to another. I do not feel that is an exaggeration. Then, perhaps, add the weight of self-delusion borne for months now on her shoulders. And so suddenly standing in front of the Hotel Ambassade—dressed as the Jewess, standing where the Jewess in the painting stood. Her fainting now almost seems like the body's logical response.

When Imogen fainted, several men and women on bicycles stopped to assist. One woman hurried into the hotel, returning with smelling salts. I held them just under Imogen's nose, and she snapped back to consciousness rather quickly. Two men helped her into the lobby, where she sat on a chair. She was handed a glass of water and drank a few sips. At first she was muttering deliriously, but nonetheless clearly, "I must see my husband, Joop Heijman." The desk clerk, a man in his fifties, was taken aback and said with incredulity, "Heijman?" He may not have fully understood the "husband" part—he simply dispatched a young bellhop to find Joop Heijman. It could not be stopped.

It turned out that Mr. Heijman was not in his rooms, for which I was grateful. Imogen was then brought a cup of tea and seemed nearly fully recovered. I implored the desk clerk to keep watch over her while I secured a room for each of us at the American Hotel, recommended by customs. Securing the rooms took all of half an hour, and I was back at the Hotel Ambassade. There the desk clerk informed me that Imogen had loudly, almost violently, protested staying in the lobby and had set out into Amsterdam, carrying her suitcase. You might well imagine, dear Helen, after not more than a couple of hours in Amsterdam, the panic I now felt. Imogen was somewhere in the city. Perhaps I should have immediately contacted the Amsterdam police (I did not know what term to use for them), but I did not. I was exhausted and did not trust my judgment. I returned to my hotel and slept.

At 7:00 a.m., or thereabouts, I went downstairs and informed the clerk that I would be paying a week's amount for both Imogen Linny and myself. He registered this without comment. I took breakfast in the dining room, then walked to the Hotel Ambassade and knocked on Joop Heijman's door. I have never seen such a broken man. He is tall, taller than I, quite haggard, and with what I immediately took as a formerly handsome face, based on a number of earlier self-portraits on the walls. He was unshaven, heavy-lidded, hair unwashed, combed haphazardly to one side of a distracted face. He walked with a very pronounced limp; I noticed several canes next to the umbrella stand. He did not wait for an introduction but walked back to his kitchen and sat down at the table. There was a breadboard of cheese and herring, mostly untouched. He beckoned me over. When I got to the table, he stood up, held out his hand, and said, "Heijman." I said who I was, and attempting an embrace, he fell into me and said, "Burn my paintings. You have my permission. They are no use to me anymore. To anyone." I am making his spoken English somewhat better than it actually was, though he made himself quite clear. "I only have the ones in my museum," I said. "I intend to mount an entire exhibition of your work." He looked dumbstruck. "Then go through the rooms here," he said, "take the paintings out, and—" He seemed exhausted and sat down. He pointed to the bedroom. "I don't sleep in there anymore. I sleep here"—he pointed to the kitchen floor.

The kitchen was cluttered. He immediately offered me a glass of vodka. It was barely 8:30 a.m. and I refused. He drank two glasses of vodka, then a glass of milk. He bit into the cheese. I began to praise his paintings, the ones I could see. They were on the walls and stacked against each other throughout the apartment. He kept shaking his head: "No, no, no, no, no." He made coffee, but kept at it with the vodka, another two glasses.

"Mr. Heijman," I said. "Joop—" and then I gave him the news about Ovid Lamartine. He said he had already read about it. "He was a hero to me," he said. "He took my paintings to Canada. The ones of Anne—I couldn't bear to look at them anymore. He knew this. But these— I no longer can paint. It's death here, in this hotel. For me, without Anne. I can't paint death, dear Edgar. To not paint is *death, and I cannot paint. Why have you come, really? Please explain. You must understand, since my wife Anne's death, I cannot pay attention to much of anything for very long, since everything reminds me of her; so attentions are painful, you see. Why have you come?"*

And so I attempted to explain. And, Helen, as I spoke, as I looked into this kind, tormented face, this soul besieged by grief, I realized with the abruptness of a heart attack that to have facilitated Imogen's desire to be in Amsterdam was more than some perverse declaration of empathy on our part —it was doom-filled. The die had been cast, and I was suddenly in Joop Heijman's dingy kitchen full of the same light as in his paintings, and my heart filled with revulsion toward myself, I was sick with it, and with honest-to-God fear for Imogen Linny. And I was filled with shame for planning to put Joop Heijman under this terrible burden, but I indeed proceeded to put him under it. I told him as much as I could about Imogen's life in Halifax, her response to Jewess on a

Street in Amsterdam, *our journey to his city. He finished the bottle of vodka. "And so you see, Mr. Heijman," I said, "you and you alone can persuade Imogen to abandon her fixation on being your wife."* Fixation, *he mumbled over and over. It may be called an illness, I said, though added that of course Imogen herself does not see it that way. "I am here on Imogen's behalf"—and when I said this, it felt like a lie, though it also felt as if I did not know the entire truth of it, either. Helen, I did not really know what I meant anymore. I asked Mr. Heijman, please—I did all but beg—as a man of artistic tolerance and imagination, try and grasp the uncanny situation, to see it as a kind of experiment which he alone could help Imogen fail at. Please, give her an audience; then, if need be, make a fool of her. Send her back home. Send her back to Halifax. Allow sheer humiliation to snap her back into reality. "Do you understand? Do you understand the predicament here?"*

What disturbed me most, then, was that Joop Heijman carefully wrapped up the cheese, the herring, the bread, and set it all on the counter. He did this with precise movements, as if setting up a still life to be painted. He composed the cheese, herring, and bread on the counter, and therefore gained his own composure, drunk as he was. Then he sat down at the table again. "Do you realize, dear Edgar, my American curator Edgar, that the Germans will eventually arrive here? They are not here yet. And God willing, they may never come. But if—if *the Germans arrive in Amsterdam, dear Edgar, my country will resist, but who can know the results of this? If this woman, this Imogen, is masquerading as my wife, as you say she is, then that* is *someone—in her mind—who is living outside of"—he pointed to his head—"how to say it, outside of her mind. I cannot help her." But now he began to pace the room, and I could see a storm cloud of thoughts filling his very face. He paced the kitchen, and then suddenly he vaulted himself at me, struck me on the shoulder—I reeled backward, but managed to stay on my chair. "This is folly!" he shouted. "My wife, Anne, was a Jewess. This other—this Imogen—is a* mockery! *I'll have none of it!"*

Now Mr. Heijman took me roughly by the arm, very roughly, and, with his other hand clamped onto my coat, shoved me toward the window. "Look out there," he said. "This is my city of Amsterdam, where I was born, and the monsters who killed my Anne are on their way here. They take their time, but they are going to arrive. There is no argument. Look out the window." He pressed my face against the glass, and I let him. "Is the monster here yet? You stupid foolish Canadian, go back aboard your ship, go home before too much time passes and Canada is too far away to get to—"

I looked down and saw Imogen standing on the narrow strip of grass between the street and the Herengracht Canal.

She was staring upward, as if listening to our argument. She was holding a loaf of bread, staring up. Joop Heijman let go of me and himself looked down through the window, and when he saw Imogen, he grew furious. Never have I seen such fury so completely take over a man's very being. He pushed me aside and ran from his apartment, and in a few moments I saw him out on the street. I followed him downstairs. By the time I got to the street, Heijman was screaming at Imogen: "Go! Go away, you hideous—" And other things, in Dutch. Then the desk clerk and several bellhops joined the onlookers, but did not intervene, not just yet. "My wife is dead!" he shouted, four, five, six times at Imogen, as if to hammer the truth of it into her heart. And Imogen—oh, Helen, how pathetic, really. She stood taking this lashing, with a look of pity and understanding—sympathy, yes, sympathy on her face. However, then Joop Heijman actually shoved her; she fell backward and to her knees, but immediately got up again and leaned against the hotel's iron fence. "You are nothing!" Heijman shouted. "You do not exist! You are nothing!" He grabbed the loaf of bread from her and crushed it under his heel. "Nothing, do you understand? Are you human? My wife is dead. You are a sick woman!" Joop Heijman then reached down, took off his shoe, and started toward Imogen with it—and it was at this point that the bellhops and desk clerk subdued him. They escorted Joop Heijman back into the hotel. Imogen, for all her passivity, now looked humiliated and quite confused, and sat down on the streetside bench. No one saw to her. A number of people stared, spoke among themselves, but no one attended to Imogen, and who could blame them? I should have. Finally, though, the desk clerk brought Imogen a drink of some sort, and without hesitation, she drank it right down. She handed him back the glass and closed her eyes.

I sat with Imogen a long while in silence. She only nodded when I asked, "Are you all right?" But would not otherwise speak to me. Not for at least half an hour. Now and then the desk clerk or a bellhop peered out the doorway at us, but kept to the hotel. No constable or policeman of any sort approached us. Bicyclists—so many—went past, passersby, the daily life of Amsterdam going on, going on, I thought, in this dark moment in history. Then, looking up, I saw Joop Hei-

man appear in his window—he opened the window and threw a soup tureen down at us. It ricocheted off the bench and into the Herengracht Canal. It floated a moment, then sank from view. Joop Heijman now flung down curses on us, then disappeared from the window. I hoped and prayed that he would not come down and out onto the street again, and he didn't.

Finally, Imogen said, "He's very angry with me. I've been away so long. I shouldn't have gone to Canada and left him for so long. He was so ill, and I left him. How could I?" She rose from the bench and started down the street. I ran alongside. She stopped, cast me the fiercest possible look, truly menacing, Helen, and said, "Leave me be! I am home now. You are not. You should go back *home!" I watched as she walked away down Herengracht, crossed over a bridge, and went down another street until I could no longer see her.*

I spent the rest of the day and night in the American Hotel, fearing to leave, lest I get a message from Imogen or miss her at the American Hotel, should she, however briefly, come to her senses. I did not know what to expect, really, so expected nothing. I simply kept to the hotel.

How to prepare you for what happened next, I do not know. Let me tell it outright as best I can.

For the rest of the week, I tried to locate Imogen. That was my sole occupation. I went to I think every modest, or less so, hotel in Amsterdam. I did not find her, but had a certain amount of luck in learning where she had been. At least such knowledge subscribed to the notion of her still being alive. How tentative my thinking had become! How provisional my optimism. I settled for whatever snippets of information were offered, of course. Yet often I felt the worst had befallen Imogen, I admit. That she was starving, had left Amsterdam, gone who knows where? That she had taken her own life. But I hoped and prayed that I had entirely underestimated her perseverance of spirit and mind. It was not terribly difficult to find people who spoke English, and I even learned a little Dutch, salutations, a few words here and there, and I got by. Awkwardly, but still. I walked the city. I found that she had slept two nights inside the synagogue of the Portuguese Jews, which is on Jonas Daniell Meijerplein. The custodian was kind enough to say that Imogen had asked to sleep there, and had gained permission to do so—he was not privy to any other knowledge of how it came about. He said it was a simple gift, "simple," he said a few times. And I also—very disturbingly—found that she had spent at least one night in the Jewish cemetery. I avoided the Hotel Ambassade for as long as possible, because I was afraid that she had indeed returned there and that violence of some sort had occurred between her and Joop Heijman. However, I did telephone the desk clerk, who assured me—I believe honestly—that Imogen had not been there.

Then eight, nine, ten days passed in Amsterdam and I decided I might best find Imogen through the police. But first—one last time—I would go to the Hotel Ambassade, to learn if Joop Heijman had seen her. And as I turned the corner onto Herengracht, I saw that a crowd had gathered in front of the Hotel Ambassade. There was an ambulance, which seemed to fill the entire width of the street. There was a police boat of some sort tied up to the railing along the canal as well. I walked closer and saw a body completely wrapped in blankets being slid into the ambulance by two medics—per-

haps a medic and a bellhop, I cannot quite remember. I had to view all of this through many people. The ambulance sped off. I was so completely convinced that—this frightening sequence unraveled in my mind, that is—I was convinced that Imogen had come to confront Joop Heijman and had been so severely rejected (on my advice) that she had thrown herself into the Herengracht Canal. I was utterly convinced that Joop Heijman had come to realize that my strategy might well rid him of Imogen for good. So convinced that I did not even ask who was in the ambulance. I simply walked up to the desk clerk and said, "Let me speak to Mr. Joop Heijman, please."

The clerk all but bellowed, "Into my office, sir, please!" I followed him into his office. The clerk, as it turned out, was also the manager, a Mr. Bilhamer. He struck me immediately as a man of very solid character—that was my first impression—and he clearly had been weeping. In well-practiced English—he did manage a hotel, after all—he said, "Why did you bring this impostor? It broke our dear Joop Heijman. The reminder of his wife broke him—" He snapped a pencil in half. "It broke him like that. Go back to Canada. We will—the employees of this hotel will gather money among ourselves to send you back. Take your witch and go back to Canada, sir. This is Amsterdam. He is a great painter. You have caused terrible things to happen. He might have drowned."

I write this, having hurried back to the American Hotel, Helen, and am now awake at 4:30 a.m. My room faces the back. Some sort of Dutch sparrows, or other small dusky birds, are constantly roosting along the ledges. The window was filthy. I cleaned it myself. I washed the outside myself, lifting it up, reaching my hand out. The birds simply carried on with their banter. And so, dear, this hotel room is where I have lain on the bed, listened to the radio (managing to get an English station), and now sit at the desk writing to you. I have contacted the police. No word yet of Imogen. Not from the bellhops or Mr. Bilhamer, at the Hotel Ambassade. Nor from the police. Nor, of course, from Imogen herself.

I will send this today. I pray that it will be delivered safely.

I kiss you.

Yours,
Edgar

January 1939

Dearest Helen,

It has been two weeks since I sat down to write to you. Two nights ago, quite cold out, I waited in front of the Portuguese synagogue, hoping against hope that I might see Imogen. That she did not appear, of course, was no surprise. I had simply chosen a night on which staying in my room at the American Hotel had become unbearable. There had been no word from the police, though they are polite and leave the message Nothing yet about Imogen Linny *at the front desk on a daily basis. There have been, as it were, no sightings; Amsterdam is a large city. Anyway, I stood there all night, pacing, collar turned up, gloves on, wearing new woolen trousers bought here, and saw the sunrise, then walked back to the hotel.*

Awake late last night, fully clothed on the bed—I have

taken to falling asleep that way, like a vagrant—I felt so distant from life in Halifax, yet, important to say, not distant from you, my dear. Yet I continually ask myself, What have we done? How to put remorse to its best use? Have I chaperoned Imogen Linny to Europe, where she, like Humanity, as Ovid Lamartine was wont to say, "is being devoured by brutal History?"

*Day to day, on the street, in overheard conversations, the expansions of Hitler's Germany are very much imposed on the consciousness of the Dutch citizens. There is a nervousness, to say the very least, tremors of foreboding, like a glimpse out of the corner of one's eye of Mr. Lamartine's "dark shroud" coming ever closer. And just last night on the English radio station, a broadcaster—name now forgotten—spoke of Hitler's purges of German art and artists. That was his word, "purges." Though it was clear, too, that much information and knowledge was quite hard to come by, filtered out by secret brave couriers at great risk. Any—*any*—natural inclination toward hope for the future is quite abruptly anesthetized by despair, born of present reports filed from deep within Hitler's domain, of atrocities and ambitions for conquest. And so here, dear Helen, in this beautiful city, I feel somewhere between a ghost and a tourist, with a kind of doom seeming to thunder in the distance. I am not a poetic man, yet "thunder" strikes me, at this moment in history, as eminently the word, for we are anticipating a storm that is building to biblical proportions. I pray not, but fear that even ceaseless prayer would be a faint voice drowned out in the maelstrom. Forgive this desperate language at 4 a.m., and a sense of decorum in language roughhoused by insomnia and much whiskey, I'm afraid. And* *the goddamn clanking of radiators—or I don't know what water pipes and such—in my room, the rooms to either side, above, below perhaps, like a hellish symphony. But I simply do not have the resources or stamina to change hotels.*

And then, Helen, this very morning as I sat in the dining room, a coffee and scone and cheese—everywhere in this city, cheeses of remarkable variety—in front of me, Imogen Linny appeared at my table! Silently, she sat down. The shock of seeing her, imagine! I'm afraid I lost all sense of where I was in public and rose from the table and embraced her. She apparently had not bathed in a good long while. She still wore the clothes of the Jewess in the painting, but now had a pitiful air. How strangely disheveled she looked; the very colors of the cloth seemed darkened by filth. How lost she looked. And yet, Helen, her first words betrayed no such notion. "I've been visiting the museums. The guards have treated me with such respect—," all in this remarkably odd accent she has affected.

The waiter brought Imogen coffee, an omelet, an assortment of cheeses—all of which I had immediately ordered for her. And we proceeded with a proper breakfast; I imagined what we might have looked like to someone across the room: perhaps a man having coffee with a woman out of a nineteenth-century daguerreotype. However, there would have been nothing eccentric or even vaguely odd about our conversation—to the eavesdropper, I mean. To me, however, this ordinariness was disturbing. How could it not be? "And how have you been spending your time in Amsterdam?" Imogen asked. I could at first only stare into my coffee. But then I thought it best to maintain a subdued tone of famil-

iarity. "I've been to see your Joop Heijman in hospital, but was turned away."

"Ah yes, turned away," she said. "Well, he's back at the Hotel Ambassade now."

"And have you been to see him?"

"No, no. He's working so hard, you see. I'm used to it by now. After all these years. Used to his needing such long periods of time for his work. Used to it."

I do not know if Imogen is actually dwelling in some shadow world between reality and illusion; yet I am certainly too limited in psychological acuity, Helen, let alone imagination, to know how else to put it. "Where are you staying?" I asked.

"I've found a room," she said.

"How are you paying for it, if I may ask?"

"I have some of my own money, in case you forgot. And a few people at the Portuguese synagogue have helped out."

"I see. But Joop Heijman hasn't given you any money."

"My husband has not sold a painting in a long time. Why don't you buy one from him, Edgar?"

"I'll look into that. Please use my bath."

"Thank you. I will."

"And have your clothes laundered. Here—at my expense, of course."

"Thank you. I've been—neglecting practical things. Having spent so much time in synagogues and museums, you see."

"Yes."

"Should I take a bath and have my clothes laundered today?"

"Yes. Right after breakfast would do nicely. Here's my room key. The number is on it. I'll—go on some errands. You'll have utter privacy."

"Thank you."

"Perfectly fine."

Imogen went up to my room. It occurred to me then that of course she had only the one set of clothes, and so I made a point of asking the laundress to hurry with Imogen's laundry—and gave her some guilders, a persuasive amount, actually. She went right up to my room with me. I knocked on the door and said, "There's a nightshirt on the bureau. Wear it—I'm going out into the city now, all right?"

"Fine. Thank you."

"The laundress is here now."

As I went down the hallway, Imogen opened the door and handed out her clothes. The laundress held them at arm's length and walked down the stairs behind me.

I did as I said I would. I simply walked the streets. It was an errand of sorts; though I felt the true errand was to fetch back some semblance of clarity and ask, "What next to do? What next to do?" As I seemed only able to react to Imogen's decisions in Amsterdam—I walked Reguliersgracht, Lijnbaansgracht, Leidsestraat, Keizersgracht, street after street, with no sense of actually learning my way around, wanting to be lost. I ended up at the Oosterdok and watched ships being loaded. Boats at anchor. Such a bitter cold day out, Helen. "I will do something ennobling"—a sentence that Imogen repeated shipboard, I in turn repeatedly heard her say in my mind, as I stood at the Amsterdam docks.

When I returned about five hours later, I was not pre-

pared at all for what Imogen told me, as we sat in my room. She was dressed in the clothes of the Jewess, of course. She had had a nap as well. "Oh, by the way, about my husband. Though he very much wanted to be alone to work, we're meeting for tea tomorrow. Eight a.m., at the café, three doors down from the Hotel Ambassade. Our favorite café."

"Of course," I said.

So, Helen, if this is truly to take place, this meeting, then it is evident that she has spoken directly with Joop Heijman, whether in hospital or at the hotel, who can say? And if the meeting is to take place, then it is equally evident that Mr. Heijman has somehow forgiven Imogen for her existence here. Or else— Speculation can drive one to madness, of course. I will be therefore obligated to station myself like a spy across the Herengracht Canal. I break this letter off until tomorrow, then.

During the night I decided it was best to try and see Joop Heijman before Imogen did this morning, if only to find out that no meeting was in fact planned. I entered the Hotel Ambassade by the back entrance like a thief. Naturally, I wanted to avoid the manager and bellhops if possible, afraid they would not let me upstairs. In fact, and much to my grateful relief, Joop Heijman was restrained, even cordial. Not terribly surprised to see me, it seemed. However, what did take me aback was that he appeared even more haggard and certainly thinner than when I had first seen him; I hardly thought this possible. I asked after his "health." He answered, "I heard you came to visit me in hospital. You, who put me in there."

But he said nothing further about it. "Well, then, come in, let's have tea." We sat at the kitchen table and drank tea, then. "Mr. Connaught," he said, "in hospital I did much thinking. And I have come to this conclusion. That I will paint this Imogen. Her last name again?"

"Linny."

"This Imogen Linny."

"I don't understand. I've come to apologize for bringing her here. It was terribly wrong. I'll try in every possible way to make her leave."

"Not yet. Not just yet."

"I don't understand."

Then we drank more tea, and he said, "I prefer this semblance of Anne to nothing at all. I grieve for her that much."

*I inquired then, did he want to have Imogen actually sit for him, pose for him, and he would paint her; did I understand that to be what he wanted? He answered, "That is precisely what I want." Imagine, dear Helen, my incredulity. Here I had come to Amsterdam blindly hopeful, with the intent to "cure" Imogen, if that is the correct word at all. And yet now Mr. Heijman obviously wanted to validate her state of delusion. He wanted her—for how long?—to remain the Jewess in the painting. Anne, his wife. At least for the course of a number of paintings. And then—then came the Devil's bargain, though Mr. Heijman is whatever is the opposite of evil. "And when I am through with the paintings," he said, "when they are done, I will—*dash *her hopes. Because, Edgar, she—this Imogen Linny—is otherwise poisonous to my—my* soul, *and life in Amsterdam may soon be threatening to her* *very life. You forget, Ovid Lamartine was my friend. He knew the world, and what he said would happen* will *happen. I have no doubt. And now that this Imogen Linny believes herself a Dutch Jew—well, God help her. Do you understand?" I said that I did understand; he was asking me to extend Imogen's stay in Amsterdam so that he could paint her, and by painting her, he would somehow finish, as he said, "my life's work."*

"And then what?" I asked.

"Who can say? But do not worry, Mr. Connaught. Do not worry."

"And so to this end, you're meeting Imogen Linny for tea this morning?"

"I will commission her. Today. Yes."

"As your—as she thinks she is your wife, she will more than likely refuse a commission."

*"I will begin by saying, 'You have always asked to be paid, like any of my models.' Which was not true of Anne, naturally. But I will say it anyway. It will work, don't you think? I did a lot of thinking in hospital. What is more, I will offer her a room here in the hotel. I have learned that she is living under—*shabby *conditions, in the prostitutes' district. Though she is not that. She is not that, of course."*

"I see."

"In the end, maybe, perhaps we will all get what we want. If that is possible. Now kindly go, Mr. Connaught."

And so I left the Hotel Ambassade.

And as you may well have supposed by now, at 8 a.m. I stood across the Herengracht Canal, and Imogen indeed appeared. In the recently laundered clothes of the Jewess. Of course, those. And having bathed the day before, hair put up nicely, no longer looking derelict. Mr. Heijman met her on the street and they repaired to the café. They sat at a table near the front window. I could observe them clearly. I sat down on a bench. Their waiter brought tea. They seemed to be talking with great animation. At one point, quite startling to me, Mr. Heijman reached across the table and took Imogen's hands in his hands and held them a long moment. I could not see the expression on Imogen's face, though.

I returned to the American Hotel. I lay on the bed and thought, I cannot blame Mr. Heijman. He is fighting his way out of the circumstances foisted on him by us. No-count immigrants from Halifax is how he might see us—or in any number of ways. He is only using said circumstances to grieve for his beloved wife, in the way he thought up in hospital. He may be about to use Imogen in a kind of séance, as it were. As she sits for him in his studio. A kind of séance. I really cannot know such a thing. But I may be correct in some of this speculation.

I will try and get this letter off to you today. I pray it arrives safely. It is impossible to overstate all my bewilderment, fear, regret, desire to be home; life in Amsterdam is highly unusual, dearest Helen. I kiss you,

Edgar

P.S. My God, I forgot to say, "Happy New Year, dearest."

January 11, 1939

Dearest Helen,

At breakfast yesterday in the hotel, I calculated that I have enough remaining funds for another month. Therefore, I have booked steerage on the SS Royalton, *leaving on March*

1. I have not received and, as we agreed upon, not expected any letters from you. I am therefore anxiously curious as to how your days go, dearest. And of course about the fate of my guard DeFoe Russet. Though knowing his personality somewhat, I expect that he confessed to stealing Jewess on a Street in Amsterdam *and may well be in prison. However, I also suspect that you may have tried to dissuade him from confessing. And that you made certain that the painting was returned to the Glace Museum the morning Imogen and I departed for Amsterdam. In addition, I am curious as to how my temporary replacement is faring. Naturally, dear, it is my hope that I will hear answers to all my questions when I return, God willing, to Halifax. Not to mention all your thoughts during these long weeks apart.*

As I finished my morning coffee and my financial jottings, a message arrived from Mr. Joop Heijman: Imogen Linny's first sitting is this morning, 9:00 a.m. You have my permission to attend. *I had just folded the note into my pocket when I looked up to see Imogen herself enter the dining room. Mornings, alas, are when she makes such appearances. And when one can see registered in her face and bearing the difficult night just past. However, she looked quite well, and "cleaned up," as it were; as if to read my thoughts, she said, "Yes, Joop is paying for my new hotel room. This isn't a surprise, husband and wife living separately. I mean, not just any husband and wife; when he's on a painting binge, it's how I best can take care of him, staying in the hotel, close by, but separately." I could only nod in understanding. She then sat down for tea. "Things are working out, then?" I ventured, affecting a half-disinterested tone.*

"Just as I'd hoped," she said. "And you've been so kind, Edgar. I want you to experience my life here in Amsterdam. I'm meeting Joop at nine o'clock this morning. Would you like to watch him draw me?"

"Very, very much," I said.

"Well, it might give you more knowledge about the family life of a Dutch painter, you know. You can tell Miss Delbo all you've seen and she can use it on her tours. This could be a once-in-a-lifetime experience for a curator, don't you think? Seeing my genius husband work close up."

I escorted Imogen to the Hotel Ambassade.

Of course, Joop Heijman was waiting for her. He could not have known whether I would be there; he could not have known that Imogen had asked me to be there, I presumed. It was a peculiar moment. Each cast a look of surprise at the other.

I followed them into Mr. Heijman's studio. Let me describe it: the ceiling is perhaps fifteen feet high. Paint is peeling in curled strips. The walls are white. Large windows look out on the Herengracht Canal and, on the opposite side, to the buildings behind the hotel. Tables, paints, brushes in jars, all the artist's tools and paraphernalia, canvases, some completed, some empty, are stacked against walls. It immediately strikes one as the most intimate sort of haphazardness; wherever the eye or hand rests is something of interest. A color used or abandoned. Dried crusts of paint along the edges of jars. It is a private world, this studio; it occurred to me that, in all my years as curator, this was the first actual studio I had ever visited. And why should that not have been so? I am not an art dealer or a fellow painter. I am a curator. The work comes to me completed. I only choose which wall. Still and all, I must confess there was something exciting about being in Mr. Heijman's studio; my tolerance and affection for even the works I liked least at first glance was widened by the privilege of close approximation. This may be a weakness.

Imogen was instructed to sit on a bench. Of course, she was wearing the clothes of the Jewess. Yet within a moment's time Mr. Heijman said, "No, no, no, no." He beckoned us to follow him again. Out to the street we went. He carried his sketchbooks, charcoal, pencils. Outside, he positioned Imogen on a bench in front of the Hotel Ambassade. It was a chilly day—Mr. Heijman and I wore overcoats. He made a number of quick sketches, then labored over a few more for much longer periods of time. Many passersby greeted Mr. Heijman, and not a few got off their bicycles to look over his shoulder, which he allowed, and which no one took advantage of for more than a quick glance. I simply stood near the front gate, observing. After perhaps an hour—Imogen, by the way, was allowed to stand and stretch now and then—Mr. Heijman said, "You may leave for the day. Back, please, the same time tomorrow morning." He allowed her then and there in public on Herengracht to kiss him on the cheek, but as he passed me on his way into the hotel, he had an expression of fierce disgust on his face. I walked Imogen to the nearby café, where we had an early lunch, tea, and then she said, "I have other appointments. Will I see you tomorrow?"

I said, "What other appointments?"

"It's not proper to ask that of another man's wife," she said. She looked quite indignant and added, "You're not my father. And we didn't sleep together aboard ship!" Here the

whole mood shifted, in fact I was struck as if by an anvil to my forehead, and after Imogen disappeared down the street, it took me a good many hours in my hotel room to regain my composure.

Make of this what you will, Helen. I can only repeat what I say to myself day and night: I expect nothing, yet life keeps taking unexpected turns.

I kiss you.
Edgar

January 18, 1939

Dearest Helen,

I am sorry not to have written in a week's time. Other than preoccupation and negligence, I have no excuse. Indeed, I have been locked into the routine of observing Mr. Heijman at work each morning promptly at 9:00 a.m. I usually arrive at Joop Heijman's studio only moments before Imogen. How strange, simply put, how strange to see a person dressed identically day after day. Yesterday Imogen was asked by Mr. Heijman to stand on the bridge spanning the canal and stare into the water. He made his sketches. He worked for longer than usual, perhaps four hours.

Last night I could no longer stand it. The days of wandering Amsterdam, hour upon hour spent in the hotel. Perhaps, too, I must add the daily reports of Hitler's psychotic Reich here in Europe—it all feels like time itself is pressing in, stifling one's very breath, forcing it back down one's throat, suffocating. It feels all too much like the world has indeed gone mad. It seems that Imogen (who says she gets her information at both the German and Portuguese synagogues) has been apprised of horrible "camps," to which Jews—all undesirables—are being herded. Just as you had begun to learn of such things in your own synagogue, dear Helen. But in our lunchtime conversations, I cannot seem to truly detect Imogen's intellectual grasp of such knowledge—because of her generally unstable "frame of mind," as it were. It is as if truth and fiction are as tightly woven together in her mind now as the dark weave of the very clothes of the Jewess she wears every day. And I am more than willing to admit that there are many components to her actions that I cannot fathom now, or ever will be able to fathom. I fully credit that possibility every minute of my thinking life here.

She continues to speak lovingly of "her husband, Joop." No change there. That has not changed in the slightest. But what has changed just over the past week or so is the intensification of a kind of willful amnesia, a kind of selective forgetfulness especially having to do with her former life in Halifax. For example, recently I mentioned your name—she replied with only a confused expression and "Yes, tell me about her. What is she like?"

Helen, I do not ever wish to lose track of the "why" of our initial presence in Amsterdam, as much as I now regret it. We felt, you and I, that it held out some little hope—the only hope—for Imogen's salvation. That sounds lofty—and you never used such a word—as I set it down on this hotel stationery, but I still feel the original emotion, the original clarity of our emotions toward that end. But now it is all too clear—and was from the first hour in Amsterdam—that the plan we set in motion in the secluded (not to mention less vulnerable to actual history) confines of the Hotel Wyatt, Halifax, Canada, with the German Army an ocean away, were not only thwarted but made to bow before the power of Imogen's own sense of personal mission. Of her desire to become, as she said again and again shipboard, "ennobled." To do something ennobling. *Forgive me, dearest, if I repeat myself, but it is only to hammer present circumstances even deeper into my consciousness. For all intents and purposes, Imogen Linny—and I say this now with shortened breath and heart pounding—is now a Jewess in Amsterdam; and what that might entail, what fate that might draw, given these perilous times, I cannot dare to predict. I shudder to think of it. I shudder to think of how correct DeFoe Russet was, when, in the heat of our brief argument in the Hotel Wyatt, he said, "You might be sending Imogen to her* real *death."*

My God, Helen, are there worse demons on earth than us, who have put Imogen Linny in this place? Have I breathed the stifling radiator air of my hotel room so that my brain is starved of all sense, Helen? Helen, I am not sleeping. I believe that DeFoe Russet spoke from his heart, and we—in the hotel room, at that moment—spoke from the high pedestal of intellect, and how ashamed I now am of that. I sit in the middle of the night at this cramped desk and write, like a student first intoxicated by philosophy, such observations as: Perhaps these moments of Imogen Linny's highest engagement in life coincide with the century's most abject dedication to terror. I am disgusted at my actual distance from events; my mind is in the way. In the English newspaper here: the terrors. On the radio here: the terrors. I sit at breakfast in the hotel, in freshly laundered clothes, toast, cheese, coffee set out in front of me on a pristine tablecloth, white cloth napkin folded neatly. Do you know, Helen, once I did fall asleep last night, perhaps at 4:00 a.m. or 5:00, whose voice entered my dream? Resounded in my dream? Edward Russet's! Yes, Edward's. He said, with a charming smile—using his language—"Had you really been transfixed by what Ovid Lamartine was saying, how could you go to Amsterdam? Weren't you listening?" *I sat bolt upright in bed and turned on every last light in my room.*

On the street, I look at men and women. They go about their day-to-day errands. They stand at the flower stalls. And yet they must feel the knot in their stomachs, their very souls knotting up with excruciating slowness.

Now it is 7:00 a.m. This very night past, I could no longer bear my hotel room, once again could not bear it. So I went to Joop Heijman's rooms. I went to the Hotel Ambassade. It was 3:00 a.m. by my watch. I knocked on his door and he answered right away. He not only was wide-awake but he had been painting. "What time is it?" he said. "Never mind, never mind. What difference does it make?" The smell of paint mixed with the smell of strong coffee, and a sweet liqueur of some sort—but mostly paint. He poured a drink for me. I sat on a chair at the back of the studio. He was working on a painting of Imogen Linny. She stood in front of a candy shop, with the Herengracht Bridge just to her right. "It's wonderful," I tried to say, but he interrupted: "You were not invited!" I sat in silence. He mixed liqueur in with his coffee and drank, and painted. "A person who is alone is even more alone in a hotel room, eh?" he finally said, without turn-

ing to look at me. "This would be true in your Halifax, Canada, as it is in my Amsterdam, Edgar."

Now, dearest Helen, please forgive me in advance for certain untoward language, but in an effort to reconstruct the hour I refer to, I report exactly what Joop Heijman said. "We are men, Edgar, and you have no doubt loved a woman and been loved, is that not true? I can see from your face that it is true. Good. I thought as much. So—let me tell you about a morning, dear Edgar. A year before my Anne was gone. The morning I speak of was a summer morning, very warm, even at five o'clock, but I was awake, beginning my day. I had in mind how my day might begin, because I lay in bed with the empty canvas in my thoughts—thinking, thinking, thinking—and the day was to begin on that canvas. But then, Edgar, then *it was not to be. Because I turned to look at my Anne. The blue sheet had slipped down, far enough so that her breast—her breast was—the sheet barely touched her nipple—and that instant the canvas I had in my mind was gone. Whoosh! Just like that—disappeared. Anne's hair had fallen loosely—how do you say it,* loosely fallen. *Along her shoulder. She moved slightly—the sheet fell away more, you see. Had I helped it fall away more or had I pulled it up around her shoulder—had I interfered, the day would have been wasted. A sin. Life would be wasted. For this was what I was* given. *Given—and no matter how many pictures I paint of her, with this one, this Imogen Linny, I can never have—and do not desire to have—such a moment. I paint this woman's clothes on her body, but there my imagination* ends. *I am very drunk now, Edgar, very very very drunk. And I have drunk everything in the room." Now Mr. Heijman sat down on his sofa and wept so loudly that a bellhop was summoned by someone living across the hall and knocked on the door. It was clear that Mr. Heijman could not bring himself to answer the door, so I opened it. The bellhop, a young man, looked at Mr. Heijman with stalwart concern and affection. Mr. Heijman heaved a sigh and shrugged, and said something in Dutch that seemed to persuade the bellhop that he was all right. But the look the bellhop gave me, Helen, was as close to being damned by a mortal as could possibly be.*

I did not know what to do next. The bellhop left and I sat down again on a chair. Mr. Heijman rose from his sofa, led me to the door. As I went down the hallway to the stairs, his bellowing sobs started up again. I set out for the American Hotel. Even at that hour, a few stray souls on bicycles could be seen along the canals.

I had an eerie thought—perhaps based on my outright ignorance of life here in Amsterdam—that people are beginning more and more to stay up all night because they feel time is running out.

I hope to get this off to you in the earliest possible post.

I kiss you.
Edgar

February 5, 1939

Dearest Helen,

And so the number of Imogen's sessions with Joop Heijman has now reached eleven. Eleven times over a period of two weeks. During this time, I have visited Joop Heijman's apartment in the middle of the night five times. I cannot say in the course of so little time that he despises me either more or less. In another life, friendship might have been possible. More sober in this life, he might despise me even more. Yet empty bottles have become almost as numerous in his rooms as jars of paint, I'm afraid. Then, two nights ago, he said, "My work with her is almost finished. One more painting. The one you see in front of you." The painting he referred to has Imogen sitting inside the bicycle shop. "Let me tell you something, Edgar. Let me tell you something," he said. "Your Canadian cemetery keeper can't ride a bicycle. She never learned. This is true. How do I know this? Because I asked her to ride and let me draw her. She said she didn't know how. What kind of place is Canada that such a thing is not learned, and how can this—this person continue to believe she is Anne? Anne rode a bicycle every day of her life." He was quite drunk, Helen, and walked then to his pantry and rolled a bicycle out and got on it and began to ride it around the kitchen, then into the studio, knocking over canvases, crashing into tables, chairs, falling, getting back up again. "Anne would ride in the rain!" he said matter-of-factly, when he finally stopped and had propped the bicycle against the pantry wall again. "Rain didn't matter, my dear Edgar. She took her students on a picnic once. All on bicycles."

He has titled the painting Bicycle Shop*—only that. It is as though he could not bear to actually name the woman he has painted.* Bicycle Shop. *In earlier paintings of Imogen, he could at least put the word "woman" in the title. Of course, he could not bring himself to put the name "Anne." He needed these past weeks to paint the idea of his wife—*

but never for a moment, Helen, did he believe he was painting Anne herself. Not even in his least sober state of mind. It is the most harrowing enterprise I shall ever witness; he goes through the motions learned in decades of painting, but his heart seems to deprive the very colors—and yet, still, the paintings, even to what I like to believe is my trained eye, are remarkably fine. It is as if he is painting the ghost of a Jewess, though, Helen: the ghost, fading; the light of the Herengracht Canal practically invading the light of Imogen's actual self. A woman fading into the light. (On your tour, should these Heijman paintings be in front of you, you, dear Helen, would put it more poignantly, I know.) The morning he made the drawings for Bicycle Shop, *he, Imogen, and I stood inside the shop on Herengracht. It is four buildings down from the Hotel Ambassade. The owner, a Mr. Paul Van Eerden, asked if he should close the shop while Joop Heijman worked. Imagine such respect. But Joop Heijman said no—"You might lose business." It was a simple daily exchange between friends, who happened to be artist and bicycle shop owner.*

We left the bicycle shop around noon. Joop Heijman carried his sketches, as usual, back to the Hotel Ambassade. I walked with Imogen to the café for lunch. In the café she said a startling thing: "Oh yes. Oh yes, of course. As anyone knows, Germany is the last place I should go just now." It was a seemingly disconnected thought, more an afterthought—picked up perhaps from a conversation she was having with herself when she first woke up, say. She then rose from the table and walked down the street. But back at the American Hotel, I could not get the sentence that Imogen had uttered out of my mind. "Germany . . . last place I should go . . . last place," et cetera. The words kept shifting, changing places in the sentence as I tried to repeat it. The days here have been filled with so many peculiar minutes it is impossible to describe them all, and equally impossible to describe how I have come to doubt my former logical way of thinking—about most anything, really. Amsterdam has not been a place that has allowed me to think straight. From my hotel late that night—two nights ago, that is—I was drawn, as if by cruel gravity or some other force, toward the Amsterdam train station. Central Station. It has an enormous façade, cathedral-like, and I hurried through it as if in a dream, not even checking the schedule clicking in on the Arrivals/Departures Board overhead. The names of European cities. I moved along, alone, but as if jostled by a crowd, though there was no crowd. Helen, how to describe the confluence of architecture, emotion, skewed time, acoustics, echoes, echoes ricocheting from the balconies and waiting rooms, trains being announced, foreign languages in the air? Instead of choosing a particular train—instead of looking for a German city on the board (could a person still actually get a train into Berlin? I could not imagine such a thing. No—impossible), I chose—quickly, quickly—a door leading down to a track. I pushed people aside. Rudely pushed them aside. Up ahead I saw Imogen, carrying the one suitcase.

All the force of convincing imagination gathered power and the woman up ahead looked *like Imogen. But as I got closer, the clothes were wrong. Nothing like our familiar Jewess. The woman was alone, up ahead only a few yards now.*

She was about to board the train. The conductor, standing by the door, saw me approach—saw something he did not like at all—and stepped in front of me. The woman turned; I saw that she was perhaps twenty years old, twenty at the most. He said something in Dutch, then, seeing my puzzled expression, said, "Your daughter?" "No—no," I said. Then the woman shrugged and stepped on board.

I hurried back to the Hotel Ambassade, hoping to speak with Joop Heijman. About what, exactly, I did not know. I simply wished to be in a familiar room other than at my hotel, no matter what might be in store for me there. When I rushed into the lobby, the bellhop—the same man who had seen Joop Heijman weeping that night—pointed to the small restaurant just up the stairs off the lobby. I walked up and saw Joop Heijman, Imogen (familiarly attired), and an elderly man, perhaps eighty years old. I immediately suspected he was the rabbi in Heijman's painting Anne and the Rabbi of Amsterdam. *Sober, Joop Heijman introduced me. The elderly man simply nodded. He and Joop spoke in Dutch. Imogen looked quite happy, truth be told. The rabbi ignored her. Entirely ignored her presence. I might say he even was disgusted by her presence, just from the way in which he squinched up his face each time he glanced at her. In the course of the next half hour, I learned through Joop's translating for me that there was to be a chance for employment at the German synagogue, this rabbi's synagogue—"for such work as the rabbi has in mind, your friend here will not need to speak Dutch or Hebrew, Edgar. It is the mop-and-pail sort of job, you see. Ya, the floor speaks no language,"*

Joop said—he laughed, and translated back for the rabbi, who half-smiled. Imogen then left the restaurant, on her way—where? I could not know.

"When does this employment begin?" I said.

"In a day, maybe two days—the synagogue needs someone to mop up, to dust, right away, dear Edgar. Jobs are difficult to find in Amsterdam, you know. Very very difficult to find. Your friend is fortunate." The rabbi shook hands with Joop Heijman, did not so much as nod at me, and then he, too, left the restaurant. I all but begged Joop Heijman to stop this from happening. I all but begged him then and there. "Edgar," he finally said. His voice was patient, controlled, and full of hatred for me. "I would like nothing more than to see this Imogen swim to Canada. Out of my sight forever. I hope never to set eyes on her again. This is—charity, dear curator. The rabbi is offering charity. That is not the word he would use—he would have his own word. I use it—charity. Let it be. He presided over my dear Anne's childhood—her spiritual life, can you understand this? The rabbi has been told about this Imogen. I told him. I told him in detail, Edgar. He—more than anyone else in my country—knows what possible fate this Imogen might meet. It may well be his own fate—he knows this, you goddamn fool, Edgar. Let it be. He will look after her. He will try to arrange papers saying she is not a Jew. He may be able to. I do not know. This rabbi cannot predict the future, Edgar. He is only giving this Imogen a job. Mops. A pail. Take her back with you to Canada if you possibly can. I hate the sight of her. But if you cannot, let the rabbi give her a way to feed herself—in the meantime . . .

In the meantime, do what you must. Do what you can. Do not—ever—come to see me again."

I am awake at 6:00 a.m., dearest. I must bathe. I have not, it suddenly occurs to me, bathed in five days, if not six. I have my inane notebook musings, nothing for posterity, to be sure, on the desk in front of me. I have always despised theories of history that elevate coincidence to a principle. *Helen, I do not believe for one moment that anything that I have reported to you from my weeks in Amsterdam is even remotely coincidental. I believe it has all been willed.*

I kiss you.
Edgar

February 12, 1939

Dearest Helen,

In the week that has passed since I last wrote to you, so much has happened, all description has to be, by definition, abbreviated. So forgive my lack of skill in conveying to you all turns of event. I visited Imogen Linny—finally—at the German synagogue, located on Jonas Daniël Meijerplein. But of course, how can such locations mean anything to you in Halifax? This is only to say, it is about a ten-minute walk from the American Hotel. I stood in the doorway and watched her scrubbing the floor. She was wearing clothes other than that of the Jewess; however, I do not think this marks a change of mind. Decidedly no, it does not. I think she now has a job and is still to her mind Joop Heijman's wife. I have no proof in conversation with her of this. I had only come to say good-

bye. Watching her, I thought that one's personal history—Imogen's, that is—is so much more immediate than History writ large. What will happen to her? I do not know. I cannot possibly know. My last sight of her—imagine this as a photograph, Helen—is of her working confidently and patiently, scrubbing along the center aisle of the beautiful synagogue, with its wooden floors. I chose, finally, not to interrupt. She seemed so fully resident in the moment, in the lifting of the scrub brush, pushing the pail along, humming or singing to herself. All done with purpose. The world can never be scrubbed clean; but this one floor, in this one synagogue in the city of Amsterdam: yes. That is what I thought—then, at that precise moment, I left the German synagogue.

Just before dinner, I decided to go to Joop Heijman's again. To accept whatever wrath, bear up, and try to convince him to allow me to carry all the most recent paintings he had done—those of Imogen, of course—back to Halifax with me. Perhaps I wanted to give myself a purpose, finally. On the way to the Hotel Ambassade, I rehearsed my pleas and arguments. As I turned the corner onto Herengracht, I experienced what can only be called a déjà-vu. Once again, there was an ambulance. Once again, a gathering of onlookers, some pressed against the windows of the ambulance. Police were holding others back. A body had been placed under a covering of some sort and was being slid into the back of the ambulance. Two bellhops and the manager of the Hotel Ambassade stood at the gate. I felt my heart sink to the pit of my stomach—all calm and hope shattered—when I heard in broken English, "He should be arrested," and saw a bellhop pointing at me. I stood in the middle of the street, knowing then that Joop

Heijman was dead. And yes, my dear Helen, it was true. Mr. Heijman had finished what he had set out to do, paint his paintings of Imogen Linny—and then leave the world. I was set on by two, then a third bellhop, thrown to the ground, kicked, rolled to the edge of the Herengracht Canal, where I saw in the distance the back of the ambulance disappear. Then a boot to my head—and I was kicked unconscious, for which, as I think back on it, I was grateful. I understand—even admire—the bellhops' point of view. They were not violent people by nature; they had lost a dear friend, and suddenly there I was, one who they felt had caused him to drown himself.

I will spare you, Helen, my brief stay in hospital, where the nurses and doctors were cordial. But I will tell you that Mr. Heijman's funeral was three days later. It was tremendously crowded, the small cemetery. Given the circumstances, I stayed well to the back, of course. Farther back, off to my left and near a tree, stood Imogen Linny, dressed as the Jewess. I did manage to move close enough to see that it was the bellhops and manager of the Hotel Ambassade who shoveled dirt over the casket—and others, too. When I next looked, Imogen Linny was gone.

For three days I took up residence—all day—at the German synagogue. But no one there had seen Imogen or heard from her. At least they said as much. I have no reason not to believe them. As for the paintings: just this morning, the manager of the Hotel Ambassade said that they were packed up and ready for me to take to Canada. He said that Joop Heijman had left a note instructing him to give them to me. From the look on his face as we stood in the lobby of the

American Hotel, I could tell it took great humility and suppression of pride for him to tell me this in person, me, whom he so hates. After telling me what he had to tell me, he looked directly into my eyes and said, "Good riddance."

Joop Heijman has bequeathed the paintings to the Glace Museum.

I fear I shall not see Imogen Linny again; at least not here, in Amsterdam.

The question I have, my dear, is not can we love each other in such a world as this but can we love each other with all we have ourselves done, all that I have described in these letters so permanently with us? Such accumulation of thoughts and incident has, I confess, left only enough room in my heart to ask, will you marry me?

I kiss you.
Edward

Acts of God notwithstanding, I arrive to Halifax on March 11.

It has been snowing two weeks straight, and the light along the wharf has been unpredictable. Sometimes it is a little ghostly, what with fog and shapes materializing, then falling away, but much of the time it is the same drab white or white-gray. Now and then there is a perfectly clear, middle-of-winter blue, with updrafts of wind making combs out of the clouds is how I can best describe it. And of course seagulls.

Ironing in the laundry room, pacing back and forth,

reading one or another book brought by Miss Delbo—and frequently in dreams—I wonder where Imogen is. No matter which dread possibility forces itself into my imagination one night, the next night I am capable of coming up with something worse. The list is pretty long by now. She has herself spun to the bottom of the Herengracht Canal; she has taken a train into Germany; she is scrubbing the floors of the German synagogue, or holed up in a heatless room —after all, her benefactors, Mr. Connaught and Mr. Heijman, are no longer there. As I said, the list is long. I have too much time to think.

I know that Mr. Connaught is back. Here in the Citadel, I read in the shipping news section of the newspaper that the SS *Royalton* arrived only a day late. I do not expect him to visit.

Five days ago, Briggs Roland tried to hang himself in his cell. He tore his shirt and braided a rope out of it, but Everett Finn cut him down. "We want him to go through a few years of hell on earth in a real prison," Everett Finn said to me, "before he goes to actual hell. Otherwise, it would've been a pleasure to watch him hang by his own shirt."

And just last evening, a Reverend Oles from a church in Halifax stopped by for a chat. He asked if I would be interested in joining a Bible study group; it meets for three hours every Sunday night, anybody can sign up, Briggs Roland signed up as he lay in the infirmary, and so did I want to be part of it? "You might come to an understanding of what put you in here," he said.

"An understanding."

"Yes. And in time, DeFoe, you might even learn to forgive Briggs Roland on behalf of your uncle. When you leave the Citadel, you'll have forgiven him. What do you say?"

"If I forgave him, life would lose all meaning for me."

I do not think he will ask me again.

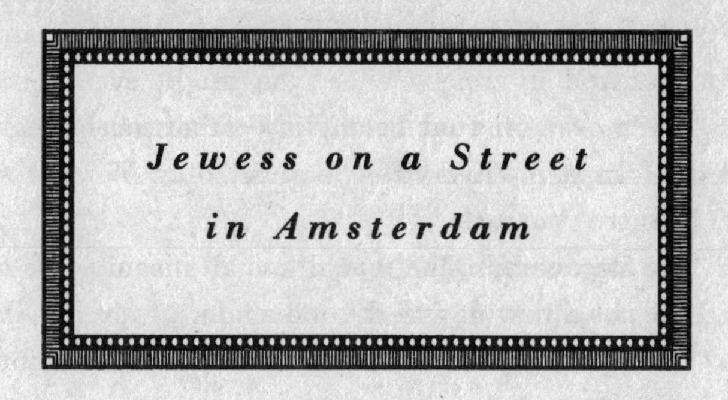

Jewess on a Street in Amsterdam

I stepped from the Citadel on March 28, 1939, with time off for good behavior. I was not a very important prisoner. They had to make room. I got dressed in the same clothes I had worn when I got there, my guard uniform, but with a flannel shirt left by Miss Delbo, not my usual white one. At the door, Everett Linn handed me my overcoat. "It's nippy out," he said in a cordial way, as if I were just leaving his house after tea. We did not shake hands. Then I was walking down the street, carrying nothing. I had the money I earned in prison in an envelope in my pocket. Naturally I went to the Lord Nelson Hotel.

Jake Kollias and Alfred Ayers were in the lobby. They greeted me warmly. We immediately sat together at the backmost table. "We've some of us got together and paid two months' rent—that is, if you want to come back into the hotel."

"I didn't make any plans," I said.

"It's Room 37," Alfred said. "We thought you might like a change."

"We moved all your belongings—that school desk included," Jake said. "Everything's in 37."

"I'll pay you back."

"Not necessary," Jake said.

"There's a new day clerk—take a look at him," Alfred said. "Name is Wallace Caine. Nice fellow. Says his ambition is to be night clerk."

"Paul's in hospital," Jake said. "But he's coming out."

They both looked me over a moment. "You seem fit," Jake said. "How'd they treat you in there?"

"Not badly," I said. "I even earned some money."

"Well, you're not a recognized-on-the-street type of criminal, DeFoe. You've got to get on with things, eh?"

"I was thinking of the train station," I said.

"Maybe get your old job back, sure," Jake said.

"The boys and I were discussing your future," Alfred said. "You know, what with Paul being pretty much out of commission—"

"I don't think I'm cut out to be a bellhop," I said. "But thanks. Thanks for looking after me."

"If you change your mind—," Jake said.

"I'll try the trains first," I said.

"No more card games," Alfred said. "Well, what with Edward—"

"Where're my uncle's belongings?" I said.

"Oh, they're packed away," Jake said. "Neatly in storage."

"Thank you for that, too."

"Don't mention it. It's almost dinner— What do you say, DeFoe? A reunion meal with us? Compared to Citadel, a hotel meal's got to seem home cooked, eh?"

"You aren't kidding," I said.

Jake handed me the key to Room 37. "Maybe you want to get out of those clothes, washed up," he said.

"By the way," I said, "did I get any mail, here at the hotel? A letter from Europe."

"Not that we know of," Jake said.

"Anybody say, 'Welcome home'?" Alfred said. "Are we forgiven for not coming to see you in Citadel?"

"I know you were thinking of me," I said.

I went upstairs. Jake and Alfred had obviously gone to the greatest possible lengths to get my new room arranged to make it seem familiar. The cleaning staff had put a bouquet of flowers on the school desk. The view was the same, too, except a floor higher. I changed into different clothes, and then joined Alfred and Jake for dinner.

The next morning before breakfast I wrote a letter to Mr. Tecosky at the train station. I outright asked for a job. I wrote, *Presently I am not otherwise employed.* I slipped the letter into the mail slot at the front desk.

Because I did not know where else in Halifax to go that day, I went to the museum. It was almost 10:30 a.m. As I approached, I saw Mr. Connaught, dressed in a gray overcoat. He was talking to two men and a woman. They all stepped from the museum, down the steps, and walked down Agricola in the opposite direction. Mr. Connaught looked as if he had aged far more, *years* more, since I had last seen him. But he was, as usual, neatly dressed, and looked to be in good cheer, excited about whatever was being discussed. He did not notice me.

I went into the Glace Museum. There was an elderly woman, not Mrs. Boardman, behind the bookstore counter. Her name tag said only VOLUNTEER. She was unpacking a box of new books. In Room A was an exhibit of architectural drawings of cathedrals from around the world. I walked through Room B. In Room C, an exhibition titled "*Jewess on a Street in Amsterdam*: The Paintings of Joop Heijman." To my right were the paintings of Anne Meijer that Ovid Lamartine had delivered. To my left were the paintings of Imogen, brought to Halifax by Mr. Connaught. As was my wont, I began on the left and slowly moved clockwise.

The Bicycle Shop; *The Herengracht Bridge*; *The Candy Store*; *In the Painter's Studio*; *At the Portuguese Synagogue*; *The Café*; *The Hotel Ambassade*; *In Dam Square*; *At the Broodjeswinkel*; *Holding Bread in Nieuwmarkt*; *On Herengracht, Morning*.

I went back to *Holding Bread in Nieuwmarkt*. I studied it closely. Imogen was in a crowd, holding a loaf of bread. I wished that my uncle were there to say, "It's stale," or, "It's new bread." It suddenly seemed the most important thing to know. I would never know it. I drew closer, trying to detect a recognizable expression. Some detail on her face that I had seen close up, in her bedroom, in the museum, on the street, at Halloran's. I reached out.

The guard—this would be Frank Oler—stepped from the Men's. He stood between Room B and C. I did not lower my hand. "Sir—" His voice had authority. He adjusted his tie. He stepped into Room C. "Don't get too close, please."